Author's Note

This is Book 3 in the 'Adventure' series, written as an offshoot from Book 2.

This novel however, uses a different style of writing in that the book is split into two different halves in an attempt to unite the saga from Book 2, bringing back into play and continuing the story about the main character of the series, John Grey from Book 1. In effect, the second half will restart the adventures of this character so the series may continue on its natural course to the end.

In the meanwhile, you will read about a cunning and ruthless man who will hopefully epitomise the dangerous underhand dealings of a certain German WW2 organisation that functioned in the ranks of the Nazi regime, which even the German's dreaded and feared their presence.

That organisation was none other than the most dreaded outfit, and I refer to the shortened and the more familiar name as given to the 'GESTAPO' and their lackeys the SS. Not even their own regular military forces could escape from them let alone any Allied personnel captured during the course of discharging their wartime duties.

As for the overall story of two halves, it's about the activities and eventual loss of a famous legendary German military unit, the **IX Legion** that was last seen in the sands of the Sahara during WW2, and the subsequent attempts to find it.

The spur to it all however, is the small matter of several hundred tons of missing Nazi gold that needed to be found, as part of Germany's secret 'gold deposits', earmarked by them to pay the Arab nations for the oil that was needed to fund their so called '*1000 years of the* THIRD REICH.'

Chapters

Prelude 1

Part One

I *Down to Business* 3
II *Peg Leg* 10
III *Sweet and Sour* 23
IV *King Canute* 32
V *Boulder Alley* 43
VI *The Eunuch Maker* 50
VII *Trouble Spots* 57
VIII *Clockwork* 73
IX *The Lake* 79
X *Ooh! La! La!* 89
XI *A Compromise* 106
XII *Something Stinks* 119
XIII *Arabs* 132
XIV *Delicate* 145
XV *Flaps and Ziffers* 153
XVI *Hissers and Moaners* 164
XVII *Hello Again* 178
XVIII *No Fear* 184

Part Two

I *Flying* 197
II *Start Digging* 216
III *Little Windmills* 226
IV *Pile of Bones* 233
V *Listening* 242
VI *Too Late* 255

Prelude

The well-equipped fighting machine defeated several armies and overran several countries in succession as the German Military forces dominated the European continent.

It was superior to any that was thrown against it, in its master's thirst to dominate the entire northern hemisphere. The German Axis forces had a willing slave in the guise of the Italian forces, but they were no match for their German counterparts. There was only one true and reliable force to help them rule the world, and they turned out to be a nation of much lesser stature in body but even more ruthless in battle. That was to be the also all-conquering Japanese in the Far Eastern nations.

The German military had their regular troops, who were treated as cannon fodder, but were strengthened by a 'Death or Glory' faction of military might, the real backbone in the German fighting machine. These were the infamous fighting units called the SS, who became the modern Guards of their beloved Fuhrer. However, in amongst the pecking order of things, was a special elite force that the Allies, and German troops alike, dreaded, and they were the special secret police, commonly known as the GESTAPO. Nobody had the right of resistance against them, not even their own military commanders, who were trying to fight a myriad of battles around the globe.

This story takes up in the time when things are still going pretty much to plan for the Germans. But even so, they still had to pay their bills and other dues to countries, which at this time were still out of reach for the Germans to seize the assets of that country. Those countries possessed the very thing that most of the civilised world needs even today, as without it, they would all grind to a halt.

That asset and most coveted commodity was OIL, and the Arabs knew how to extract as much wealth as they could from those countries desperate to obtain it.

The Germans normally had their oil from the Arab world of Algeria, Tunisia and Ethiopia in the Near East, with the Persians, Yemeni and other Arab Nations further to the East again, but not so far as to upset their Japanese Allies, whose warriors were of a different culture and race that the Germans aspired to.

The Germans decided to model themselves on a Saxon race called the Aryans. Their stereotyped image of a tall beefy man with blond hair and blue eyes, and a well-endowed female of similar grace, was their idea of producing a Master Race that would rule the whole of the European and Asian continents for the next millennium. Little did they know of a certain black man, that showed them otherwise, during their 1936 Munich Olympics. Perhaps that was the final straw for them to take stock and rid the world of such creatures let alone put the blame for everything onto the Jewish communities that thrived in most parts of their country.

Unfortunately, there were specimens of this so-called Master Race that could not fit into the idyll of things and therefore could not cut the mustard with those who did.

For those unfortunates, they had to rely on their own special brand of courage and devious cunning of operendi to survive their own rat race. It is to such a person that this part of the book is attributed to.

Part One

Chapter I
Down to Business

The black and chrome saloon slid to a halt on the gravel pathway before wide concrete steps leading up to the entrance of a very ornate and massive building. Graceful figurines flanked these steps, which led up to the entrance with an ornate gantry overhanging it. The carved livery of the erstwhile nobility, who once owned the building, revealed that it was also one of the most elegant and now it was festooned in the regalia of its current occupants, whose large red, yellow and black flag with a roundel showing a large gold Swastika on it, declaring it was now in NAZI hands.

Alighting from the car, the man looked up at the building, then passing two guards, began to climb the steps for him only to be confronted by two more, who stopped him from entering the place.

"You're supposed to salute an officer not get in his way!"

The two burly guards duly saluted and let him pass into the ornate reception room where the receptionist, who in fact was a scar-faced Sergeant apparently in a bad mood, met him.

"Stand still that officer, and identify yourself. Show me your papers!" the sergeant snarled, and clicked his fingers to induce a quick responds from the man.

"I'm Captain…!" he started.

"Hah! He's only a Captain! You lot are just the same as the Generals in this place, 12 a Pfennig! Not worth a dog's bollock." the sergeant sneered, then rose from his seat to accept the papers. "Captain! You are late and also out of dress. Get yourself to the cloakroom and prepare yourself for your appointment. I will tell General Hanschel you have arrived!" the sergeant directed, and dismissed the insignificant looking man away.

The man prepared himself for his long awaited meeting with

his revered idol General Von Hanschel, mastermind of the Jewish Extermination and Wipe-out System (J.E.W.S.).

"Come in Captain Luchens! You have travelled a long way and perhaps you are weary from it.

It explains your delay, but have some of this delicious vintage wine, and you can have something to eat if you're hungry, no?" Hanschel invited, acknowledging the standard Nazi salute with a wave of his own.

Luchens was given a large goblet of bubbling red wine and a richly ornate chair to sit on.

"These French lived well even after they beheaded their king and all the rest of his kind. Mind you they certainly knew how to look after their own. Until we showed them, just who is the master race on this continent!" Hanschel stated, and with a wave of his arm, indicating that he was allowed to sit down and relax.
Luchens looked around the room at the fabulous paintings and the rest of the matching furniture.

"I see what you mean Herr General! This wine is very much at home too!" he said as he drained his glass and found it was promptly refilled by one of the stewards.

"Now you are settled, I will tell you why I have sent for you." Hanschel said, and opened up a large map that had several details marked on it.

"According to my records, you have done an excellent job with the J.E.W.S. project, which means that you are the only man to carry out a special mission, that only myself and the Fuhrer himself knows about it.

In recognition of your work, I do hereby promote you to Major, and also by proclamation, you will not be going to join our victorious army in Russia, but you are earmarked for subsequent operations of this kind, already in the planning stages." Hanschel announced, opening the desk drawer and pulling out a crimson coloured box, which he brought over for Luchens to see.

"It even has your name on the box. Our Fuhrer has such knowledge to detail, which makes him truly great."

Luchens opened it and saw two gold badges that he would wear on his lapels, and managed to read the citation quickly, before he stood up for Hanschel to pin them upon him.

"Congratulations Herr Major!" Hanschel said magnanimously and gave him a salute

"This may be the only time you'll ever be saluted by a General. But if you succeed then we'll all be saluting you!" Hanschel smiled self-consciously, and sat down heavily in his chair.

"Thank you Herr General! I always strive to do our Leader's bidding, even though I doubt the wisdom of some of his messengers who pass on his orders." Luchens said with a smile, as if to alleviate the insubordination he was showing his general.

"Yes Major! I agree! But now down to business!" Hanschel stated, before starting a lengthy narrative and explanation of several photographs, places and other details.

"In short Herr General. I am to take a snowball and roll it across two continents. By the time I get it there it will be much bigger, and should arrive just in time for the next round." Luchens said after a while.

"This 'snowball' as you call it, means that we ensure our next years supply of oil from our Arab friends. And yes, if all goes well, you can be relieved for someone else to do the job, whilst you enjoy your next exalted rank in charge of your very own regiment."

"Then when do I start, Herr General?" Luchens asked eagerly as he looked over his route and other detailed plans.

"You will be taken by special plane then by car to your start address tomorrow morning. But in the meantime, enjoy the freedom of the chateaux, and if you want a bed warmer, just ask the waiter. He can supply you with one of your choice, be it girl or boy!" Hanschel said, flicking his eyebrows at the suggestion of 'boys'.

"Not for me Herr General! In fact I demand that the soldiers you give me, are such that no distraction of that kind will present itself as a threat to my operations."

"Well said Herr Major! I had anticipated your wish for such soldiers, and have already assigned a group of them to meet up with you as you go along. They are the specially, shall we say, adapted men, and have been trained up with our own SS troops. You will find them big, mean, and with a death wish attitude. Each one of them has been created to form the famous and special guard of Eunuchs." Hanschel said with a smile, and showed an explicit picture of these special guards.

"Lets hope they fight as good as they look mean!" Luchens replied, handing back the photos of the soldiers.

"Be off now Major! But I shall see you in the morning before you leave."

Luchens nodded his head and clicked the heels of his boots before walking out of the Generals study and made his way to his room.

"Follow me, Major!" a steward said courteously as he ushered Luchens up the red carpeted stairway and along a corridor that had several famous paintings adorning the length of it.

He found that his room was just as richly decorated as what he had already observed, including the large 4 poster canopied bed along one side of the room.

It was a freezing night so he sat by the log fire to eat his food that was brought into him on a trolley.

"If you need anything else Herr Major! Just pull the cord by your bedside." the steward declared, as he bowed his head and left discreetly, shutting the ornately carved door behind him.

He rose early and managed to have his early morning run around the chateaux grounds, before he allowed himself the luxury of a hot shower and got ready for the start of his next adventure. He decided it might be a lucrative venture, but only as a sideline from his already highly profitable dealings in two very different places literally an ocean apart from each other.

"Hope you slept well Herr Major!" Hanschel greeted when Luchens presented himself to the General.

"Yes thank you General! But too much luxury would spoil your appetite for the more strenuous aspects of our work."

"Well said again! No wonder you were hand picked for this operation!" Hanschel said jovially, before he scowled and handed over a large sack.

"Here are your written instructions. All the necessary passes, letters of authority and your special code words to use, as and when. You are warned that nobody is to approach you, nor pull rank on you. You are also warned that you have special instructions that you must effect immediately, should your operation become untenable or compromised. Failure is not an option." Hanschel said ominously, patting his holstered machine pistol meaningfully.

Luchens smiled, and quipped.

"Failure? That's not even in my vocabulary Herr General."

"Good. Because the last person only got as far as the Swiss border before our Deputy Leader's man-eating Stepdaughter made his genitals into trophies. She, by the way, will be keeping a special watch out to see that you do not do the same."

"Yes! I've heard of her, a good-looking wench! Bit of a lesbian too, as I'm led to believe. Still, you can't have everything can you!" he said philosophically, to which Hanschel agreed by nodding his head.

"Off you go now Major! Your first rendezvous will be at point Bravo. Good luck, and keep in touch at the stipulated times. If you don't then I'll have the entire SS army onto you." Hanschel said, as Luchens saluted and left in the same car he arrived in.

"You must have a golden arse or something! You came as a Captain now leave as a Major. The last lot of Captains and Majors I took there had hot lead in their ears for their breakfast. You fail, and you get the same!" the driver growled as he looked at Luchens through the car's internal mirror.

Luchens gazed at the changing scenery as the car made its way to his first contact with his men. The journey to the waiting aircraft was quick, but the flight took several hours before it landed in a field, close to the side of a building that backed onto a river.

Luchens was a weedy looking man who was not exactly an example of the much portrayed, Aryan master race of Man. But what he lacked in looks and other outward signs of such image, he more than made up for in other ways.

He was manipulative and cunning to others much bigger in stature than himself, and was merciless to others under his influential powers. This was his only single success in life keeping him alive and ahead of the others in the pack.

"Here you are Major! You'll find people inside waiting for you. Good luck!" the pilot said, leaving Luchens on his own, before taking off again.

He picked up his suitcase and his sack of instructions and walked slowly along the wooden veranda to the doorway of this ramshackle building.

He opened the door to find several burly, scruffily dressed men lounging around in a large barn-like room, with a roaring fire belching out smoke up an equally large open chimney.

"Who's in charge here!" he demanded.

A well-built man stood up from a chair he was reclining in and replied with his own question in a belligerent manner.

"Who the bloody hell is asking!"

"Stand to attention when you speak to an officer!" Luchens snarled back.

"I'm Major Luchens. When I ask who's in charge, I expect a proper answer."

Another man stood up and walked slowly up to him, saluted and in a soft voice said.

"Don't mind Pfaltz, he's a bit sore hanging around this bloody place. My name is Sergeant Kretshmer. These are my men, only six of us that are left from an entire company.

We have a barge tied up alongside this building, and we're standing by to move off, sir!"

"That's better Sergeant! We will move off just as soon as I've had some of that coffee you've got on the fire." he replied, as he went over and helped himself to a mug of coffee warming himself by the fire.

Kretshmer got the men organised and had the fire doused before clearing the place to look as if nobody was ever there. Luchens followed the men down to the barge and waiting until everybody was on board, had the craft cast off and sail along the river.

Chapter II
Peg Leg

It was nearly dark when the barge arrived at its first rendezvous point, and Luchens ordered each man to keep as quiet as possible when their load was being stowed in the belly of the empty barge.

"Ten boxes in total, is all we brought. Sign here and here, Major!" the agent said softly as Luchens signed the papers under the light of a dimmed torch.

"Here is your token to match the receipt. Return it to the Chateau Flavot immediately." Luchens responded sharply then handed the man a small brass key.

The man saluted and climbed back into his lorry and drove off into the night.

"Sergeant! Make sure we have enough room to move around in, before you put those sacks over the hatch covers. Also make sure the tarpaulins are over properly to hide any light. Only the barge hazard lights will be showing, and even then only if another barge is spotted coming towards us.

We have a long way to go on this barge, and it's going to take us a good two weeks or so. So get yourselves settled down as best as you can." Luchens said quietly.

Luchens turned to look at a white-bearded man, with a peg leg and whose weather worn skin was as brown as a nut, standing just inside the wheelhouse.

"You must be the Bargee! I need you to sail up river without stop until we reach Cologne. In the meantime you will instruct two of my men on how to handle this craft, save for the navigation of it. That will be done between yourself and your own cargo handler. I will have the men rotate duties so that everybody can have time on deck. Other than that, my men will be kept out of sight and allow you to carry out your duties in peace." Luchens stated pompously, whilst peering into the Bargee's face.

"If you don't get your scrawny face out of my beard right now, you'll end up swimming all the way." The skipper grunted.

"Now look here old man!" Luchens started to say.

The Bargee raised his peg leg up and kicked Luchens so hard in his crotch that he was lifted off his feet and fell overboard, spluttering and coughing and trying to swim back to the craft.

Before the Bargee had time to reach over the side to grab hold of the spluttering man with his boat hook, two of the burly soldiers grabbed him and pinned him to his steering wheel.

"You do that one more time and you're dead old man!" one of them rasped.

"In that case, I go no further. Take your boxes off my craft and find someone else. I do not take kindly to jumped up messenger boys trying to act the all conquering hero."

"What is your problem old man?" Kretshmer snarled.

"I'm an ex-Battleship Captain, and fought in the Battle of Jutland! I have the Iron Cross with Oak Leaves and cross swords, as given me by the Kaiser himself! I don't take kindly to upstarts such as him telling me how to run my own barge." the bargee said indignantly.

Luchens clambered on board and heard the bargee's statement.

"My apologies for any untoward insult to you Herr Capitan! But I can assure you that will be the last time you do that. Just get this vessel going up stream, as I have a tight schedule to stick to. I need to be in Cologne by this time tomorrow night!" He snarled, rubbing his sore genitals.

"Very well Major. Just remember, I am the skipper on board, and what I say goes. I understand your instructions and you shall get to wherever you wish. Providing you keep yourself and all your men off my deck. And by the way, just for the record, it will take us longer to get that far up river." the bargee said gruffly.

"How long that is I don't know, but that will have to do. Just one thing you will keep in mind and that is you're under my orders.

So let's agree on that!" Luchens replied, before he climbed down into the tiny cabin below the small wheelhouse of the motorised barge.

The barge was a 60-foot flat-bottomed craft that had a small cabin, with room enough for the skipper, and just two others. Luchens chose the best bunk and took up most of the space for himself; only to find that he had taken the skipper's bunk and that the other two were hard pressed to make room for them. This again caused trouble, and the cargo-handler dumped him off the bunk telling him that it was the skipper's, and absolutely nobody was to go near it. If he wanted more space he should join his men in the cargo hold.

Luchens told the cargo handler if he knew what was good for him, he would go and join the men in the cargo hold. Under the threat of a waving luger pistol, the cargo handler reluctantly left and went forward as ordered.

Luchens had the luxury of the boiler and the stove that the cook used for their meals, to keep him warm. Whereas the men were staying at the bottom of the freezing cargo hold with the wooden crates. This was to be their cramped home for the next couple of weeks.

Luchens ensured that he ate his food in company with Kretshmer, but kept his conversation to a minimum except when he had orders or other items to divulge.

"We shall be moving upriver without stop. But we will be taking on different deck cargo as our disguise, every day. The men will have their food here, before they do their stint on deck. I want one man up on deck at the front to keep a lookout. He can keep his weapon by him but out of sight. You will have them changed every two hours, and anybody else is to stay quiet. I intend to stop from time to time to get fresh food provisions etc, but that will be in the planned stops. No smoking in the hold, but feel free when on deck. Any questions Sergeant?"

"Yes Major. Where will you be all this time?"

"I shall be right here, planning our next stop and who I shall be meeting. I have a small radio transceiver to use in case we run into difficulty or unwanted attention. I have to make sure we arrive at each r/v point within our allotted time. Otherwise we'll have the entire combined forces after us, and we can all look out if that happens. Anything else?"

"What about toilet facilities. Are we stopping at the waterside beer cellars and cafes like all the other barges, or at some bushy part of the riverbank?"

"We'll get a slop bucket for the day, to be ditched as each watch come on deck. But at night, the men can do it over the side. If we have to stay longer at the planned stops, we can always have time for a campsite meal, stretch our legs and have a smoke. Weather permitting of course! Just one thing though! The men will remain in civvies at all times. Their uniforms can be folded neatly and used as pillows or whatever for the duration. If we decide to stop at a waterfront beer hall, then all the men are to keep to themselves. Nobody is to find out what we're doing. Any loose tongue will be cut off, along with other useless bits. Do I make that clear Kretshmer?"

Kretshmer looked at this pimply faced person who dared to come amongst him and his veteran troops, and decided that he was not worth the bother of slitting his throat.

"All that suits just fine Major. How far upriver are we going?"

"I'll let you know when we get there Sergeant. Can't have any loose tongues just yet. Sufficient to say, there could possibly be a change of crew, or the same again in manpower addition, but I won't know that until tomorrow evening."

"I'll go and tell the men now Major." Kretshmer said as he left the warmth of the cabin.

The skipper came below and was given a bowl of broth before sitting down at the table. He ate his meal without a look or word towards Luchens, before he sat back and started to smoke a large wooden pipe stuffed with several handfuls of tobacco.

He puffed and snorted for a while, which made Luchens almost retch with the smoke.

"Do you really have to smoke that bloody awful thing down here skipper? Some of us are trying to read!" Luchens said annoyingly.

The skipper took no notice, but reached over into a hidden compartment and drew out a very large pistol, which he pointed menacingly towards Luchens.

"Look here you scumbag! I've already done my bit for the Fatherland in the last lot. This vessel belongs to me and is my home. Not you nor any of your lily-livered cowards that rape, rob, and murder poor innocent people just because they are Jews or Romany's or do not fit into your so-called Master race, can take it away from me. If you don't like me smoking, then get up on deck out of my way."

Luchens looked down the barrel of the heavy navy colt and saw a bullet waiting to be fired.

"It appears that you don't get the picture old man. You're from the old days where all of you were cowards who ran away when trouble started, and sued for peace at the Versailles Treaty. I'm the new breed that will rule the world for another 1000 years. If you look under the table I have my luger machine pistol pointing at your fat gut and unless you put that pipe out it will be your last breath." He snarled.

The skipper looked under the table to see the pistol but got hit over the head with a heavy wooden cudgel, which knocked him out.

When he woke up, he found himself tied to his chair and saw Luchens smashing up his favourite pipe.

"You had me cold, old man, until you looked the other way. I asked you not to smoke but now you can't as I've just smashed it for you. Now what do you say?" Luchens sneered with satisfaction, then gazed into the skipper's face.

The skipper raised his peg leg and stabbed Luchens in the groin with it once again, making him shout and groan with pain before he fainted.

The cook untied the skipper and helped him to his feet as Kretshmer arrived with a machine gun in his hands.

"What's all the noise here skipper? What have you done to the Major? He better not be hurt or you'll swing for it."

"I am the skipper on here. This is my home and has been since the Battle of Jutland! Nobody comes on board my vessel and tells me what I can or can't do! I don't give a monkeys' toss who it is either. Not even that shit Hitler can order me around." the skipper growled and threw Kretshmer an expensive looking wooden box.

Kretshmer opened it and saw the medal contained inside, which made him whistle softly and said.

"My father had one of them, exactly the same. And I've got the next one down from that! I shall see that the Major will not bother you again Herr Capitan!"

"Then you must be the Grandson of my old friend Grand Admiral Hippenfeltz. I thought I recognised you, but I couldn't be certain. I was expecting a naval tradition, but you're obviously regular army." The skipper said, holding out the gun for Kretshmer to see.

"Yes Capitan! That pistol you've got was one of a pair that my Grandfather had given out. I have the other one at home. I was regular army but got transferred to the SS Battalions as part of the Special Guards. The work is pretty much the same except its on land."

"Well! As long as you keep this so called officer off my back, we can get along just fine."

"Just as long as you don't provoke him anymore with that ancient musket of yours!" Kretshmer chuckled, returning the weapon back to its owner.

Luchens woke up to find Kretshmer fussing around him.

"He tried to kill me. Have him thrown overboard with a weight around his neck!" Luchens whined and cursed, as he rubbed his crotch again.

"Now then Major! We need this man to get us to our destination. Besides had he wanted to kill you, he would have done long before now. For God's sake let the man smoke if he wants, besides, its part of our subterfuge. Without him we'd not get another day up-stream, because he's well known and well respected by all the other bargees. Think about it Major!"

"Very well!" Luchens conceded as he stood up and went up on deck to get some fresh air.

The barge sailed up the Rhine at its constant slow speed, before it stopped at a small landing jetty with an open barn next to it, and adjoining waterside pub.

The skipper went below and kicked Luchens awake; saying that it was six o'clock in the morning and that they had arrived at the first r/v point. He also told them that there was apparently nobody around and that the pub would be open shortly, as some of the other barges that were coming upstream, would arrive within the hour.

Luchens rose swiftly and went up on deck to raise his men.
"Skipper! We have to move over to the other side and wait for a truck to arrive. It should be here in about fifteen minutes, and we must have it unloaded with the boxes stowed below in a further ten minutes. We can't be seen nor can the cargo."

The skipper had his barge moved to the opposite river bank and alongside another jetty as a covered lorry arrived.

Each box weighed 80 kgs, and every man had to carry one each into the cargo hold. Luchens had the men working hard as they sweated and grunted with their boxes, whilst Kretshmer had a machine gun nestling in his arms just in case of trouble.

The transfer took less than ten minutes, as Luchens signed the driver's receipt, for the lorry to disappear and the first downstream barge to appear slowly around the bend.

The men lay panting and gasping for breath in the cargo hold, as the handler covered up the hold. Kretshmer and the handler put a couple of grain sacks back onto the cargo hatches to complete the disguise before the skipper received greetings and calls from the passing barges.

"Hello Admiral! Got a couple of trainee deckhands I see." came a greeting.

"Hello Otto! Have you got my tobacco?"

"Yes! I'm calling in for some schnapps! We'll have a glass and a smoke, yes?"

"Thanks for the offer, must get upstream as soon as I've finished here."

The other bargee nodded and steered his barge right alongside to hand over the tobacco.

"Thanks Otto! Got a spare pipe? Mine went fishing awhile back there. Must have dozed off at the tiller."

The bargee laughed briefly, but gave him one from his topcoat pocket.

"I've been breaking this one in. It's still a bit hot!"

"Thanks! I'll cure it with some cabbage leaf!" the skipper said, taking the pipe and tobacco, before steering his barge away from the other one and upriver again.

Luchens looked through the small porthole at this interchange and at the other barges that were now approaching them.

"Keep away from them. Keep going and don't stop!" he hissed.

The skipper looked down at him and slammed the cabin door in his face.

"I've told you before. Keep your nose out!" he growled.

"Morning Skipper! Heading upstream a bit more this trip?" came a question.

"Morning Siegfried! Yes, taking this load of grain over to Cologne. I've got a load of coal to take further upstream before coming back with straw. Why?"

"Couldn't pick up a ton of beet could you? Only my bottom timbers are a bit thin to take the extra."

"Where do you want it dropped off, Weselstad?"

"Aye, that'll do. Thanks!"

The skipper tooted his horn and steered his barge past all the others, before he was finally on his own again in a lonely stretch of the river.

Luchens climbed up on deck to look around, and saw the majestic countryside slide slowly past him, with only the low throb of the engine to break the silence.

"You did well back there skipper. But don't offer any more favours, as you might not be able to make them. And before you reach for that blunderbuss of yours again, I meant that we might have to go further upriver than you think."

"I can navigate up as far as Mulhousen, and on to Basle. What have you in mind?"

"I won't know until we reach Seitzenhoff. That's all I'm prepared to tell you."

"Fair enough! We have to stop long before then to take on fuel and stores."

"Our next stop will be a small village at Remagen and we'll be there for a couple of hours."

"I know just the place to land. Out of the way, yet pleasant enough to enjoy some decent hospitality!"

"Anything just as long as we're not late in getting to that next r/v. But any trouble, or questions why we've turned up, we'd better move on with or without fuel."

The skipper merely nodded his answer and puffed on his borrowed pipe, happy in steering his barge along the narrow ribbon of water.

The barge passed through the bustling waterway of Cologne, and sailed straight past until they were almost out of the area before pulling up alongside a stone wharf, that had a large hotel next to it.

Luchens looked at all the barges' tied up, and at the men drinking large steins of beer, which made him decide that this was a well-chosen place, but demanded that the barge be tied up slightly apart from the others.

"Can't do that. Must tie up outboard of the uppermost, as its

The Lost Legion

customary for us bargees to swap cargoes now and then. I have grain, and could swap it for some timber, that sort of thing!" the skipper advised.

"And before you say anything. I'll only take a small load due to the shallow area we're about to go through. I'm already on two feet, and won't be able to take on more than another foot, until we get back into deeper water again. Then I would happily take on a further one foot." he added.

Luchens scratched his head and asked what the significance of each foot.

The skipper smiled and decided to confuse him with naval slang.

"I can take up to 70 tons in the much deeper salt water reaches of the lower parts of the rivers, and using my maximum draught of six feet. But canals and the rivers upstream are shallower and fresh water, which restricts me to just three feet. The vessel when empty has its own one-foot draught. Or if you like, I have 220 cubic metres of cargo space but can only carry 20 tons at this stretch of the river."

Luchens was still nonplussed and demanded a straight answer. "It's simply this, Herr Major. My vessel carries 10 ton per foot deep." he said in between puffs of his pipe.

"Why didn't you say then. You will only be carrying 150 of these boxes, plus my men." Luchens stated with a nod, and went forward to tell Kretshmer and his men to prepare for a short stay ashore.

"Stretch your legs. Have fun, but keep together. Any sign of trouble, just back away. Remember, you're just civilians taking a ride upstream for a razzle with the local farm girls." he advised, as the men climbed up onto the deck.

"No weapons of any kind." Kretshmer added, removing a dagger from the pocket of one of the men.

The men went into the pub and joined in with the merriment and had a few beers before they all made their way back to the barge.

All except one, who somehow got into an argument with one of the barge cargo handlers.

"What's the matter with you lot, queer or something? Prefer little boy's winkles, yes?" the bargee taunted.

The soldier just laughed and went to turn away as the bargee grabbed hold of the soldier's genitals. The soldier grabbed his attacker's arm and threw him judo style across the room before he leapt after the bargee and started to kick his head like a football. The others took exception to this unsportsmanlike fighting and tried to take hold of the soldier.

Kretshmer and the other five soldiers arrived and waded into the bargees, in a one sided fight. Within a few minutes, the soldiers were walking slowly away from a pile of groaning and injured bargees lying all over the place.

Luchens was livid when he heard the noise of the fighting, and ordered the soldiers to get back on board.

"I told you lot not to get into trouble. Now we've got to lie low for a while, which means that we'll be behind schedule. Kretshmer, you promised me they'd behave if I gave them the time off. You've broken your word. I'll have you lot relieved and go on with a fresh crew that I can rely upon."

"But Major! It was that bargee that started it." the offending soldier said truculently.

"I don't care a damn. It was only a few names they called you. Yet you fell for the bait. I'll deal with you later. Now get on board." Luchens shouted and waved his pistol at them.

"Skipper! Get this barge away from here as quick as possible. We don't want any police or military poking their noses in over it. We're all dead otherwise."

"Cast off for'ard! Stand by with your pole. We've got a sand bar up ahead!" the skipper said calmly as he steered the barge into mid-stream again.

"I need more fuel and fresh supplies. The chandler was shut for the day, so we've got to pull in somewhere else." The skipper advised.

"Let's hope your next place will be less occupied. I have to report my position by telephone when we get there."

"It's just up the next creek junction. We can hide there for a few hours if you want. Only I've got to be seen on the river and not ashore, otherwise my friends will think something was up."

"Okay! We'll take on supplies and fuel and extra men at Koblenz when we take on the next load."

"How many more loads are you getting?"

"Not to worry skipper! I told you that my full load of boxes won't exceed 150, and I will eventually have 15 men on this part of my trip." Luchens said swiftly, and went forward to the cargo hold.

The skipper heard a single gunshot, and saw a body being dumped overboard before Luchens came back with his smoking pistol.

"Mutiny in the ranks Major?" he asked.

"Something like that skipper! Remember, you're just as liable to get shot as that idiot Pfaltz was." Luchens retorted.

The skipper tut-tutted and carried on smoking his pipe as Luchens went back down into the little cabin again.

It was getting dark as the barge arrived at their next r/v stage.

Luchens had the men load up with the fresh provisions and the fuelling of the barge, before he slipped away to make his radio contact.

When he came back he told Kretshmer that a fresh section of men would be joining them when they arrived at the Brubenstat Kamp. But that he was to remain on board as 2nd in command.

"I've been with these men since our Narvik campaign, and would much prefer I stayed with them, Major."

"You'll do as I say. I want real SS troopers, not like the one I had to shoot back there." Luchens growled, patting his holstered luger.

"He was just a new replacement, but pity you shot him, because he was reputed to be the Divisions' top sniper."

"Well he should have kept his mouth quiet, as he's now a dead top sniper." Luchens replied sarcastically and left Kretshmer to go back to the cabin.

The barge arrived late the following afternoon and tied up alongside several other barges so as not to look inconspicuous.

"Right skipper. We shall be here for a few hours to refuel and for you to get your fresh provisions.

I have a change of men and an extra ton of cargo to load and sail at midnight."

"That suits me! I'll be ashore in that tavern just down the river. I'll see you then!" the skipper said nonchalantly before going below to the cabin.

"Sergeant! There is a lorry over there with supplies and drums of fuel. Get the barge fuelled and loaded with the fresh supplies. Then put them in a defensive position around the barge to protect it from would be thieves and other scum." Luchens ordered, then added.

"I shall be leaving on that truck to get my own orders from the garrison Kommandant. So you see Kretshmer, even I have to obey orders."

Kretshmer just nodded and got the men working on re-supplying the barge.

Chapter III
Sweet and Sour

The truck made its way through a maze of barbed wire and several heavily armed guards before it stopped at the guardhouse, where Luchens got out and strode into the building.

"Major Luchens to see General Klammer!" he announced pompously, only to find an SS Colonel standing there looking sharply at him.

"You will follow me Major! The General has been relieved of duty and I'm now in command of this camp!"

"That sounds about par for the course then Colonel! It seems that our regular army officers cannot be trusted to do even a simple job like running this backwater of a camp!" Luchens crowed, striding purposefully alongside the colonel.

They went into another building and down a poorly lit tunnel before the colonel opened a large metal doorway, which revealed a well-lit cavern of a room.

Luchens saw several men busy at their desks, and several women lounging about. He heard muffled screams and other sounds, which told him that he was in one of the interrogation units that were spreading right across the continent, like the bubonic plague.

A much larger scream was heard which became muffled before complete silence reigned once more.

"That was the General you were asking about. It seems he's bitten more than he can chew now!" the colonel said with a faint smile, as a tall, slender, neatly dressed woman entered from a side door, carrying something that was dripping blood all over the place.

She walked over to the colonel and threw a complete set of genitals onto the table.

"One more for my collection Colonel! Have you brought another for me? Only I'm running out of men with balls!" she purred.

The colonel shook his head and introduced Luchens to this woman.

"You are witnessing our top double agent at work. Major Luchens, meet Fraulein Wintermann. It is best to meet her after her work, otherwise you could be her next victim." the colonel said as Luchens bowed slightly as his acknowledgement to the woman.

"So you are the new rabbit. How far can you run before you too

"My orders are to reach a certain destination within four weeks. the woman.

"Operation Snowballs. In fact it's Operations No balls. I have literally hand picked these men. They were once distinguished officers now they are mere privates without their privates.

That My operation is called…" Luchens began but was butted in by is because I have personally removed the testicles from all of your end up on this table next to the General?" men, and some who, shall we say, got too greedy just like the General was."
Luchens smiled and asked.

"I take it you have started a collection of them, and stacked in a row of pickling jars. Which set is your favourite Fraulein Wintermann?"

"I have a large nigger's dick that I took great pleasure of sampling before it ended up in its jar. A sweet and sour process if you like Herr Major!" she giggled, then snarled instantly at him.

"Just you make sure I don't get yours, little man!"
Luchens chuckled and responded by asking her to show him her interrogation technique and how she achieve her trophies!"

The colonel was sounding slightly alarmed at this request, but Wintermann merely stated that it would be her pleasure and his pain if he was not careful.

"Major Luchens has to change his guards, but have you got fifteen suitable men available for him Fraulein Wintermann?"

"I only have four here and a further five waiting further down the line. The Major will have to keep the ones he's got, as I need to follow up the information the General imparted before he was separated from his genitals."

"I had to shoot one of them for a slight misunderstanding of my orders. For that reason I felt that the rest of the men had compromised my mission." Luchens stated, and went on to tell about the incident.

"We appear to be two of a kind, Major. I'd like to come along some of the way with you, as I have to be in a certain place at a certain time too. Very close to where you're going, actually. But that won't be until you reach the 5th pick up point."

"You are more than welcome Ms Wintermann!" Luchens said, using his best charm on her, and only receiving a frosty smile in return for his troubles.

"I have a new set of orders for you Major, which countermands all previous orders. In fact your orders will be changed about three times before your mission is completed." the Colonel announced, before going into detail with him.

"It seems pretty straight forward Colonel, but I will take exception to anybody coming near me unannounced. If they do, then they will suffer the consequences." Luchens avowed as Wintermann kept looking at him throughout the entire briefing.

"You are only a little man, how did you get yourself into the SS?" she asked curiously, as she lit up a cigarette in a long ebony holder.

"I happen to be involved with the J.E.W.S. project both here and abroad. My recent escapades have somehow been recognized by the Fuhrer himself, as I happened to be with a daring sea Captain at the time." Luchens answered quietly, looking at this very feminine yet deadly person.

"Ah yes! I remember. I can feel safe with you then Major, as a girl can't be too careful who she meets up with." Wintermann said coyly, patting her large and very sharp dagger.

"Will you have something to eat in the officers mess before you go Major?" the colonel asked.

"Yes that's kind of you! Care to join me Fraulein?" Luchens

invited, holding out the crook of his arm for Wintermann to link her arm into.

"Why thank you dear sir, are you coming too Colonel?" she asked.

"No, I have to tidy up the place for our next guest. You two go and enjoy yourselves!" the colonel said, watching them happily leave the room.

Luchens looked at this flaxen haired female, who looked at him with piercing blue eyes, yet with a thin-lipped smile on her face.

"You have something to eat in the officers mess before you go Major?" the colonel asked.

"You can call me Lenka and I shall call you Lucky! And I think I will have the measure of you before too long, providing you play your cards right!" she giggled as Luchens offered her a glass of wine.

"Here's to the success of my mission!" he toasted, and commenced to enjoy the ambience of the well-appointed saloon that had several other high ranking officers and their female companions.

They dined on a feast that would keep an entire family for weeks, as their first course was a delicious prawn cocktail followed by a fillet minion with all the trimmings.

"Mmmm, haven't tasted steak this good since leaving the chateaux. The wine is also very, shall we say, excellent. Goes to show how these Frogs knew how to live in style. Until most of their heads got chopped off that is." Luchens said, swallowing yet another tasty morsel.

"The French are but pawns in our overall plan to rule the world. Mind you the Italians are not far behind.

We of the Germanic race will always dominate all these inferior races including those stupid British who think that they are the only ones to rule anything. They've got another think coming even if it does take us the next 1000 years to do get them to comply, you just mark my words. I mean we're talking about a new era of a total European dominance with our Fuhrer at the head. The only fly in the ointmen, are those funny little men out in the Orient. They might be our, shall we say, allies, but they will need to be brought under control at certain boundaries so as not to incur the wrath of our invincible forces that are crushing any army that comes in its way."

"You seem to disregard the fighting British spirit as we well know from the last war. What makes you think that they will heed our words." Luchens asked as he opened yet another bottle of priceless vintage wine from the well stocked French chateaux wine cellar.

"The thing is dear Lucky, it is the long term solution that we're talking about. We are winning this war all hands down at the moment, but it only takes a certain fluke of the war from our enemies to turn things around. Therefore we are now preparing for some sort of an end game plan that will guarantee us the supremacy we are currently striving towards.

In plain terms, win or lose this war, I predict that we will eventually gain the upper hand and rule the world and thanks to the stupid and gullible French, Spanish, Belgian and all the other countries that we've already conquered so far, and it will be an easy victory without any further lives being lost. As far as the British are concerned, we will take them slowly by underhand guises, and by any subtle means at our disposal so that in the end they will not have anything left to offer any resistance. It will take the greed of self- aggrandisement of just one or two of their, er, prime ministers I think you call them, to hoodwink their people to do so. I mean, one of them was gullible enough to declare to his people that there would be 'Peace in our time', the stupid fool that he was.

However, by that time when the people realise what took place, it will be too late. A creeping dictatorship just like we're doing with the Danish and other weak-minded countries. Mind you though, when that happens we will have wiped out all the rotten elements such as the sick, infirm, Romany's, non Aryans and especially every nigger and Jew of the world." she stated with relish, as she held out her empty glass for yet another measure of wine.

"So it seems that you are in a very privileged position to decide as to just who will run the show, no matter how that person has shown loyalty to our leader."

"Yes dear Lucky! But make sure you keep yourself 100% loyal to our exalted leaders, then nothing, will befall you." She giggled, as she showed him her curved dagger that has already cut the life from many a hapless man.

Luchens did the honours again and offered a small toast to their success

"Here's to our successful conclusion of my mission dear Lenka!" he said as the clinked glasses once more.

"It's time now that I must leave you dear Lenka. Mustn't run behind schedule and all that." Luchens said after a little while, checking the time from the grandfather clock standing in a recess of the room.

"Yes Lucky! I'll probably meet you further down the line, whatever you do. So make it the right way, otherwise!" Wintermann said, winking at him and patting the sheathed dagger.

"Providing you play your cards right all will be well!" she giggled as Luchens offered her yet another glass of wine, but was refused by her.

Luchens drained his glass and wiped his face with a silk serviette and started to leave.

The two walked arm in arm slowly out of the big house to find an awaiting truck in front of them.

"That must be my next load. Better make sure there's the right number of boxes and men on guard. We can't be too careful." Luchens said as he held up Wintermann's hand and kissed it bidding her farewell. She stood waving at the disappearing lorry before she went back to complete her work.

* * *

The lorry arrived alongside the barge and was surrounded by the heavily armed men.

Luchens climbed out of the cabin of the lorry and directed the men to get the boxes on board as quickly and as quietly as possible, to prevent any discovery of what they were doing.

"Kretshmer. Its midnight, where is the skipper?" Luchens whispered, looking around the after end of the barge.

"I'm right here, with my gun ready to repel boarders. Where else do you think I'd be Major?" the skipper said softly, appearing out of the darkness, and poked his navy colt in Luchens ear.

The cold steel of the gun made Luchens flinch before he went to grab his luger.

"Easy Major. You don't want to shoot yourself in the foot with that toy pistol. I'm fully loaded and ready when you are. Next time you disappear make certain you arrive when you should do. That way you don't get another loaded revolver in your ear!"

Luchens turned brushed the weapon away from his head.

"Just get this barge moving skipper!" he hissed, signing his piece of paper of receipt for the lorry driver.

Both the lorry and the barge melted back into the night again, going their separate ways.

The barge carried on its lonely way up the river until dawn, when the skipper pulled alongside a stone jetty, and tied his barge beside an empty one.

"Cook. Time to get breakfast on the go, but I'm going ashore to for a while. Tell the Major the warehouse has a washing facility for the men to use, only they'd better be quick before the down traffic arrive here shortly."

"You're not going anywhere skipper. You will remain with the rest of us, so I can keep this operation under wraps." Luchens said sleepily, as he arrived on deck.

"Major, your secret trip is not really a secret. For as long as I'm master on this barge, where it goes so do I, and vice versa. This is one of my resting-places, and if I should pass it without any reasonable excuse, then people will start getting suspicious about my health or whatever. Better let me take a stroll and say good morning to the local postmaster and his missus. They've got a pedigree Labrador I gave them as a pup, so I always call by and say hello to them and the dog." the skipper said holding up a large bone, and a couple of freshly caught fish.

Luchens looked with astonishment at the skipper, at his logic and his devil-may-care attitude, and let the man wander off without any further challenge from him.

"Well, be back in one hour!" Luchens shouted after the departing figure.

"Sergeant! Get the men over to that warehouse and take a shower. After breakfast they can see to their weapons and tidy up their living space. Cook, have breakfast for us all in twenty minutes!" Luchens ordered, as he went below again.

The skipper arrived within the hour, carrying the local newspapers and a small hamper.

"Here are yet more glorious victories our fighting men have won, I don't think!" he snorted, handing Luchens the papers.

"If you believe all that the papers say then you're a fool Major!" he added, as Luchens was cooing and marvelling at the crushing victories the German forces were still enjoying.

"You had better start believing it skipper, or I'll have you shot as a traitor."

"I'll only believe it when I see it. Besides, unless you are totally stupid and can't count beyond single figures, then tell me. How come the entire British Navy was sunk last year, yet the papers state that it has been sunk yet again somewhere else later on? The British Navy are worth more than those petty lies!" the skipper scoffed.

"It appears that you need to be re-enlightened Herr skipper. That usually takes the form of special treatment at the hands of the GESTAPO, and a certain Fraulein that I happen to know."

"Pah! If the might of the British Navy couldn't scupper me, what chance have you brown shirt brigade boys got!" the skipper replied and started to eat a large piece of cake that he took out of the hamper.

Luchens just sighed and let the incident go, vowing to get the skipper fixed before he was finished with him.

"Kretshmer! Get the men below and ready for sailing again. We still have a long way to go." Luchens said with full venom in his voice.

Chapter IV
King Canute

The next few days of quietly sailing up the magnificently scenic river, had begun to become painfully monotonous and slow for Luchens and his men, when the craft finally arrived at its next point and yet another change of plans.

"You will stop here for two hours skipper, as I've got a r/v to make ashore. Pull up in this creek so as to keep us from prying eyes." Luchens sighed with total lack of enthusiasm.

"I'll secure my vessel where I always do. I know these waters better than most, and if I do what you ask, we'd be stuck high and dry after a few minutes. That creek is only an overflow and only weekend sailors use it for their craft." the skipper said quietly, steering his vessel to where he had previously pointed.

But Luchens had got tired of the skipper countermanding his every word these last few days and cursing vehemently, he drew his pistol out and pointed it at the skipper.

"You do exactly what I tell you. Unless you pull into that creek I will shoot you here and now!" he shouted.

The skipper simply shrugged his shoulders and turned the vessel to where Luchens demanded they go. The vessel chugged slowly alongside a wooden jetty and was tied up to it before Luchens re-holstered his pistol and jumped ashore.

"Kretshmer! Get the men organised into a defensive position in case we have unwelcome guests. We mustn't be seen or boarded by anybody. I'll be back within the hour." Luchens ordered swiftly, then disappearing among the trees and bushes that lined the creek.

"Skipper! You have pushed the Major too far now, I won't be surprised if he has you shot before we leave this place." Kretshmer said, shaking his head disapprovingly, before mustering his men.

"Right you two. Get over there with your heavy machine gun. You two stay down in the cargo hold. Corporal Lutz, take two men and keep a lookout at the entrance to this creek. Any vessel coming towards us let me know. Skipper, get your men doing whatever they are supposed to do alongside a jetty!" Kretshmer ordered.

"That will be a very hard thing to do Sergeant. I normally tie up over yonder and have a few beers with whoever is around. Mix with the other bargees and generally take note of what cargo I can swap with and the like. I have already been spotted coming into this creek and I'm expecting a few visitors and questions as to why I came into this place." The skipper advised quietly, whilst smoking his pipe.

"Be that as it may, but we can't move now until the Major arrives."

"Lets see how he manages when he does comes back then." the skipper replied knowingly and went below into the crews cabin.

Luchens did come back with the hour and ordered the men back onto the barge.

"Right you scum of a skipper. Get this wreck of a barge of yours out of this creek and back into the river again. You've already taken longer to get here than was planned, and we've got a detour and must be at Rheisfeld to hand over our cargo. Then it's back again and into the canal that's only a few kilometres up from here." Luchens hissed as he pointed his luger at him.

The skipper looked at this weedy person and at the pistol pointing to him and started to laugh almost uncontrollably.

Kretshmer came running aft to see what the commotion was. "What the bloody hell is he laughing for? Has he gone stark raving mad? I want to shoot him as a traitor but we've nobody to take us any further." Luchens whispered.

Kretshmer grabbed hold of the skipper and thumped him so hard that he fell down into the wheelhouse.

When the skipper got up again and rubbed his chin, he grabbed Luchens by the scruff of the neck and by the seat of his trousers and threw him effortlessly into the deep mud that was now the creek, saying.

"If you're so bloody clever Luchens, start digging a channel to get us out. Better get some water under us first, you stupid bastard. I'm going ashore for a few beers, let me know when we can float off again."

Kretshmer looked over the side of the barge and saw that the water from the creek had gone, and that Luchens was almost up to his knees in slimy mud.

Luchens was beside himself with terror, and screamed for the men to get him out of the mud.

The men finally dragged the mud-caked major back onto the barge and hosed him down to get rid of the stinking mud, and vowing to shoot the skipper when he came back.

"This is all your fault Kretshmer. You should have told me this creek was only a sluice. If we're late again for our next r/v point then it's your balls the Gestapo will be cutting off not mine." he snarled angrily.

Kretshmer grabbed hold of Luchens and threw him back into the mud again, shouting,

"You're a fucking asshole, Major. The skipper told you, but you decided you knew better. Get yourself out of your own mess!"

It was dark when the skipper and his crew arrived back onto the barge, and as the creek started filling up again. The soldiers were sitting around waiting for their return and cheered them before they lined up and asked for the cook to feed them.

Luchens was to be found huddled in a blanket, coughing and wheezing and warming himself by the stove when the skipper came down into the cabin.

"Well if it ain't King Canute! Found a new way of getting a twenty-ton barge out of a muddy creek yet? And here's me thinking you knew all about the river and bargeman ship. Still I have to hand it to you, your complexion is much prettier now that you've washed all that mud off."

"I will have you shot when we get to the other end, that's a promise. Now just get this craft moving. We have our orders. It should take you about five days providing you get that bloody engine going properly." Luchens said during a bout of sniffling and coughing.

"That's where you're wrong yet again, and I still don't understand how you rose up to the dizzy heights of a Major. If we've got to go down that canal system, although it is a deep one, it has a speed restriction of four knots, and I'm over half its width. If we meet any similar vessel coming towards us, we'll have to back off to the next passing point, and even then we'd be down to a passing speed of just two knots. Therefore Major, you can add an extra day at least to your plans."

"You're out to deliberately sabotage my mission, by your delays and other excuses." Luchens hissed, reaching for his pistol again.

The skipper sneered at this gesture and turning his back, went to go up the steps to the wheelhouse.

"Stand still you traitor!" Luchens snarled, cocking his pistol ready to fire.

The skipper turned round calmly and levelled a brass cannon at Luchens whispering.

"This is an old naval cannon that I use to repel boarders and pirates and other scum of the earth that dare to come aboard my vessel. You had better put that pistol down before I use it to blow your head off, and heavens know why I haven't done so before now, you miserable excuse of an officer. You will need me more on that canal and the other adjoining rivers, than at any other time so far. I'm not fussed one way or the other, but what's it to be Major? Me blow your head off or you being smart and staying alive to fulfil this mission of yours?"

Luchens licked his lips nervously and decided to lower his pistol in a feint to put the skipper off guard and then shoot him when his back was turned.

The skipper lashed out with his wooden leg and knocked the luger from Luchens hand, as it flew across the cabin and landed under the steps where the skipper was standing.

"Now we can get somewhere. I care naught for you, but as far as I'm concerned I too have a pride in what I do, and that is to get your ungrateful, snivelling arsehole to wherever you are going, whether I like it or not. I know exactly where you are going and I know exactly what's in those crates. And if I know, so do several other interested parties just waiting their chance to relieve you of them. That canal is known for its river pirates and bandits, that's the reason why I've got this cannon. They've tried it on a few times and have come off the worse, they don't like my cannon they don't. But just maybe, you as some sort of an officer, and the fighting men in my cargo hold, might be able to give them enough of a surprise to put them out of action for a few months. And again, just maybe, we poor bargees can enjoy a peaceful transit for once."

Luchens rubbed his sore hand where the skipper kicked him, and listened intently at what he was told.

"How do they know what's on board, unless you've blabbed off in the local beer halls?"

The skipper sighed and put his cannon down.

"It doesn't matter what we've got on board. But just to enlighten somebody who thinks he's God's gift to the human race, let me tell you this. The pirates always demand a toll or 'river tax' as they like to call it. Every bargee has to give some if not all of his cargo to them otherwise they will be killed.

Apart from me, the last bargee who managed to get through found when he got back to his home wharf again, his missus and daughter raped and the home ransacked. So Major, unless you know who they are or where they will attack, then you need every gun on board ready for them, including me and my old cannon."

"Very well skipper. Just get this barge moving and try to make up some lost time. We have taken over eight days to get this far. And we've only got another five to reach Chalons with two pick ups on the way." Luchens agreed with great reluctance, conceding the skipper's logic.

"Just so that we understand one another Major, I trust you as far as I can throw this barge of mine. My own men will man this end of the barge so I want you up front with your men where I can keep my eye on you. That way Major, I won't have a miserable luger bullet in my back." the skipper replied with venom, taking hold of his cannon again as if to underline his total dominance.

Luchens looked at the menacing weapon and nodding meekly in agreement, sat back down on his bunk still nursing his sore hand.

"Good, that's settled then. I suggest you get yourself fed and a suitable change of clothes for night time engagements of the enemy kind." the skipper concluded and climbed out of the cabin, shutting the door behind him.

Kretshmer came into the wheelhouse and asked if all was well, before he was told about the trouble that was waiting for them, after they went along the canal.

"I have my bows specially re-inforced, that I use for ramming their craft, just like the Phoenicians and their Tri-reems. I also have this cannon that I introduced the major to, and a twin barrelled Spandau machine gun hidden under the tarpaulins by the for'ard capstan. But they don't know you're on board, so maybe your men will give them something to think about, and even put them out of business for a long time."

"We are only half a platoon of men but we are capable of taking on a whole company. That is, as long as the Major leaves the tactics to me."

"Speaking of which, make sure he is up with you with his pistol in his hand, and pointing it at them and not me. I'm the only one that knows their tricks and hideouts, so if he shoots me then you lot will be in dead trouble with your mission controllers."

"Don't you worry skipper, I have just the place for him, you just watch." Kretshmer smiled in offering his assurances to the skipper.

"We have a detour to the Swiss border. Luchens is to hand over the boxes to their guards for onward placement in Zurich, thank god. Maybe we can get to somewhere where there is some real soldiering rather than riding shot gun to these boxes."

"Yes Kretshmer. They're full of Jew gold. So called because it is taken from our erstwhile Jewish countrymen before they somehow disappear into thin air. Maybe that's the Corporals way of paying for his little escapades in France and other places."

"That's not my concern skipper, and I'd advise you to train your tongue not to speak of such things, or Luchens will definitely have you shot or emasculated just like my men."

"I'm too old for all this caper. I'm only a bargee trying to earn a decent living from the river, that's all." the skipper said stoically and manoeuvred his barge back into the river again.

The short detour that took them further up river went without a hitch and they arrived at a small creek that was fenced off with reels of rusty barbed wire.

"Here we are skipper. I'll have the wire removed for you to enter the creek. It's No Mans Land between us and the Swiss, and just the place for our transfer." Luchens said with a grin, waving to a plain clothed man standing on the wooden jetty the barge was heading for.

"Morning Mr Klinschaff! Waiting long?" Luchens asked politely in his best Swiss language.

"Morning Herr Luchens. You are a day late. How many boxes have you brought?"

"I have exactly 150 boxes."

"150? My orders say that I only get 140."

"I know! It was a change of orders. Just give me my receipt for the 140 and let me send my signal before I leave."

"Very good Luchens. Have your men unload the boxes onto the jetty. My men will load them onto the lorries."

Luchens had the men stack the heavy crates neatly in big columns, which they did as if the boxes were empty.

The Swiss guards grunted and sweated and had to carry one between two of them to load them onto the trucks. Luchens saw the obvious dilemma and delay and ordered his men to help out.

"You do not set one foot off the jetty. If you do, you will be arrested and interred until the rest of your hostilities have stopped." Klinschaff shouted, and waved his hand above his head.

Before Luchens or the rest of the men could blink an eye, several machine guns were pointed at them.

"You must respect our neutrality Luchens. These border guards have orders to shoot anybody trying to enter the country without express permission or notice."

Kretshmer calmed his uneasy men down and ordered them to finish their work quietly before he had them back on board the barge again.

Luchens got his receipt and sent his message off before waving goodbye to Klinshcaff, and his still grunting and groaning men who were trying to load the heavy boxes onto the back of their trucks.

"Skipper. We still have 10 boxes to deliver. But we'll be collecting a further fifty on our way, lets get going." Luchens ordered, folding his order papers up and stuffed them into his coat again.

"We have to stop off at the village of Krozengin for me to get my fuel and supplies. I also have to report to the Canal master so that he can have my vessel registered and accepted through the canal lock systems. I have twenty sacks of grain to pick up and take to Becoux, so your ten boxes can be hidden under them for a while."

"How long will it take you to do this?"

"About four hours. I must obey the law of the land too, war or no war, Major."

"Very well. If there is a quiet discreet spot for my men to get off and relax for a while then let's go."

"Yes Major. There's a very good bierkeller nearby, but I'd need a couple of your men to help load up the fuel and other provisions, including a few rounds for my empty cannon."

Luchens swore loudly when he realised that the skipper had tricked him with his empty cannon, making Kretshmer chuckle.

"You see what I mean Sergeant!" the skipper said with a smile and a wink, as he steered the barge down the fast flowing river.

The barge glided down the river, until they reached the canal turn off, when the skipper started his engine again and steered it to one of his regular stop off places.

"Luchens. This is it, so enjoy a couple of hours whilst I get my business sorted. There's a local garrison just down the road if you want to do yours. I'll be back in two hours with the provisions first, then move up lock to get my fuel and authorisation papers."

Luchens in turn, told Kretshmer that he was going ashore to the garrison the men were to stay out of sight until he came back. And that only when it got dark, were the men to be allowed ashore to sample the local beers.

Kretshmer had the men fed and gave them some money each to spend in the bier keller.

"This will be deducted from your pay when we reach the other end. Remember, stay together and pretend to be part of the local garrison. No fighting or you'll end up like poor Pfaltz!"

Kretshmer was a car mechanic before the war, and during the passage upriver, had struck up a friendship with the barge's engineer, who was trying to repair a faulty gasket. As there were only the two of them on board now, both men relaxed and worked together to fix the engine.

"She's an old Werkenspall two stroke, Sergeant. We were supposed to have it overhauled last month before we came up here.

Unless we get it working properly, and as I haven't got the proper material to use as for the head gasket, we won't be going anywhere. Mind you, I noticed you have rubber oilskins in with your kit, any chance of using one?"

"We most certainly can. Here, have the majors. It also has a soft doe-skin inner lining that we could use too." Kretshmer said, taking out his commando knife and slashed the coat into the shape that was needed.

The engineer smiled at the sheer vandalism of such a fine coat, rubbing his greasy hands over the material. It didn't take them long to do the repair and have the engine tested before they were satisfied enough to go up on deck and have a brew up.

The skipper arrived back driving a horse and cart full of provisions.

"There's enough there to feed an army!" the skipper said, jumping down off the cart.

"Isn't it just skipper, a platoon of men anyway!" Kretshmer laughed, and helped to offload the cart.

"Where did you get the transport skipper? Somebody coming back for the animal?" Kretshmer asked politely as the last of the provisions got stowed away.

"No Sergeant. The horse will make its own way back home, it knows the way blindfolded!" The skipper responded, feeding the horse an apple and a sugar lump before he turned it round and patted its rump for it to trot away.

The horse and cart had no sooner disappeared before the men started to filter back from their little forage into the bier keller. Kretshmer looked at them walking back and spotted that one of their men was missing.

"Where is Becker?" he demanded, as the last man passed over the small gangway.

"He's gone. We all looked for him but couldn't find him anywhere, Sergeant!" some of them said in unison.

Kretshmer swore and cursed the men before he detailed four of them to come with him as he led them ashore to look for the missing man. Kretshmer and his men crept around the buildings like ghosts, searching and looking in every nook and cranny, but to no avail. He quietly signalled the men to return back as he saw Luchens walking purposefully along the footpath, blissfully unaware of what was going on around him.

Luchens walked over the gangway, humming to himself.

"Skipper, time for us to get onto the canal system."

"About time too! What took you so long? We've been loaded up with provisions for ages now and must get upstream before the down convoy arrives." the skipper said with annoyance but gave Kretshmer a crafty wink.

"I'm picking up my fuel on the other side of the lock, and my grain a few kilometres further along the canal." he volunteered.

"That's okay skipper, we're already overdue at our final destination. In the meantime, I've been briefed on the perils of this canal, and you will find my men very handy on this trip." Luchens smiled uncharacteristically towards the skipper.

The skipper noted the change of attitude and guessed that someone had serviced him for once, but kept it to himself to muse upon during the long lonely small hours of the morning, steering a silent barge along a silent canal.

They arrived at the small fuelling jetty, where the skipper had some of the soldiers carry a couple of oil drums on board and lashed down for immediate use.

Whilst the fuel was embarked, they had to wait until morning before the grain arrived in a much smaller barge.

"Morning Verner! How is the canal upstream?" the skipper asked casually as another barge floated past them.

"The water tax men are out in force, took half my cargo they did, so be careful." the bargee said glumly.

"Well, they'll have a tough time getting any more." the skipper said, brandishing his brass cannon.

"Be careful, as they've got hold of a few machine guns from somewhere. Must be going as I'm due downstream before now."

"Thanks for the warning." The skipper said and waved the other bargee goodbye.

Chapter V
Boulder Alley

"Hello skipper! Didn't recognise your vessel, new paint work?" an arriving bargee asked.

The skipper replied courteously to the Frenchman in the same language, as they exchanged bottles of wine.

"Yes! Had a special cargo on board last week, from Rotterdam to Basel. A heavy load, but it will pay for my hull repairs and refurbishment to my engine."

"Sounds good. You're lucky you've got a good cargo hold. Are you picking up cargo on your way across? Maybe go all the way to Chalon?"

"Don't know! It all depends on what I can pick up! If not, then I'll turn around on the Lac du Pont and head back again. Cologne is looking for small barges to send up the Ems canal system, if you're interested."

The two bargees talked shop for a little while longer as the deck hands transferred the grain sacks onto the bigger barge. Once the transfer was completed they waved each other goodbye and went their separate ways again.

Luchens was sitting on the cabin stairway listening to this conversation, but had to wait until the barge was clear from the wharf and any other prying eyes that lurking behind the curtains of the houses that flanked that part of the canal.

"Didn't know you spoke fluent French, skipper. I was available in case you had problems. Anyway, we have a man missing and I just have the feeling he'll turn up with some of his friends to highjack us. So be extra vigilant in case he shows up." Luchens commanded.

"There's a lot more you don't know about me and that's the way I like it. Your man is probably long gone from this country, so I won't expect him. In any case, we're all right for another ten kilometres yet Major.

If you keep your head down just below my steering wheel,

and look out ahead of us, I will show you what to look out for.

You will then tell your men as they come up for a smoke. But relax for now and get me a coffee from the stove if you would." the skipper replied with a grin, holding out a large empty mug.

"Very well skipper, coffee it is." Luchens agreed amiably, before going down the steps to get the coffee.

Kretshmer arrived into the wheelhouse with his machine gun and sat down beside skipper.

"You certainly know how to court danger skipper, but just watch him as he's a very dangerous man to have hanging around you."

"Him? That pile of boils! Just how the hell did he make officer material? Now you I understand and can parley with, but he's a totally different can of worms."

"It appears that our Major has had a very lucky escape from the infamous eunuch maker, Fraulein Wintermann from what he has told me, it appears that somebody is sabotaging our mission and he was literally hauled by the goolies to account of some gold we supposed we've had delivered back there on the Swiss border, but in fact were lumps of iron. Somebody somewhere must have switched the boxes over and he thinks that you and your crew might just be the prime suspects. He doesn't know it, but I already know that the Reich Police General Gueller is your guarantor and your passport to safety, which lets you off the hook. But a few more eunochs will be made by Frau Wintermann by the time she is finished, I'll warrant."

"How you know of such things I will never know. But my gamble is that that asshole of a so-called major doesn't know. If anything should happen to me during this trip then the asshole will literally be in shit-street."

"So how come you know the Reich's chief of Police then, skipper?"

"Simple dear Kretshmer. He and I were on a certain battleship in 1918.

Instead of surrendering our entire battle fleet and the rest of our heavy naval vessels to the British, we both secretly arranged the scuttling of them, right in the middle of their anchorage and right under the noses of the British Admiralty. Our action had created such a furore and embarrassment for the British Navy and their Admiralty in that we achieved more success in scuppering more of their admirals and staff than we could have done at battle stations at sea. We managed to survive the sinking and got taken ashore by the British sailors.

That was our 'after dinner' speeches for quite a while until a stupid jumped up paper hanger decided to declare himself undisputed Corporal of the New Third Reich!"

"Yes, well you'd better keep your opinions to yourself skipper, else our friend Luchens will put a bullet in both our heads if he hears any more antisocialism."

The skipper looked at the sergeant and smiled slowly as he drew on his smokestack of a pipe.

"Indeed Sergeant. You have the makings of a good leader once all this stupidity is over and if you survive. The last war was a waste of good men on both sides of the wire, especially when nothing was ever gained by either side. The only people making a decent living out of all that lot were the local undertakers. Lets hope for our sake we win this one even though we are doing so at the moment. Watch out for those Yanks, though. They're all mouth and trousers, but they more than make up for it by their limitless manpower and equipment. That was what done it for us last time, at least." the skipper said slowly, tapping out the ashes from his pipe before recharging it with new tobacco.

"Thanks for the history lesson skipper. Like you, I too have misgivings just like my father had explained. However, I have a job to do no matter what the devil gets up to." Kretshmer concluded, then got up and strolled over the cargo deck coverings.

* * *

The barge made its slow but sure way along the almost still waters of the canal, as the kilometres of open countryside slid by like an ever-changing painting.

These were idyllic times for the bargemen and their trade, as they enjoyed a quiet time in transiting from one river system to another via the canal networks that was to make up for the hustle and bustle of the busy waterways that normally surround large cities and the industrial urban sprawl.

"Major. We are about to enter a known trouble area. Do you see that bend in the canal flanked by cliffs either side of it?" the skipper asked, and offered Luchens his binoculars to look through.

Luchens had a good look before handing them back.

"Seems perfectly normal to me. Looks peaceful enough anyway. So what's the problem?"

"This is exactly the reason why I am still here. There is a shoal on one side of that bend in front of us, which means that we have to go close to the cliff on the other side. That's where we can expect a load of boulders to come our way. The plan is not to sink us, but to force us to turn and run aground on the shoal area of the opposite bank. Now that's where we'd meet several gun-toting pirates looking to help themselves to our cargo.

If they fail in driving me aground, they have another ambush place a few kilometres further along where you'd also least expect them. They still don't know its me otherwise they'd normally let me through without hindrance, only to let me go onto a totally different set of thieves they know who are also waiting for more fat pickings."

Luchens looked at the skipper for a moment then decided to get Kretshmer and his men ready for a welcoming party.

"I'll see to the men Major. But I need you in the bow compartment to man the machine gun. You will be responsible to check any forward movement onto the vessel from the intruders. Keep hidden and listen to my 'Open fire' signal." Kretshmer nodded, directing the others to similar positions around the vessel.

Luchens merely nodded and went swiftly towards the bow hatchway, as the other men scampered to their designated defence positions.

The skipper managed to exchange a glance with Kretshmer and nodded his approval at the cunning way he handled the major, then got his own weapons ready for action.

"Sergeant!" the skipper called softly.

"We'll be on the bend in about five minutes. This place is called 'Boulder alley'. So make sure your men are covered over, or the bandits on the cliff top will see them.

There will be lots of waterspouts but none of the rocks are designed to hit us. But should one hit, nobody is to cry out until I pretend to make for the shoals. I will give you the word to commence firing when I'm clear of the hazards."

"You've got it skipper!" Kretshmer replied as he went round the men informing them of the skipper's orders, before he came back and took up his own position.

The barge rounded the bend, coming very close to the 50foot cliff, leaving the shallow water as far to port as possible. Within moments, a hail of heavy boulders came crashing down around the barge, creating large columns of water all around it.

The skipper pretended to be alarmed and turned his rudder over so that the barge moved towards the shallow side, before quickly turning the rudder and had the vessel return back into the deeper water again.

Just as he had done that, several men rushed into the water firing guns at the vessel and shouting for the skipper to stop immediately else he'd get killed.

The skipper gave his signal to Kretshmer who shouted his own command for his men to commence firing.

The bandits were taken by total surprise and were slaughtered in a hail of machine gun fire. Even the men on the cliff-top were shot to pieces and fell like rain into the canal, turning the blue-green waters into crimson. When Kretshmer was satisfied he had them all, he called the cease-fire.

"Skipper. Stop the barge for us to gather up the dead men and hide them somewhere.

We used silencers on our weapons, so nobody further up could hear us. If there are others then they'll assume that this bunch had been successful in raiding us. The only fly in the ointment is that arsehole with the vintage machine gun in the bow compartment. He made enough noise to waken the dead with it." Kretshmer said quietly, as he looked around to see that his men were okay.

"Not to worry about the noise. These idiots were using old cannons and weapons, but any new weaponry heard by the next lot would have tipped them off. So the arsehole of a major has done something good for a change." the skipper said with a grin, as he steered his vessel back into the main channel of water again.

The skipper brought them to a wooded area of the canal that was used as a passing point, with a natural toilet area for the bargemen.

"We can stop here for a couple of hours to have dinner and let the men stretch their legs, Major. It is a good time for latrine functions too."

"Very thoughtful of you skipper, but we must be pressing on, as I have to be checking in at our next r/v by nightfall."

"Remember me telling you about passing points and possible delays? Well this is one of them. See that smoke over there to the right of that small wood next to the cornfield? Well that's a barge coming our way and negotiating a series of bends. Rules of the canal mean that he has right of way even though he will take about forty minutes to reach this point."

Luchens looked over and saw the faint wisp of smoke from the direction the skipper pointed to, and shrugged his shoulders.

"Very well skipper. But we move off as soon as it passes us, agreed?"

The skipper nodded his agreement and shouted to the cook to get the dinner on the go.

The Lost Legion

Kretshmer had his men ashore making good use of the time and had them fed and back on board again before the oncoming barge reached them.

The passing bargee shouted over that there were two more barges about fifteen minutes behind him, and he was going to wait here until they caught up before going in convoy through Boulder Alley.

The skipper told him that there were no signs of the bandits at Boulder Alley, but look out for some fresh boulders and rocks in midstream anyway.

The bargee thanked the skipper and stated that he decided to carry on, but asked that he tell the others the same.

Luchens was starting to curse and get angry at these slow moving barges that were now coming into view from the river bends.

"No good losing your temper Major. Once I get into this section, anybody else will have to go astern until the next passing point some three kilometres at the other end from here. They have their schedules to keep too you know. Besides, did you see the mess on the lead barge? Bullet holes everywhere, and judging by his load, I'd say he's a good twenty sacks of coal lighter than he should be."

Kretshmer nodded at the mention of bullet holes in the wooden barge, and also pointed to the same state of the other smaller barges that passed them.

The skipper exchanged greetings and information with these bargees as they passed by, who were more cheerful at the news of a clear passage through the Boulder Alley.

"Time we went, skipper. This is only day two on the canal and I have a load to pick up by nightfall." Luchens urged, going below into the crew's cabin.

Chapter VI
The Eunuch Maker

"**S**ergeant! Surround the lorry and disarm the guards. I want them all lined up and the Officer in charge to come with me. But let them unload the boxes off the lorry and get them opened for my inspection first. Make sure you have a defensive cordon around the jetty in case we have uninvited guests. Skipper, have your men armed and keep a watch out for any approaching river craft. Shoot anybody that approaches too closely." Luchens ordered, as the lorry arrived with the next consignment of boxes.

The lorry guards unloaded the boxes quickly and were surprised to find themselves surrounded and relieved of their weapons.

"Captain! You will open each box for me to inspect the contents. If I find anything not correct you will be shot." Luchens said coldly, pointing his pistol at the officer.

"I do not understand Major! What is it you're looking for that I am not supposed to have?" the captain asked in total surprise and nonplussed.

"Just do as you're told Captain!" Luchens growled, and handed over a crowbar and pointed to the pile of boxes.

Luchens inspected each box until he was satisfied before he had the lorry guards re-seal the boxes again and loaded onto the barge.

"Just as well for you all is in order, Captain. You would have been shot by me or had your balls removed by Frau Wintermann."

The captain looked at Luchens with alarm and asked with a stammer, "Frau Wintermann the eunuch maker?"

"Yes the very one. If any of the boxes were found not correct in their contents as stated on your manifesto sheet, then she would have been your next visitor. But instead, I would have shot you and all your men, if only to put you out of your misery." Luchens stated, re-holstering his pistol.

The Lost Legion

"Here is your receipt for the boxes Captain. You and your men can go now, but go quietly as there are bandits in the area."

"Thank you Major." the captain said gratefully, ordering his men back into the lorry and left.

"Sergeant. Feed the men before you get them below again. We will be moving off very soon." Luchens ordered, walking across the barge gangway to see the skipper.

"Skipper, we have to move off within the hour. If you need fuel and water, better get it now, I'll have some of the men to help you."

"We need fresh provisions too, Major. But we can get that in the morning when we arrive at the first set of locks. Meanwhile, there's some suspicious movement in those on the opposite bank. I thought I saw two men spying on us from that clump of bushes. I don't think they saw you and your men though. But I suggest you have a couple of men armed and ready in case they decide to try their luck with me." the skipper said, pointing to the area, and handed his binoculars over for Luchens to see for himself.

Luchens looked intently for a moment.

"Sergeant! Get some of the men on guard around the barge, but do it quietly and discreetly, we appear to have nosey neighbours." Luchens whispered to Kretshmer who was standing by him.

"Corporal Lutz! Get a mortar loaded and stood by. Then get a man up front with the machine gun and have four men with silenced weapons along each side of the barge. But keep out of sight and do it quietly." Kretshmer whispered to his men before coming back to the crew's cabin again.

The skipper had the empty fuel drums and water barrels off the barge and replaced with full ones, then returned to the barge to sail again.

"Any sign of our nosey neighbours Major?"

"No skipper. Just as well, as he or they would walk right into our little trap." Luchens replied, nodding his head towards the waiting soldiers.

"That means that we've been given the once over for them to size up their next move. Their next two ideal spots for an ambush are about two hours and a further five hours from here. Beyond that there is the first system of locks that they control, and incidentally is where we'll be getting our next lot of fresh provisions.

I normally trade a barrel of wine for my supplies, but perhaps it's going to be a few pounds of Krupp lead this time."

"As it's night time, can you speed up a bit to make the lock by daybreak?"

"Yes for the first part, and no for the second. We'd arrive at the locks an hour or so before we're due, so there wouldn't be anybody to operate the system for us."

"How many times have you gone through this canal system skipper?"

"Quite a few, but only as far as the lake. But from what I gather, they've upgraded the lock systems."

"Yes, that might be so skipper. But surely, a man with your experience and knowledge, can't you operate the locks yourself?"

The skipper sucked on his pipe for a moment before giving his reply:

"I have the know-how and experience to do just that. But then, had you had your way the other day, you would have shot me without a thought as to how you would get up the waterway safely. True?"

It was Luchens turn to think for an answer.

"That's very true skipper. But this trip is not over yet, and I may do so anyway. So I think you'd better do as you're told just for once."

"It's no good threatening me Major. I have a sick engine below us that might just pack in for good, at any time. Ask your Sergeant if you don't believe me, as he's been kind enough to help my engineer to nurse it up to now."

Luchens cursed and muttered to himself and called for Kretshmer.

"Sergeant! The skipper tells me that you've been helping the engineer to keep his engine going. Is this true?"

Kretshmer looked puzzled at this question coming out of the blue.

"Yes that is correct! It's an old..." Kretschmer started but was shouted down by Luchens.

"All right, I get the picture. You can go now Sergeant and dismiss the men. I want them ready for combat in about two hours from now."

Kretshmer shrugged his shoulders and left as ordered.

The skipper was humming to himself and looking straight ahead as he steered the barge along the narrow canal.

"Major, I need a man up in the bow with a pole to fend us off in case we move too close to the canal bank. And a man on the stern to keep a watch out for any sneaky river craft trying to come up on us."

"Pah! That's all I get from you, skipper. I want this, or I need that. Its' about time your men earned their living now, so get them to do it." Luchens exploded vehemently.

The skipper looked at Luchens and shook his head slowly.

"Very well Major if that's the way if it. Cook! Bring up the men's supper and ditch it overboard. Then stay aft and keep a look out. Engines! Come up on deck and get a pole up onto the bows in case we run aground. If the engine stops just leave it." He commanded.

Luchens looked at the cook throwing the food over the side and as the engineer came up from his little engine room, the engine failed and stopped.

"Engines. Just get forward with a barge pole and fend us off gently when we hit the bank." the skipper said softly as Luchens started to rant and rave at him.

Luchens took out his revolver and held it to the skipper's head and swore at him.

"I knew all along it! It is you who is trying to sabotage my operational mission. You have three seconds to get your men back to where they belong." he snarled, as great globules of saliva dribbled down his chin.

"Major! You can shoot me now if you like. But I was only obeying the specific orders you had just given me." the skipper said quietly, whilst manoeuvring his vessel neatly alongside the canal bank where it stopped.

"Go on then Major shoot me! I obeyed your orders, so go on. Come on man what's keeping you?" the skipper goaded.

Kretshmer had arrived on the scene and observed all what went on. He prodded his machine gun hard into Luchens back and whispered.

"His orders come direct from the Reich's Police, General Gueller. If you harm him in anyway, or he fails to complete his side of this mission then you had better kiss your bollocks goodbye now. So just put your weapon away and get hold of yourself Major. He's been around long enough to know to always obey the last order. As it was you that gave the last order, all he was doing was to carry out those orders. Now unless you get your brain back into order, we'll all end up dead." Kreshmer hissed.

Luchens felt the cold steel ram into his back and turned swiftly to see Kretshmer behind him, and gasped out the name of Gueller.

"But how does the general know of my mission? How is the skipper involved with the general? Why wasn't I told of these things?" Luchens ranted.

"In the big scheme of things, you are just one little insignificant jumped up pen-pusher, with no particular value to the Reich. Therefore you got the job of cruising along the continental waterways on a mission that was doomed to failure had not the skipper volunteered his services. It's thanks to him we've got this far, and probably will be thanks to him again that we arrive at our destination on the Mediterranean coast. My job is to see that our skipper completes his mission that far, and for you to reach your destination." Kretshmer said with a whisper.

Luchens looked at his gun for a moment before he finally handed it to Kretshmer.

"Nobody tells me anything. As far as I was concerned, the skipper was one of the saboteurs of my mission whom I had every right to shoot. Now it looks as if you're the real one in charge, not me." he said petulantly.

"All your duty and total concern is, to make sure that we get all the boxes with the correct filling in them, and get them delivered within the time schedules. We know there is a conspiracy, so if the contents of the boxes don't add up to the value of each consignment, then as each consignment is taken on board, we can pin-point to just who has been helping themselves. As stated, and as you've already had a Frau Wintermann experience, you know the consequences if you are found to be one of the conspirators or prevent the operation reaching its proper conclusion. The other side of the coin is that if we succeed in a triumphant fashion, then there'll be promotions and medals all round. This is the last time I shall speak of this Major, so you had better buck your ideas up and be more conducive to the well-being of the rest of my men."

Luchens stood mesmerised at Kretshmer and shook his head in disbelief at the thought of a mere Sergeant lecturing a Major of the SS.

The skipper called the cook and engineer back to resume their duties, saying sarcastically to Luchens.

"I was looking forward to our beef and wine casserole too. Shame it got ditched, Sergeant. It looks as if the men will have to starve tonight until I get fresh provisions at the lock house in the morning.

In the meantime, there's a jug of hot coffee for the men to enjoy before they're needed at action stations again."

"Thank you skipper. But get the engine started and try to make up some extra speed, we're a sitting duck in the pond otherwise." Kretshmer responded evenly, observing that Luchens had now gone quiet and standing quite still.

"Major! We have a possible ambush ahead of us in about an hour or so.

I suggest that you get some warm liquid inside you and prepare to take up your position with the machine gun again." he said gently, and handed back his luger pistol.

"Here Major, you'll be needing this. Use it on the enemy and not us, your friends."

Luchens looked his pistol as if it was a strange object, before putting it away.

"It appears Sergeant, that I owe the skipper an apology. Knowing that General Gueller is his guarantor and that you are part of his staff, will make all the difference when I speak to Frau Wintermannnnn again." he said sombrely.

"Don't dwell on this too hard Major! I would probably have done the same given the same circumstances!" the skipper said in a forgiving manner.

"Besides, I'd rather be shot, hung from the nearest yardarm, anything, rather than be de- bollocked." he quipped.

Luchens smiled at that and replied before he went below into the cabin.

"And that's a fact too skipper."

Chapter VII
Trouble Spots

The engineer smiled as the engine coughed and spluttered back into life, and for the barge to finally gets itself under way again.

"Good. Maybe you'll put a bit of speed on now, skipper." Luchens sighed, observing the barge move gracefully along the ribbon of water.

The skipper ordered a speed of six knots, which wasn't good enough for Luchens.

"Any more than that Major, the speed will create a wash that will swamp the banks. If that happens the water level will be reduced too much for even a duck to keep afloat."

"We will probably meet the first ambush, but are likely to miss the second as we'd pass them before they were ready." Luchens said almost absent-mindedly.

"There again Major, we might be lucky on both. But as they control the double drop locks, we'd certainly get nabbed going through them."

"What exactly is this double lock skipper?"

"We have two double locks to go through to drop us down fifty feet. That will take us to the next river and canal system, which has a further thirty feet drop into the Saonne. In other words Major, it's the only way we can go up or down hills. The Rhine is some eighty feet higher than the Saonne which is another ten feet higher than the Rhone where we're heading."

Luchens thought for a moment and tried to work out a plan for the swift clearance through.

"So these waterway stairs must be on a bit of a hill. Therefore we'd be able to see if anybody was waiting below us. If not you could operate the lock system yourself, with some help from my men, and we could be through and on our way before they realised anything. Our early arrival would take them by surprise."

"Not so fast Major. I'm too big for one lock, and there might be other barges waiting at both ends to come through. It would mean that we'd have to clear the waterway and even then it could take us a good two hours to get through the second double one. On top of that, there are sirens warning the other craft coming the other way to pull into the passing points so I can pass them. Any collision or vessel sinking in mid channel and we'd be stuck fast not able to move either way."

"You can stop there, I get the picture! For once I see what you mean, skipper."

Both men lapsed into silence, both in deep thought. But the skipper's mind was on his steering and which part of the canal he was actually at.

"Major, I think we're about fifteen minutes from the first danger sector. We shall be turning into a tight right hand arc, which means that due to my length, we'll be almost scraping the banks to get through. It will be on both sides of the canal and at both ends of the bend where we'll meet our intruders." the skipper said softly, and prepared his cannon for firing.

Luchens called Kretshmer and told him what the skipper said, then after telling his men the same, got them into various firing positions.

Kretshmer went swiftly and quietly back to the wheelhouse and saw the skipper point to something ahead of them.

"I can't see any signs of them Sergeant, better take a good look yourself." he announced and handed the powerful binoculars over.

Kretshmer scanned around slowly for several minutes before he was satisfied and handed back the binoculars, saying:

"I've spotted four men on the left bank on the bend, hiding under a willow tree. When I give you the order skipper, you will fire one round of your cannon at them. If there are others waiting, they'll realise it was you and will pounce before you reload your piece again. But they will get a nice surprise when they do try it."

"They might have a line across the canal to snag me, Sergeant. In which case, I need a man in the bow compartment with an axe to cut it."

"If we snag a line then it means that there are others involved. But as you have your lights switched off, we might just sneak through before they have a chance to spot us passing them. How much time are we ahead of normal sailing skipper?"

"I make it about half an hour. But these bastards could have been here for ages waiting for some oncoming craft, and if so would have another line to snag them too."

"Very well skipper. We'll try and sneak through, but as soon as you feel the snag-line fire that cannon of yours. We will see to the rest!"

"I shall have to slow right down to get around this bend, but once done so, I'll make a full speed dash along the straight section to make our getaway. The thing is Sergeant, we're only about ten kilometres away from the next ambush area and your fireworks might alert them. If they only hear my cannon then they'll be ready for me."

"We'll try the silent approach first as plan A. Plan B for the rest." Kretshmer concluded, leaving to go onto the cargo hatches.

The skipper had the barge slow right down when it started to enter the first bend, and spun his steering wheel hard over. He turned the long barge neatly around the tight bend and pointed it towards the straight section before he whispered for the engineer to put on full speed again. The craft seemed to roar back into life as it raced along the canal, leaving a large bow wave that washed right over both banks.

The skipper started to hum and pat his cannon when he heard the crackling of rifle fire behind him.

Both the major and the sergeant came running aft to the wheelhouse to see the skipper smoking his large pipe.

"We surprised the bastards good and proper this time Major.

They weren't ready for us, but pity the next poor devil that comes along." The skipper chuckled.

"Well done skipper. Maybe we can have a cuppa and relax until the next time." Luchens said grudgingly, and went below into the cabin.

"Sergeant. I recognised one of the bandits as their leader. He's a well-known criminal, and part of the gang that stays around the lock houses. The whole gang is around thirty of them, and the next set is a rival gang of about twenty. Maybe, before we get to Lac du Pont we can take them all out and give us bargemen some peace on the canal for a change."

"How many gangs are there and how long has this being going on skipper?"

"It's been going on steadily for years now, with the original gang on the Chalon side of the system. They're about twenty in number. There's another gang of about thirty on the lake. Both double lock systems have a resident gang of roughly twenty on each. But as I've just said, they're are the ones we've just met and due shortly to meet up with the rest of them."

"All Frenchmen, skipper?"

"Mostly, although I have shot a few Spaniards and Germans on the way."

"We have a platoon of heavily armed men on board skipper. We'll put them all out of business for you, so you are able to return in safety."

"Thank you Sergeant. Me and my trusty cannon are getting too old and tired to cope any longer." the skipper said after taking a long draw from his pipe.

"Call it payment for services rendered skipper." Kretshmer smiled, and went forward to see to his men.

"That sergeant is a bit of all right skipper!" the cook whispered, handing him a large mug of coffee.

"With men like him, is it any wonder we're winning the war. On the other hand, it's no wonder everybody hates the likes of Luchens." the skipper said philosophically.

"Here, take over for me for a while. We're doing the regulatory four knots, but keep the navigational lights off. Call me when we get to the bridge." he added, climbing down the steps into the cabin.

"Major. Here is where we are now and here is where our next gang is waiting!" the skipper said as he unfurled a large map and pointed to it.

"What are these different coloured lines marked on the map, skipper!" Luchens asked, leaning over the table and looking intently at the map.

"Those are my trading routes. Each colour means different weights. The round spots mean refuelling and stopover points. The diamond shaped ones, are for loading or unloading cargo. The square ones mean border checkpoints. The triangle ones, are the trouble spots such as we've just come through!"

"And the cross-swords? What about these little stars?"

"Each cross-sword means military garrisons or police units, in case we need help from those bloody pirates. The cross-swords with the ring around them indicate our r/v points."

"This sort of map could be of great use to the enemy, skipper. You are to remove the references to the units." Luchens ordered sharply.

"On the contrary Major. I showed you this map to let you know where your next r/v will be. If you notice, it has cross swords with a ring around it. This is all you will be permitted to see. If you don't believe me, just use your transmitter. Besides, once you've passed your last point of contact, it gets rubbed off, just like the first ones. See? No trace." the skipper said, quickly rolling his map back up again.

"It seems skipper, that you're more informed than even my controller, and that can be very dangerous for you.

You will have those symbols removed by the time we reach our destination, or I will have the map destroyed."

"That is a map that I took several years to create. There is a duplicate of it in General Gueller's office that's used for river and canal policing. The army also uses it for cross-country waterway networks to shift their heavy loads with. So it's thanks to me Major, the Reich has such a valuable document to use, rather than rely on old or useless public maps."

Luchens sighed and shook his head.

"Be that as it may, but you will erase those symbols non-the-less."

"If it makes you happy I'll do it right now Major. But you won't be able to report or meet your next r/v if I do rub out the offending symbols for future r/v positions. If you get lost even for just one day, then its your firing squad not mine."

When the skipper was finished, Luchens stood up and said quietly:

"Thank you skipper. That's the first order you've obeyed from me since we met."

"Not at all Major. It's a pity as if even some of your orders made sense, then you'd be well away. As it is, as the skipper of this barge I have to ensure your safe delivery, otherwise you'd have tasted the river long before you did. We have a war on Major, and we need as many fighting men as possible. Believe it or not that also includes you but not me." the skipper said softly, climbing back up to the wheelhouse again.

The skipper lit his pipe and took a few puffs of it before he calmed down and took the wheel over from the cook.

"That major is in for big trouble if he's not careful."

"He has said just the same about you. He keeps mentioning Wintermann and execution squads, skipper." the cook said quietly.

"If anything should happen to me, try and get a message to the missus, and to a special address I have hidden in the centre wheel spoke. You will then become the master, and if I were you, learn decent French and base your operations from the Med." the skipper said slowly as he peered into the darkness.

"Thank you skipper, but you'll be still sailing the Rhine long after the Major and his men have gone." The cook replied, patting his skipper gently on his shoulder.

"Better get for'ard with a fender, there's another barge ahead coming towards us. Engineer! Slow to two knots. Major! Alert your men for possible collision." the skipper called urgently.

Luchens went and spoke to his men and came back with the Sergeant.

"Sergeant! It happens that we're near a passing point with an oncoming barge already there. We might ground at that point and at the same time we might collide with the other barge. Get some of your men along the side with bales of straw to fend that barge off with, and we'll deal with the grounding later. But also make sure you have some men armed in case this barge contains hostiles." The skipper said quietly, pointing to the pinpricks of coloured lights ahead of them.

Kretshmer grabbed the binoculars and scanned ahead of them quickly.

"It's a small barge and it's already into the opposite passing point. We seem clear to pass through, look!" he said, handing back the binoculars.

"I don't recognise that type of barge, probably a new Froggie one. It looks too quiet and unlit for me." The skipper said, looking at the strange barge for a moment longer.

"Forget the straw, get your men armed and ready. We have a barge full of hostiles, as I can see at least six of them profiled in the moonlight. We're in the shade and won't be seen until we're opposite them. We'll give them a good old naval broadside as we pass." he said with a chuckle.

Kretshmer also chuckled at the skipper's remark and went forward to get his men ready.

"Engine room, make two knots. Major, you will have the honour of hoisting my little pennant on the flagpole astern.

Must be under our proper battle flag and also make a good impression you know." he ordered, handing Luchens the little flag that declared the vessel was a German warship.

When the two barges were almost right opposite each other, the skipper fired his cannon and blew a big hole into the bow of the other barge. That was the signal for Kretshmer and his men to send a murderous hail of bullets and hand grenades into the unsuspecting bandits. Not one shot was fired back in return.

Such was the surprise and ferocity of the broadside, that within the brief time it took their barge to finally pass it by, the other flimsy barge was literally shredded into matchwood from stem to stern, and all the men on it were blown into little body parts. The skipper fired one more shell into it, which was the signal to cease firing.

Luchens came back carrying the little flag, and met up with the Sergeant who was standing talking to the skipper.

"That was a good example of German firepower, Sergeant. Here skipper, have your little flag back. It was a pleasure to watch a German gunship in action." he said happily, handing the battle pennant back to the skipper.

"It felt good! Just like old times!" the skipper said, still full of exhilaration and with a big smile on his face.

"Those bandits we have just annihilated, must have been getting ready for another ambush. And because they came towards us, it must be some of the bunch from the next lot waiting for us. If we keep on like this, the gang on the locks will be a lot fewer for us to deal with." the cook quipped, joining the group.

"Which is only about another ten kilometres away, Major." the skipper added.

"I'll get the men some coffee, Sergeant, it's going to be a long night." the cook volunteered.

"Thanks cook. I'll get the men stood down, Major." Kretshmer added, then left.

Luchens stood looking at the now burning but half-sunken wreck behind him for a while, before he shivered with the cold and decided to go down into the snug cabin.

The barge made its weary way along the canal, as the soldiers prepared themselves for another skirmish.

"Sergeant, we're about to meet another natural stop, but one where our bandits normally have the upper hand. It's an old drawbridge that carries a busy railway line over it. The railway has priority and we normally have to wait until it is quiet before the bridge is raised again to allow us to pass. During the day the railway gets quite busy, and it's only during the evening we get a real chance to move through it. The only thing is, we bargemen never sail more than four hours at a stretch, and especially never overnight. So there might be several barges on both sides waiting to move when the bridge is open.

So what they do is wait until the new arrivals tie up alongside the long quayside, then pounce on them as they tie up. Or, if it's a quiet period, wait until a barge passes underneath the bridge, then drop down onto it and force the skipper to stop. If there's a barge moving in the opposite way as well, they double up and get both barges at the same time. So watch out for the gang on the other side too." The skipper advised.

"How many of them skipper?" Luchens asked quickly.

"Depends on the barges tied up waiting for the bridge to open, but given that we've bagged some of them, I'd guess about ten. That would be five per barge, as most barges only have the skipper and his family on board."

"How long have we got skipper?" Luchens asked eagerly, grabbing a nearby heavy axe.

"About ten minutes, if that."

"Major, we shall be using hand weapons and unarmed combat, so I need you to stay guard in the wheelhouse. If you feel you need something more substantial than your pistol then tell me now." Kretshmer ordered.

Luchens stated that he was happy with his machine pistol but demanded that one soldier was posted on the stern end by the flag-pole in case.

"There's just one thing I nearly forgot. If there is a barge in the way, I might have to ram my way through. Tell your men to be aware of this in case some of them happen to fall overboard." the skipper added.

***

The soldiers got themselves in position, as the skipper ordered the speed to ten knots.

"Not many barges can do this speed, Major. Then again, not many have three inches of battleship armour plate to re-inforce their bow, let alone a cargo full of armed men." the skipper chuckled, as Luchens peered into the darkness and at the ever-nearing bridge.

"Major, the bridge is raised only halfway up and nobody is coming towards. So I need you to climb on top of the wheelhouse and literally pull my mast out of its socket and lay it flat until we get clear of the bridge again. Likewise the funnel if you please."

Luchens climbed on top of the wheelhouse and removed the mast, then scrambled back to remove the black funnel. He grabbed the funnel and swore loudly as the hot metal seared his hands. He tossed the offending object away from him, which flew over the side and entered the water with a large splosh and a hissing noise.

"Thank you Major!" the skipper whispered as Luchens came back blowing on his burned hands.

"Major, you're a fucking arsehole! You've just spoilt our surprise by advertising our presence, now we have to fight our way through." the skipper snarled at him.

"Why didn't you tell me the funnel was going to be hot?" Luchens said, blowing hard onto his hands as if to cool them down.

The skipper sighed and grabbing Luchens by the collar, threw him towards the cargo hold.

"You are an out and out imbecile. I'd have you keel hauled in my days. Now go and tell the sergeant, you've just blown our cover and he is to arm his men immediately."

***

The Lost Legion

The barge had just slid under the bridge when bullets and men started to rain down on them. Kretshmer had his men return their fire whilst the skipper zig-zagged the barge through the gap, thus causing several bandits to fall straight into the canal, and be shot by the soldiers.

Luchens came back to his post in time for two bandits to land on top of the wheelhouse demanding the skipper stop or he would be shot.

Instead of which, they were surprised when they felt a tap on their shoulders and saw Luchens behind them with a pistol in his hand, who, with a sadistic smile, shot the two of them.

"Stowaways are not permitted on this cruise!" he cackled, and kicked them over the side and watched the bodies drift away.

They were now clear of the bridge and the shooting had stopped, but the skipper was facing a barge that was right across their path.

"Stand by for collision. Sergeant, get some men forward with their weapons in case the barge has men on it." The skipper shouted.

The skipper fired his cannon, blasting a hole in the side of the flimsy barge just before he rammed right through it without stopping, just like a hot knife through butter. Several men that were on the other barge were thrown overboard by the collision, and got swiftly dispatched by Kretshmer and his men.

The entire incident only took ten minutes, before the bridge was lowered again, just in time for a long train loaded with tanks and artillery pieces, to pass over it.

"There you are Sergeant! Typical German efficiency!" Luchens cooed, watching the last wagon clear the bridge.

"Don't let our beloved leader find out about your own recent effort on efficiency, Major!" the skipper said sarcastically, as Kretshmer came into the wheelhouse, and heard the remarks.

"Yes Major. You might be good at organising Jews for the gas chamber, but you're no soldier. Knives are no match for machine guns and it's just as well I heard the skipper or we'd have lost a few good men, thanks to you."

"Sergeant! You are getting too insolent for my liking. Get the men back below at once and prepare for this lock system ahead." Luchens replied angrily, as if to re-assert his authority over the sergeant.

"Sergeant! We'll reach the lock in little under two hours!" the skipper called to the departing Sergeant, who just waved his acknowledgement.

"Major! We really must stop at the next r/v for me to have the engine fixed. Plus the fact that I have a change of deck cargo and need supplies for the next part of our voyage!"

"No stopping skipper. We only stop to pick up another consignment of boxes, some more men and my orders, that's all." Luchens snapped, as he tried to wrest his dwindling authority.

"As skipper of this vessel…!" the skipper started to say, when Luchens rudely interrupted him.

"I don't care what or who you are! I have a schedule to keep and I intend keeping it, bandits or no bandits, engine or no engine!" he snarled.

"Whatever you say Major!" the skipper said nonchalantly, manoeuvring the barge round a bend.

This reply seemed to give Luchens the idea that he was finally winning the battle of authority over the mission and decided to enlarge on it.

"And another thing skipper. You will inform only me of anything that you deem a threat to our mission, and not the sergeant. Is that clear?"

But the skipper said nothing and let the man rant on.

"Now you're beginning to see sense. It's a pity all you navy men don't listen a little more to those much superior to you. That means SS officers such as myself." Luchens droned on.

The skipper steered the barge into the bough of a tree that was sticking out into the canal. This caused the barge to lurch violently over to one side, making Luchens fall overboard.

The Lost Legion

Luchens screamed as he fell overboard, but the skipper carried on steering the barge down the canal. He stopped the engine and pulled the barge into one of the passing points before calling for Kretshmer.

"It seems that our major has taken his leave and gone swimming. Last I saw of him was back there, just beyond that tree sticking out over the canal. You can get your men ashore here and go looking for him. I'll wait here until you come back. Take as long as you like, as our engine needs seeing to again. The lock is only another three kilometres away."

Kretshmer looked at the skipper and smiled.

"He's pulling this SS Officer thing again isn't he skipper! You and I know he is an out-and-out arsehole, but you really must stop teasing the man. After all, he has an important job to do you know."

"Aye Sergeant! I suppose your right." the skipper replied with a grin and started to smoke his pipe again.

Kretshmer and some of the men swam to the other bank and ran back along the towpath to see if they could find Luchens.

It took several minutes for Kretshmer to locate Luchens, who was sitting on a fallen tree trunk, sneezing and coughing whilst wringing out his clothes.

"Sergeant! I want that man arrested and shot when we arrive at our destination. He has caused us too much time delays, and now he wants to stop again to get his engine fixed." Luchens said crossly between his bouts of sneezing.

"I'll see to that when the time comes Major! In the meantime, we had better get back on board again. Are you fit to travel?" Kretshmer replied diplomatically.

"Of course I bloody well am! Lead on at the double, Sergeant!" Luchens replied with venom, pulling his boots on and donning his soggy cap.

The sergeant and his men doubled back to the barge, where the cook had some food and drink waiting for them. This cheered the men up, as they had been fighting all night, and thanked the cook for the meagre rations that were dished out, for they knew it was the Major's fault that they had to starve in the first place.

"You deliberately went into that tree didn't you! Why didn't you stop for me when I fell overboard!" Luchens growled and swearing angrily at the skipper.

"You're lucky we haven't crashed several times before now Major. No bargeman sails at night, as he can't see to navigate. If you fell overboard then, I certainly didn't hear you. I just kept on sailing forward without wasting any more of your precious time.

Besides, I'm not in the middle of the ocean and able to turn around to pick you up. In other words you asshole, my barge is over sixty feet long, in a fifteen-foot wide canal. So what else did you expect me to do?"

Luchens was left speechless at this fundamental logic from the skipper, who left him to go down into the warmth of the cabin.

"The engine bearings have been cooled down sufficiently for us to carry on Sergeant. We need new ones when we reach the next stopover point, but they must be marine engine bearings. The engine has been virtually non-stop for over ten days now and can't take much more punishment. There's a marine engine place on the lake where we could stop and change engines, other than that the major will have to fly the rest of the way, boxes and all." the engineer said after a while.

"Yes, I agree with you. But how would you change it if you could, engineer?" Kretshmer asked

"Simple. Do you see those two rails under the engine? Well, we uncouple the engine from the propeller shaft, then open this hatch which leads out into the cargo hold. All we do then is slide the engine along the rails and have it hoisted out. The new one comes in the same way.

It's a three tonner and too heavy for a man to lift, but I have a lifting boom here that I use to do it, in case there's not one available on the jetty." the engineer said pointing to the arched boom and rails.

"Clever stuff engineer. Your ideas?"

"No, the skipper's actually. I can replace an engine in about one hour providing I have one ready for me, and it doesn't matter if its diesel or petrol. But I prefer diesel, as it's easier to get than petrol."

"Right, leave it with me engineer." Kretshmer said evenly, leaving the engine room and went into the cabin where he saw Luchens trying to listen into their conversation, and the skipper relaxing on his bunk.

"A bit of an engineer are you Sergeant? I could do with another one, once this trip is over.

Mind you though, the pay isn't all that great as I haven't been paid for my efforts so far!" the skipper said slowly and winked slyly at Kretshmer.

"You'll get your just reward when I reach my destination skipper, and not before. What have you learned from the engineer, Sergeant?" Luchens replied sharply.

"This engine has had it, and we need a new one sooner than later. The engineer can manage until we get to the lake, but after that you'd better start thinking of road transport. Failing that, start growing wings, because the engine will not make it beyond that." Kretshmer stated.

"I know of a refit yard on the lake where we can get one. But we've still got the locks to get through first." the skipper said.

"What? How long will it take you to change the engine, four hours or more?" Luchens asked with alarm in his voice.

"Calm down Major, you really must learn to control your impatience. We can effect a change in about an hour, providing we have one waiting for us.

I suggest that when you check in at your next r/v point, you arrange to have one available and waiting for us at the lake's lock gates at this end. We have about four hours before reaching that point, so whoever you see had better get a move on." the skipper said calmly, drinking form his cup of coffee.

"It's still dark, and according to you we are the only ones on the canal. How far is the lock from here, and from the lock to the r/v position?" Luchens asked.

"We've got about three hours of darkness, but we should arrive onto the locks sooner than you think. Your r/v point is about a further one hour from there, but I can't swear on that as you made me rub out the symbol for your position."

Luchens glowered angrily at the skipper for that remark but decided to leave it.

"Given that we were supposed to arrive at the lock at dawn, and the time now makes us three hours ahead of schedule, yes? Which means that I will have to contact the agent for the next r/v in time for them to meet us. If the engine can last to the lake and we get a new one, how much more time can we make up?"

"Once we get onto the Saonne and then onto the much faster Rhone, we could make up a good 100 kilometres, or in canal terms, about two days. Mind you, it would take the replacement engine to be there on time to make it possible." the skipper said, as he pulled out his waterway maps, and traced the route still facing them.

"Fortunately we have only two more pick ups before we finish this trip. I'll agree to this plan and have the engine ready for you skipper. Now perhaps you can get us going again." Luchens concluded.

Chapter VIII
Clockwork

Yet again they were under way in the dark, as the skipper strained through his binoculars to see what bend or turn the canal had in store for him.

"The light is starting to fade now Major. If you put someone up in the bow to signal when we meet a bend or an obstruction it will save us a little more time and me a lot less work spinning this wheel."

The skipper advised for Luchens to go forward and bring back a soldier with him.

"He has learned the river craft you taught him over these past days, so he'll be your lookout." Luchens said, pointing to the man.

"Ah good, it's you Hartman! Here's a small signalling torch so you know what to do. You will remain on the bows until it's daybreak again. You will man the machine gun in the bow compartment and ready for action at the locks. Before you go, get yourself a cup of coffee from the stove below, I need you wide eyed and fully alert." the skipper ordered, as Hartman did as he was told.

"He'd make a good sailor that lad would, Major. I could do with him on my other barge up on the Rotterdam delta." the skipper said softly to Luchens, who was also busy scanning the canal banks with a borrowed pair of binoculars.

"Yes, they are all good men. Each one is worth at least three Tommies, and definitely twenty Italians, and that's why I have them specially picked for this assignment."

"Lucky for some, Major." the skipper concluded as both men stood silently together, but each taking care of their own ends.

The barge went under several overhanging trees before the skipper broke the silence between them.

"Major! The lookout is signalling a left-hand bend ahead about a hundred metres away. These trees confirm that we're about to approach the double lock."

"Better get the sergeant then." Luchens agreed and went forward to get him.

"There will be nobody in the lock system, either end. But I need one man on each side to swing open the lock gates and operate the pump levers. Here is a picture of what they will be using." the skipper said, handing the Sergeant a photo of the area.

"See those buildings down there, that's where the bandits hang out. The pump houses are those near the jetty. That big building in the middle is a beer hall and the two long buildings opposite is where the bandits stash cargo looted from us bargemen. The little houses you see at each end of the lock system, is where the engineers who look after the locks, live. But see that shed out the back of that building set away into the trees?

Well, that's where the bandits keep their ammunition and other weapons. If that was knocked out, and the bandits seen to as they come out of their buildings, then the cook and I can get the boat organised through the lifts." the skipper explained at length.

"Major, we'll get the men ashore before the barge gets into the first lock. You lead the first section to knock out the ammo dump and destroy their store of loot. But keep a close eye in case some of the bandits are on your side as well. I'll lead the second section on this side and take out the bandits where they sleep. Corporal Lutz will take the 3rd section to get the lock engineers out and also operate the machinery for the skipper. Skipper, you will have the lookout up front manning the machine gun to cover us, but keep your cannon handy as support fire for the Major. Major! Better take a machine gun with you and a red flare to let off when you have completed your action. Once done then return to the barge and defend it in case the bandits have friends nearby who might want to get involved." Kretcshmer directed, as Luchens nodded in compliance.

"Yes Sergeant! But what if there's a boatload of them coming up behind us? I'd much rather take up position at the top of the hill than be picked off in the barge below." Luchens said swiftly,

The Lost Legion

but not wanting to seem too reluctant as he did, to take part.

"How long would it take to go straight through if you know what I mean skipper?"

"The actual double lock from one end to the other is only about 300 metres, but as long as someone operates the other end at the same time, about thirty minutes.

But you'd need to get both lock engineers out to do that, as the time taken is up to the pumps. I can operate the middle section myself."

"Right then. Major, you take your men to the exit end of the lock and set up a position there. I'll have my men guarding our rear, and catch up with you as you leave the complex." Kretshmer concluded.

The three men agreed on the plan and started to prepare for their part in the action, as the barge finally arrived at the locks.

The skipper stopped the barge gently at the lock gates for the men to disembark.

The place was in total darkness and silent, as Luchens led his men across the wooden bridge to the other side of the lock, whilst Kretshmer and his men ran silently along towards the buildings that housed the bandits.

Within moments several grenade explosions and machine gun fire shattered that silence, as lights, first from the buildings were switched on, then as if by magic the entire complex was lit up by several large overhead floodlights.

The skipper saw and heard the lock engineers being bullied and shoved towards the barge, and started to operate the heavy gates to shut the barge into its first lock.

"Get these locks operated, I want to pass through right now." the skipper shouted in French.

"But M'seur, it is only very early. The Taxman hasn't arrived yet!" one of the engineers complained as he was shoved roughly from behind by one of the soldiers.

"You had better do as you're told M'seur. As you can see,

the taxman is too busy paying his own dues now!" the skipper replied pointing towards the barn full of loot that was burning away merrily and the bandits being mowed down by the soldiers.

This was the incentive the engineers needed to rush to comply with the skipper's orders, but pleading that they should not be shot in the process.

The plan went like clockwork, and within ten minutes, everything was quiet save the crying from children and wails from the women folk who grieved over their shot men-folk.

The barge made its way along the lock system and was ready for leaving out the other end before the skipper blew his barge horn as the signal for the men to return back on board.

Luchens seemed to be missing, but arrived a few minutes later after everybody else was on board and accounted for. If it hadn't been for the skipper who saw him running across the cobble stoned jetty he would have been left behind.

"Managed to phone through to my next agent." Luchens gasped, trying to catch his breath again.

"He's getting an engine for you as you wanted skipper, but we'd better get from here as there's several personnel carriers coming our way."

"Oh! What do they want Major?" the skipper asked calmly.

"Probably coming to investigate the noise we made, thinking there's an enemy raid on."

"Maybe your agent will put them wise then Major, as we're sitting ducks on this open stretch of canal. At our speed, even a walking blind man can overtake us on the tow paths."

"Better get a few of the men in full uniform and sitting on deck in case, Major. But keep most of your men below and ready for action in case. I'll put my little flag up as well for them to see us. If any shots come our way then you'll know it's not our forces but the Free Frenchies." The skipper countered.

Luchens nodded his agreement and directed Kretshmer accordingly.

The men sat on deck in full uniform, as the dawn lit up the

skies and an armoured vehicle to arrive alongside them.

"Who are you? Who is in charge? You Sergeant! Who are you and what regiment are you?" a metallic voice demanded from the armoured vehicle.

"You in the back. Stop this craft or I will blow it out of the water!" the insistent voice shouted, as the vehicle's cannon pointed ominously at them.

The skipper was about to obey when the major whispered to him not to do so. Instead he stood up and went up onto the cargo deck with his pistol in his hand and demanded the person making the orders to show himself.

A man's head and shoulders appeared out from the top of the vehicle, put his cap on and looked at the barge through his field binoculars.

"What regiment are you from Major?" the man asked pertinently.

Luchens saw that the man was of the same rank but noted that he was a regular soldier.

"Never mind who I am Major, I am no concern of yours. Suggest you contact your commander first before you engage my men. You are obviously keen to track down bandits and saboteurs, in which case you'll find a whole cartload of dead ones back there at the locks. Call it a present off me." Luchens said calmly.

The other major did not reply as he was listening to his radio earphones.

"You are Major Luchens, yes?" he asked curtly.

"You have obviously checked up on me, so now you can leave yes?" Luchens replied in equal manner.

"Yes Major Luchens. I will inform my men further down the canal to let you pass, good day." the other major said as the vehicle stopped and turned around to drive back towards the locks.

"What was all that about Major?" the skipper asked as Luchens arrived into the wheelhouse.

"It appears that either my agent at the local garrison did not inform anybody of our presence in the area, or that someone else is trying to trace us for something other than mail from mother. But we've got another pick-up in this area and I don't like nosey neighbours around when we do." Luchens said coldly.

Kretshmer had arrived and heard the major, saying.

"If we've just been spotted then we've no chance of another surprise on whomever is waiting for us. Unless we could speed up and be at the r/v point before we're supposed to be and be ready for them. Or…"

"Or we can just stop here and ask your agent to come to us. That passing point ahead is pretty secluded and screened with bushes and trees, we could wait there. We have a push bike that's stowed in the bow compartment to use in such times as these " the skipper added.

Luchens stood in thought for a moment then looked at his watch.

"How long to full daylight skipper?"

"About another half hour. We could make the next passing point, or even with luck make our r/v jetty by then if you want Major. What have you in mind?"

"The trucks are already on their way by now, and there's no way I can contact them unless I send a messenger on ahead. So we'll have to try and get to the r/v point as planned, and meet any trouble when we get there."

"In that case, we'll have a quick breakfast before we get there." the skipper said cheerfully, but added.

"We need to stop at the next jetty to get our fuel and supplies anyway. That should take us onto the lake and get our new engine, before needing more supplies."

Luchens nodded his consent and told Kretshmer to get the men fed, but to check on their ammunition, in case they needed a supply of that too.

Chapter IX
The Lake

Luck was finally fortuous towards Luchens and his mission, as when they arrived at the r/v point, they witnessed that the Major and his light tanks had surrounded the place to ensure the next shipment of boxes.

"Major! I did not realise how dangerous your assignment was, and the immense pressure you have upon you and your men to complete your mission. I went back to the locks as you pointed out, and shall we say 'cleaned up the mess, after you!"

"Glad you appreciated my calling card. Maybe you would care to investigate the various bodies I have left along the entire canal stretch. Here are the map co-ordinances and other details for you." Luchens replied calmly and threw a container towards him.

"It is good to do business with you Major. Let me know when you have re-supplied your barge and are able to continue. You have a squad of men joining you when you stop for your engine, so look out for them." the other Major replied, as he had a man pick up the document thrown onto the towpath.

"We have a long journey ahead of us Major. Please contact Frau Wintermann for me, and ask her to join me before I move off. She will know what I mean."

The other major looked at Luchens and shuddered violently enough for Luchens to see the effect the name of Wintermann had on him.

"Now I know the score Herr Major, you poor bastard. That is one person that me and my men have had the luck to avoid thus far."

"Then you'd better keep questions and prying eyes away from us, else you will end up like the rest of us. Just keep a safe distance from us and make certain we survive the transit."

"That is good enough for me Luchens!" the other major said quickly, as his light tank slewed away towards the towpath and the vegetation that hid it from view.

"About time we had some landlubbers with the savvy to realise how dangerous and vulnerable we have been all this time. Better make capital out of this Luchens, or we'll all be swinging from the nearest tree, minus our bollocks!" the skipper said, as he wincing at the prospect.

Luchens laughed at the skipper at his uncommon show of feeling.

"I didn't know you old sailors were so attached to your appendages!"

"Oh that! No not really! I don't fancy swinging off the nearest yardarm like a common tar. I have my pride you know. I'd rather blow my head off with my old brass cannon than have my brass knockers cut off by a bloody dyke!"

"Now then skipper. Frau Wintermann is our illustrious Deputy Leaders step daughter, and a model of the Aryan race, and don't you forget that it's our true race that has all the qualities to be the most superior race on earth"

"Pah! The little Nipponese Army could show you lot a few things or two, and they are only half your height. Lets hope they remain friendly for your own particular sake. I have no fear of the future as I have already done my bit in the last war. So much for our sacrifices, as you stupid lot are trying to re-write the history of Europe once again!"

"Skipper, I have already warned you of your loose-lipped opinions, so you had better cease now whilst you're ahead. Next time, I'll have no compunction in shooting you like a dog."

"Major! That to me is old hat now! Tell me something new. Better still; show me your authority that countermands General Guellers orders. Just you ensure you meet your own deadlines and promises to the Fuhrer before you condemn me to a lousy luger bullet."

"Major! We have the last lock system in sight! What is your plan?" Kretshmer interjected hastily as if to play down the deadly mood of the conversation.

"What? Don't ruddy well ask me Sergeant! How am I

expected to conduct my mission if I'm always keeping an eye on this stupid bargeman!" Luchens snarled.

"But Major!" Kretshmer insisted.

"No buts Sergeant! Better ask this stupid bargee."

The skipper shrugged his shoulders again pretending not to take any notice of these now, very familiar situations between himself and Luchens.

When the skipper refused to answer, Kretshmer sighed, cocked his machine gun and pointed to both the skipper and Luchens.

"Now look here you two! I've had just about enough of you two bickering like little schoolgirls. I want straight answers from both of you, and now is the time to give them." he shouted angrily.

Luchens went for his luger, but Kretshmer simply put the point of his gun under his chin and said.

"Just you try it Major. I've served under far better officers much junior to you. You really are just a pain in the neck and the cause of the problems for all of us. As for you skipper, I'd expect better from you. After all, you're supposed to be one of our model heroes. We all have a role to play, and its about time you, Herr Major, showed us just how you gained your exalted rank in the SS. My men have seen more action than you've read in the local propaganda press, so as of now I want straight answers to my questions!" Kretshmer whispered, and cocked his gun.

Luchens started to stammer, before going a whiter shade of pale.

"You are in subordination of a superior officer for the last time, Sergeant. I will see you shot before we finish this assignment, mark my words!"

"Just tell me what the score is for the next phase of our trip, that's all. If you can't, then I will get the message out that its you who's sabotaging our mission, and of course you know what that means!" Kretshmer said, drawing his finger across his own throat to indicate the severity of his words.

"I know exactly what is to happen Sergeant! But then, it's the Major who's supposed to be in charge.

However, as you've asked me, then I will tell you that we're about to get a new engine and then race across the lake before we enter the Loirens waterway and then into the Rhone river system. We have another gang of brigands waiting for us, and I suspect you need further ammo to cope with the extra guests."

"That's exactly the sort of answer I was expecting from you, Major Luchens." Kretshmer scowled, looking scathingly at Luchens.

Luchens just stood quietly as if mesmerised by the end of Kretshmer's machine gun as it waved right under his nose.

"Right then skipper! Lets get to work and get ourselves onto the next phase before we have any more bouts of madness from our commander, Major Luchens!" Kretshmer ordered sarcastically.

Luchens glowered at the both of them, and resolved that they would pay for their belittlement of him and his exalted rank in the glorious 9th SS Legion. He also vowed that in time, he would take all the credit for the success of the mission and at the same time ensure that everybody on board the barge will be shot for their insubordination. Thus ensuing that only he gets a higher promotion than the rest of his erstwhile 'Gung-Ho' Officer class students who were more substantial in build, and better academically qualified than him. Such was his lust and thirst for supremacy and power over all.

The final lock of the canal swung open as the skipper eased the barge gently out of the canal and glided into the shallow freshwater lake. He turned the barge and lined up his approach to a stone jetty that had some men standing around watching them.

"Major! There's our welcoming committee, and replacement engine. It looks as if we've got more stores to load up." the skipper said smoothly as the barge was tied up neatly alongside.

Luchens called Kretshmer to get the men organised and help to load the stores, whilst he went over to the squad of men standing idly by.

"You men! Stand to attention. I want your name rank and number. Who has your transit papers?" he shouted crossly at the slovenly men.

The men stood up swiftly and stood to a ramrod straight attention, each calling out their particulars. One of them held out the paperwork saying that he was the one in charge of the detail. Luchens peered into each mans face and inspected them before he was satisfied that all was in order.

"Get yourselves and your equipment on board and report to the Sergeant. We move as soon as the stores are loaded." he ordered sharply, for the men to rush away in their obedience to his orders.

"Pull! Pull! It's nearly there Sergeant!" the engineer shouted.

"Come on you men! Its only a three tonner, you can do better than that!" Kretshmer goaded, as the burly soldiers shoved the engine along its rails and into position for the engineer to connect up.

"Stop now! It's in position, thank you men!" the engineer said, before he took over and had it harnessed ready for testing.

"Ready to test, skipper!" the engineer shouted.

"Very well!" the skipper said, untying the barge from the jetty.

"Slow ahead for two minutes, then slow astern!" he ordered.

The engine spluttered into life and performed its simple slow task before the skipper ordered full speed and had the barge go round in a big circle, then stopped the engine and tied up alongside the jetty again.

"Everything had better be in order skipper." Luchens said icily, as the other soldiers sat on deck mystified as to why they just went round in a circle.

The skipper took no notice but shouted down to the engineer to come up on deck, who did so with a cheerful voice.

"Always fancied one of those Stollers, skipper. She is just perfect and goes like a dream. Mind you, we'll need extra fuel, as she is a thirsty engine. It can outperform our old one even when it was new, which means we can have an extra push upstream or a lower idling speed for going down." said the engineer as he gave them his verdict and confirmation that all was well.

"Did you get and understand all that Major? It appears that your agent has spared no expense or effort in getting me this engine. Now what do you say?" the skipper asked with smug satisfaction.

"German organisation at its best again skipper. Now get us moving in the right direction this time." Luchens said with a grin.

"Let go both ends Sergeant! Full ahead engineer! Next stop one hour ahead of us. Hartman! Come and take over for a spell." the skipper called out, puffing on his pipe.

Hartman rushed into the wheelhouse and eagerly steered the barge on the course the skipper showed him to take.

"Makes a difference steering in open waters skipper!" he said cheerfully, taking his stint on the wheel.

"Keep one eye on the course, and another two out for any strange craft that looks to be acting strange towards us! And another eye on the Major." the skipper said gently, as he went below into the cabin, followed by Luchens.

"We can have some fresh food now Major, but I'll have the men fed first if you don't mind."

For once Luchens was feeling in a good mood as he agreed to the skipper's statement.

"I have a full platoon now skipper, and you've got a new engine. Maybe we can achieve this part of the mission in a better frame of mind, no?"

"Funny how different things can upset people in different ways. You with your shortage of men and an increasingly bigger pile of boxes, and me with an engine that had the guts flogged out of it." the engineer said philosophically, handing Luchens a large mug of coffee.

"Indeed. But this mission is not over yet by a long shot so don't get too carried away. But it's nice to have some of your plans working the way they should." Luchens agreed.

The skipper sat on his bunk smoking his pipe and scanning his maps with a pointed finger as he looked at them.

"Major. Here is something you might be interested in, look." he invited.

Luchens moved over and sat by the skipper to see what it was.

"We can take a short cut from Dormein to cut out this big dog-leg in the canal, and end up just south of Chaloix. That will mean that we can enter the Rhone further down and give you a further day to make up the time we've lost." the skipper said quietly, tracing the line of the canal across the map

Luchens looked at the proposed alteration carefully and asked a couple of questions, which the skipper answered to his satisfaction.

"I will inform my controller on the next pick up point. That way we can be monitored all the way, instead of seemingly disappearing off the map and unaccounted for." Luchens said after a while.

"As long as you meet your r/v points and complete this section of your mission on time then who would care Major. It would show initiative on your behalf and besides, we get to miss the next stretch of bandits I told you about." the skipper replied.

Luchens looked at the skipper with a sideways glance, as if to suspect something untoward.

"If you're up to something skipper!..." Luchens started to say

"Here's me trying to help you and all you do is think evil of me. Besides, why should I hurry my date with your threatened firing squad?"

Luchens felt unsure but gave into yet another piece of simple logic from the skipper.

"Fast speedboats approaching from our right skipper!" Hartman shouted down to them.

"Major, go through the engineers hatchway to the cargo hold and get your men organised. I'm expecting at least three fast boats full of bandits wanting to board me. You have about three minutes before I fire my cannon into them, which is your signal to do your bit." the skipper prompted, ascending swiftly up the ladder into the wheelhouse.

"There's that one over there, and by the look of it, two more behind us." Hartman said excitedly.

"Get yourself up into the bows and man that machine gun. Don't fire until the Sergeant tells you. You must walk forward slowly as if you're enjoying the cruise, so as not to tip them off we've spotted them. Get the Sergeant to come and see me, and ask the Major to man the flagpole again but with a machine gun."

"I heard that, and it's exactly what I intend doing skipper!" Luchens said quietly, as Kretshmer arrived with his machine gun.

"Ah Sergeant! I'll wait until that front launch is near enough for me to fire a salvo at him. I will purposefully miss, for him to think that I'm some old duffer.

It won't approach until the two behind have reached us at the same time. When that happens, I'll fire another round at the same launch which will be your men's cue to use their mortars and heavy machine guns on them."

"Sounds good to me. But what I can't understand is, if they pirate a barge, what or where do they put their loot? And where are the river police when all this is happening?"

"No police on this lake Sergeant. There's a barge following behind the one ahead, which will be here in about another ten minutes. That's about as long as the pirates take to get alongside and stop the barges. Mind you, I'm about to double my speed which will surprise them and make them more aggressive in their chase. So stand by both sides for your broadside Sergeant!" the skipper said with a grin, as he shouted down to the engineer to go full speed.

The launch ahead of the barge slowed down and began to turn, to make its run at the barge.

The skipper fired his cannon, as the barge began to make its way much faster in the water.

"Take that you robbing bastards!" the skipper laughed, as the fast launch turned full circle to get out of the way of the cannon ball.

The Lost Legion

* * *

He saw the men on the launches behind getting ready to approach and told the major to remain hidden until Kretshmer started to fire.

The front launch raced towards the barge with the bandits firing their weapons at it.

"Stand by Sergeant! Wait until all three are almost by us. On my cannon signal, stand by." the skipper shouted.

Within a few seconds of his order, the skipper fired his cannon, taking a big chunk out of the nearest launch's bows as it closed within metres of the barge.

Kretshmer had his men unleash a hail of bullets and grenades at the unsuspecting bandits, who were shot to pieces and died with surprise written on their faces. The barge left the wrecked launches behind and ploughed on towards the oncoming pirates' barge that was to take on the loot.

"Stand by to ram!" the skipper shouted, as the oncoming barge tried to get out of the way. The skipper fired his cannon, blowing the bandits' wheelhouse to pieces as his barge sliced their boat into two neat halves.

"Cease firing!" the skipper ordered.

Luchens came back into the wheelhouse with the little flag again as the sergeant arrived.

"I've been wanting to do that for years. Now we can have a peaceful passage across this lake." the skipper said exuberantly.

"I must confess I enjoyed that action too skipper. No wonder you naval men like to sail into battle. It makes us infantrymen appreciate the fact that there's no hiding place on the water!" Kretshmer said with a smile, as he saw the big grin on the skipper's face.

"Indeed Sergeant. Just like a game of chess, it's your tactics and your counter moves against your enemy that wins the day." the skipper replied as he waved his cannon, over the now desolate area to where his erstwhile attackers should have been.

"I'd like to keep this little flag of yours skipper, it seems to bring me luck." Luchens said, examining it.

"That's fine by me, Major. You make your own luck during a fire fight, lucky mascots come as a bonus." the skipper replied jovially, as the soldiers started to come up on deck for a breather.

"The lake is seven kilometres long, but at this speed we'll reach the other end in about twenty minutes, Major. If you've no business at this point, then we can proceed onto the next stretch of navigable river." the skipper said after a little while and when everybody had calmed down from their little bout of euphoria.

"Next stop should be about four hours from now, skipper. If we do take that short cut, we can stop at that r/v for a couple of hours rest." Luchens said magnanimously, and went below into the cabin.

Chapter X
Ooh! La! La!

The mood and attitudes of the men on board was now relaxed and high-spirited, as everybody talked about the impromptu barbeque at the last r/v point. It was also a Major factor in the well being of the skipper and his crew, as Luchens also lightened up enough to share a few jokes and laughs with them.

The skipper put it down to the fact that they were now on a change of route and that much nearer for Luchens to complete this gruelling part of his mission, to which he had agreed and quite bluntly too: "Yes skipper. We're about to come onto the last lap of this part of my journey, and I agree that a train or even a cargo plane would have been much quicker. But this was a covert operation to find out who was robbing the State. We have suspicions of a conspiracy plot that is or at least was aided and abetted by several high-ranking officers. This part of the mission is to find out exactly who is where and how they are involved even though we have to make sure the consignment makes its safe passage. I have an important meeting with some of them soon, concerning the second stage of my mission, which terminates your involvement and you can return to Cologne or wherever your home wharf is."

"As I've told you Major my job ends when my old friend takes over, he will help you to make your mission a success as I have tried to thus far." the skipper replied quietly as they ate their evening meal.

"But this barge is big enough for sea surely?"

"No Major. I've a flat bottom and a narrow beam, only suitable for rivers and canals. In deep open waters of the seas or oceans, any decent wave would capsize me no problem, that's why you'll be transferred over to my old friend to take you."

Luchens scowled at first, then brightened up by saying,

"Oh well! I'll be glad to see a clean-shaven man behind the wheel, who will do as he's told for once, skipper."

The skipper just grinned at the remark and climbed slowly up the steps to take over the wheel again.

It was the fourth day when they arrived into the famous Rhone valley just above Lyons, where the barge had to stop for its last pick up.

"Here we are Major, the famous Rhone. Once we've gone through the waterway system at Lyon and reached our jetty at Pont du Valons, it's only a few hundred kilometres from there, then on to the river mouth. We'll be going down a fast moving river, which means that we'll be able to make a faster transit.

Tell your friends where we are now and to expect us in about five days, although my orders state that I'll be handing you over in about six. So you've got some leeway to play around with if you need it once we get there."

"Glad you told me skipper, because I have a meeting with Frau Wintermann who might just stop the mission there and then."

"So long as you dance well and keep your appendages intact, then I can go home too." the skipper replied, steering the barge onto its allocated jetty.

"Here's our reception committee. We'll be here for about two hours, so I intend going ashore to drum up some business ready for my return trip, Major. Our Fatherland needs as many supplies as possible, and I am needed to continue bringing these supplies in long after you have left these shores."

"That's about right skipper. But make sure you're fully refuelled and fresh supplies on board before you go." Luchens replied, stepping ashore to greet his agent.

The skipper watched Luchens climb into a sleek limousine and drive off before he tended to his duties.

"Sergeant! We have a two-hour stopover. Get me refuelled and loaded with supplies before you and your men step ashore.

But I'll expect at least six men on board to stand guard." the skipper ordered.

"What's this place like skipper?" Kretshmer asked in bewilderment, watching several very unattached young ladies parading about in the sunshine.

"Plenty of 'Ooh! La! La!' and don't forget the delicious wine too. But watch out for any onion sellers as they are usually a sign that the Free French are about and ready to blow up or shoot some poor unsuspecting person or other."

"You can forget the 'Ooh! La! La!' stuff. Maybe a little tour around the sights, or better still, a good old lederhosen booze up. Where do you suggest?"

"In that case, there's a football stadium only a kilometre from here, and several good Bistros on the way. Try the Rue de Garrands to start off with."

"That sounds just right for my men, but I'm still blessed with my tackle. Oh, never mind that palaver skipper. I might just stay on board to keep an eye on things, and have a nice quiet time"

"That's up to you Sergeant, but if I was you, I'd use it as much as possible. Otherwise Frau Wintermann will get it if things go kaput with this mission."

Kretshmer merely nodded and went for'ard to sort out the men for those to stay on guard and those who went ashore.

The short time spent in Lyons proved to be very productive in the surge of morale in the men, even though it was the local brandy and the excellent Rhone wine that solved their problems, albeit short term. Kretshmer came back with a very broad grin, but Luchens came back with an even bigger one.

"It looks as if your mission is going better than you dare admit Major!" the skipper said genially.

"Yes skipper. You did say that if all went well and if I managed to get to my final allocated destination on time, I'd be promoted to a colonel and given a proper command of my own. Well, it was well spoken even from an ancient mariner such as yourself.

My controller agreed with my switch of plan, and us taking the short cut that we did from the lake. Because when we did, my support troops nailed a few more conspirators who were waiting for us in Chalons. I like it when a plan comes together, don't you." Luchens said with relish.

The skipper smiled and blew a large puff of smoke from his pipe before answering.

"There you are then Major, us old ones are still good for something. You have conned your superiors by using my planning and foresight to get your own way. Therefore in the field of battle, you owe me plenty. In the meantime I have already sent my report which makes your new promotion suspect. But unless we have an agreement on this, as soon as you give the firing squad the command, then you too will feel the bullets."

Luchens glowered at the skipper and tried to dismiss him.

"You'll never get away with this blackmail skipper. Your foul mouth and seditious ranting have branded you a traitor to the Reich. I have you dead to rights and well you know it, unless you can change my mind that is."

"Wrong again Major. Just remember who it is, that's on your tail and not mine. You Major, are unfortunately damned if you do shoot me, and damned if you don't. You really must learn the value of your troops and how to treat them. And you'd better start learning fast from the person nearest to you, and that happens to be the sergeant, not me. For it'll be him that will get you out of the shit, not me."

"Kretshmer? Pah! He might know his tactics in the field, but what does he know of the real art of living in the politics of the Reich. He's just cannon fodder for us 'Chosen' legions." Luchens said vehemently.

"The thing is Major. It's the likes of me, and Kretshmer who win the battlefields for the Fatherland, not pillow fights with arse bandits or painted tarts like your lot. You still have a lot to learn before you earn your Iron Cross and your spurs as a Colonel. In the meantime, I suggest that you go up forward and give the men a good stirring speech on the merits of being on the winning side of the war so far. That way, your own indoctrination will have more effect on those who've been there and done it all long before you were shitting your nappies."

Luchens looked daggers at the skipper, but gave him a brief wry smile and said.

"You may be of the old generation, but it's us that are calling the shots. And I literally do mean by the bullet and by the political process. Unlike me, you are not indispensable as you were in the old days."

The skipper shrugged his shoulders and commenced to get ready for sea, but gave Luchens a parting word, as Luchens left to speak to the soldiers.

"That maybe so Major. But even you need us so-called disposable bits of cannon fodder to get you where you want to go. Without us, you lot would still be playing funny leap-frog games with the Brown Shirt Lifters' brigade."

Luchens scowled at that turn of phrase but decided not to respond to the skipper's obvious wind up.

The barge cast off from the bustling jetty in Lyons and made its way down the majestic but very windy valley of the Rhone, on its last lap to the sea.

"Ever since we blew up those launches on that lake, we've underlined just what we are, a boat load of heavily armed soldiers. Therefore Sergeant, I suggest that during the next few days going down-stream, your men can stay on deck and enjoy the scenery."

"That's just what I came to see you about skipper. But aren't we stopping here and there for us to stretch our legs?" Kretshmer asked quietly, watching Luchens sitting broodily on top of the fuel drums.

"Yes Sergeant, every night for about four hours. I need my sleep too you know."

"I'd been wondering about that skipper. Just how have you managed to keep going these last fourteen days or so?"

"I am used to a ten hour shift at the wheel, but I've been forced to be doing about eighteen hours or so on this trip. Thanks to Hartman and my deckhand, I've managed the odd hour or two in between sorting out my navigational routes and so on. My biggest nightmare and cause for concern was the antics of that bloody fool Luchens. The only good thing that I might take comfort from is perhaps Luchens might grant me a decent wish other than to be lined up and shot in some back alleyway somewhere. And even then it's only that I could keep Hartman. He'd make me a good bargee partner he would. Somebody to hand over my barge to when the time comes."

"Unfortunately life isn't that simple skipper. I'd much prefer to go back and start up my own racing car company again than look after this arsehole of a major." Kretshmer said with a sigh.

"I know exactly what you mean Sergeant. Still, if the powers that be say that we've won the war and it will all be over by Christmas, then who am I to say otherwise."

Kretshmer gave a throaty laugh and whispered.

"Not even in the famous 1000 years. This mission of ours will end up in disaster if we have the likes of Major Luchens in charge."

"Soon to become Colonel!" the skipper corrected.

"Colonel? Who in their right mind would promote him beyond a bloody latrine digger? You do realise that if he becomes colonel, then he gets a regiment of his own. Pity the poor men who are forced to join him."

"Well Sergeant. It looks as if your baby-sitting job is not over yet, because it seems as if you're stuck with him until the end of the war. Mind you, you'll get promoted to the exalted ranks of captain or even major too."

Kretshmer swore softly as he looked towards the Major.

"May the Gods help us all! Here I was looking forward to being relieved by the time we got this far. It goes to show just who is shafting who to get on in this world."

"Well, never mind Sergeant. If he doesn't pick up his promotion by the time you reach your next leg of the operations, then you can safely say you're off the hook and homeward bound. Perhaps the Russian front would be more in your style?"

"No. I'd rather stay in warmer climes in around the Med. Greece or Italy even, but not there."

"Such is life for a soldier then. We navy men can only go where there is deep water, and plenty of it."

"I don't know, skipper. That lake was fairly shallow but you certainly had your share of action."

The skipper grinned and concluded their little conversation by saying.

"Ah yes! That's true, but then I did have you and your cavalry to back me up. Honours even shall we say!"

Kretshmer smiled as Hartman came up and relieved the skipper for a while.

"Just keep a little to the left of the centre of the river and make sure you don't bump into any of these lights on your port side. If you want to pass a slower craft ahead of you, make sure you show your red light to their green one. And always show your green light to their green light if one comes towards you, but slow down when you do pass on both occasions."

Hartman repeated his orders and thanked the skipper for the honour opf steering the barge once more.

"Keep me informed of any strangers trying to nose around." Kretshmer said quietly, leaving the soldier on his own in the wheelhouse.

Apart from the wonderful scenery gliding past the barge, the next few days were more monotonous for the soldiers than ever before, if it wasn't for the fact that the skipper insisted on a brief overnight stop for the soldiers to stretch their legs.

"We'll stop here for the night Major. There's a quiet little village only a few hundred metres from here, if you wish to check in with your agents. I need more provisions and fuel for our last lap anyway, so lets make the most of it shall we?"

"That's fine by me skipper, as long as we make the transfer deadline tomorrow."

"I'm off ashore to get some return cargo. No point sailing all that way back up the river without one. I have to pay for my fuel and provisions somehow Major."

"Indeed not skipper. But as I said to you almost three weeks ago, you'll get your just rewards and payments." Luchens replied coldly, which made the skipper stop in his stride.

"Major, after all this time and what I've done for you. I don't understand why you are still threatening me. I was hoping that you'd at least offer me an advance, to tide me over so to speak, so that I can get my return trip groceries organised."

Luchens sneered at the skipper, for his briefest show of reliance on someone else.

"This mission is still not decided yet skipper. I'll tell you when we get there."

The skipper sighed loudly as he ordered the barge to be tied up alongside the wooden jetty.

"Right then Sergeant. Half you men can go ashore to the village for half the time then swap over so that everybody gets time off. I'm going to report to my agent at the local police station. Make sure there is a sufficient security perimeter around the barge, with absolutely nobody be allowed entry other than our own." Luchens ordered gruffly, before striding over the gangway and ashore.

The skipper arrived back to the barge with the fuel and supplies and was allowed through by the sentry on guard.

"Just as well the soldiers knows us both cook, or we'd be dead meat like what we've got on the wheelbarrow."

"Aye skipper. Let's hope they don't recognise the Major, or he'd be shot on sight." the cook replied with a chuckle.

"You've always been a daydreamer cook, but on this occasion I'm inclined to agree with you."

"Welcome back on board skipper. The second batch of the men should be making their way back from the village about now. Any signs of the major?" Kretshmer asked politely.

"Let's hope the men enjoyed the local delights, as there's plenty of good food and wine to be had in this area. And no I haven't seen him since leaving. Maybe gone to the nearest town which is some three kilometres away. Let's hope he gets lost, better still ambushed by the Free Froggies!"

"That would be the answer to all our problems, but only in dreamland. Anyway lets get stored up again." Kretshmer replied, as he helped the men carry the provisions on board.

It was nearly sunrise when Luchens appeared and was surrounded by several of the sentries.

"Let go of me you stupid idiots. Don't you know its me?" Luchens shouted, wrestling himself free from the men who hustled him on towards the barge.

"Stop! Who are you?" Kretshmer challenged, raising his machine gun at the major.

"You're a dumkopft! I am your commanding officer. Who do you think it is Sergeant Kretshmer, Marlene Deitrich?"

"You obviously have a conflict of character. Come forward and show me your papers and be recognised." Kretshmer insisted.

Luchens swore loudly and went to put his hand into his pockets whereupon four machine guns were pointed at various parts of his body.

"Slowly! Keep your hands where I can see them."

"Sergeant Kretshmer! It's me Major Luchens! Can't you even recognise your own commanding officer?" Luchens asked in exasperation.

Kretshmer walked slowly up to Luchens and shone a very powerful torch right into his face, making Luchens cover his eyes from the glare.

"If you take your hands down maybe I can see just who you are." Kretshmer ordered, holding out his hands to receive the documents, then added

"Now hand me your papers, I must make sure you are who you say you are."

He looked at the documents very slowly and carefully, knowing full well it was Luchens, before ordering the sentries to stand back and allow Luchens to advance onto the barge.

"Welcome aboard Major!" Kretshmer said without any emotion in his voice.

"Just doing your duty and obeying orders Sergeant? Remember that in times to come." Luchens replied irately, finally stepping on board the barge.

"Just like the skipper when you were about to shoot him when he was only obeying yours!" Kretshmer muttered to himself, but Luchens heard him.

"Indeed Sergeant! You can't be too careful or you'll get shot along with him." he said angrily, descending into the cabin to rest before his next appearance.

"Let go both ends, and let's get to it!" the skipper ordered, as the barge slipped away from its berth and headed swiftly down stream again.

It was another full day downriver before the barge arrived at the bustling fishing port near Arles, for the skipper to call the Major to come up into the wheelhouse.

"Right then Major, we will be going down a canal to reach Marseilles. Have you got an r/v there, or do I make my own r/v and your departure point?"

"That depends on your r/v skipper. It makes no difference to me either way." Luchens replied in a non-committal tone of voice.

"In that case Major, I will proceed to the Red Point, where I have papers to get you through the security system and onto the next phase of your operations."

"That concurs with my instructions too."

As the skipper manoeuvred the barge into the approach of the canal, Kretshmer came into the wheelhouse and asked what was happening.

"I am taking a short cut to my disembarkation point, but within my own interpretation of my orders, Sergeant."

Kretshmer raised his eyebrows at this declaration.

"You are able to interpret your orders skipper? Does that mean that you are given a free hand on your orders providing that all goes well?" he asked in surprise.

"Yes Sergeant. We officers in command of a warship at sea have our orders, but its up to us to interpret them to our best advantage. As you say, if all goes well, then we win a sea battle, and the Kaiser bestows lots of honours and favours upon you. If not then we get it in the neck literally, for not reading our instructions properly and for losing the battle too. A double kick in the teeth if you like, if you get it wrong."

"Sounds a lot of rubbish to me!" Luchens expostulated, sneering at the explanation given to Kretshmer.

"Pretty much the same in the field of battle then skipper. If your tactics dooes not suit the terrain or the situation in front of you, then you lose the day and probably your life. More's the pity we didn't keep your kind in our mob, instead of executing them willy-nilly and replacing them with the propaganda hyped pen-pushers of today." Kretshmer said angrily as he stood up and faced Luchens.

Luchens shrugged off this statement with nonchalant disdain.

"I'm still a Major whereas you used to be one. Tell me just who is the smartest then Sergeant!"

Kretshmer lowered his machine gun to point towards Luchens and replied so quietly that even the skipper could hardly hear him, even though they stood besides each other.

"I'm SS the same as you Luchens. The difference between us is that I know I'm a soldier, you only pretend to be one. Just like the skipper, I don't have to prove my Iron Cross with Oak leaves. Whereas the likes of you can only gain a brass one over the dead bodies of men from whom you've pinched their glory to achieve it. Anybody can massacre innocent women and children at the gas chambers Luchens, but it's a different story fighting your way through to safety."

Luchens paled and started to tremble at this insult he had to endure without taking retribution. Instead, he pointed to his major's epaulettes.

"You will soon see that I don't need these to hide behind, Sergeant. I do my battles in different combat zones than yours. Mine is the more delicate and more sophisticated method of achieving my battle aims. Which means that you'll always be cannon fodder for me to decide where or when you die, and I will survive and continue to enjoy the finer things of life beyond your grave."

"Pilot launch approaching skipper!" Hartman shouted, pointing to the fast approaching launch. His intervention to the tense scene was a timely one, as feelings between the three principle characters on board were getting back to its deadly word and mind games again.

The skipper looked through his binoculars for a moment and told the engineer to slow down.

"Ahoy there! What barge and where are you from?" a loud voice said with the aid of a loudhailer.

The skipper grabbed his megaphone and replied.

"Motor barge *Hippleschaff*, from Lyons."

"We require you to show your full steaming lights in these waters. Where are you bound?"

"Bound for the canal and onwards to the grain silos at the Grand Juliette Basin."

"Thank you skipper! You have a four-hour wait at the incoming canal locks. Suggest you move through the bay, but keep to the temporary buoys on your starboard side. Good luck!" the voice said, as the launch turned full circle and sped away in spumes of white wake.

"That means, we're forced to take another detour if we're to make our r/vs, Major."

"Do whatever you think is necessary. Interpret your own orders skipper, not mine." Luchens said sarcastically, before going below into the cabin again.

The skipper gave Luchens a helping hand down the ladder by prodding him in the back with his peg leg, which resulted in

Luchens falling down the ladders instead of walking down them. He landed heavily onto the cabin deck and bumped his head on the table leg, which knocked him out for a few moments.

Kretshmer went below to tend to him as he came around.

"What happened there, Sergeant?"

"You must have shut the door too smartly behind you, causing it to knock you down the steps. It appears that when you bumped your head and knocked yourself out, you gashed your forehead slightly. I'll put a plaster over it to stop its bleeding." Kretshmer said soothingly, administering First Aid to him.

"For a moment I thought the skipper kicked me again with his peg leg. If that's so then he will not be going home in his barge, but in a wooden overcoat." Luchens said angrily.

"No Major. The skipper was nowhere near you. In fact he was up on deck checking the navigation lights." Kretshmer lied.

"Okay, that's enough! I'm all right now." Luchens said impatiently, as Kretshmer wiped the rest of the blood from Luchens eyebrows.

"I'm going forward to get the men fed now Major, as it looks as if we'll be needed before long." Kretshmer said brusquely, leaving the major looking and feeling sorry for himself.

"Skipper, the major is someone who does exactly what he says he's going to do. He's getting near his own showdown with his controllers and Frau Wintermann. So for God's sake, watch your step very closely and keep your opinions to yourself from now on." he whispered to the skipper, passing through the wheelhouse to get down into the cargo hold.

The skipper nodded but told Kretshmer that it was the major, who was on dodgy ground not him, but thanked him for his concern anyway.

The bay was calm and almost free of vessels when they eventually arrived at their destination r/v, on the shores of the Mediterranean Sea.

"Major, here we are. The Red Point Naval Base." the skipper announced, as he had the barge tied up neatly alongside the jetty. Luchens came up on deck and looked around slowly then back to the barge.

"We're about 30 kilometres short of our target of Toulon, skipper. Why have you brought me here?"

"Do not alarm yourself Major. This is as far as I can take you. I am a river barge and would capsize in these open waters. If you care to wait a couple of hours, you will meet someone who will take you directly over to your next port of call, never mind pratting about in Toulon. Remember what I said about initiative and interpretation of orders? Well this is yet another example for you to learn from. So sit back and enjoy your last decent meal before you hit the wide ocean waves again."

"I know all about ocean waves skipper, as I have sailed the Atlantic with a certain naval Captain who is carving his own glory out of virtually nothing." Luchens bragged.

"In that case Major, you will stay with me for your hand-over to my relief." the skipper concluded, waving to a man in uniform coming towards the barge's gangway.

"Hello Skipper! You're about one day ahead of schedule. Fortunately my pilot launch, the one that met you earlier, was able to tell me you were approaching, otherwise my squadron would have gone onto the next r/v point."

The skipper and Luchens went over the gangway to meet the naval officer.

"Nice to see you again Helmut! Yes, I'd guessed it was one of yours. I have ten tonnes of cargo, and seventeen men for you this time."

"No problem. Who's the rabbit this time?"

"Here he is. Captain Hartz meet Major Luchens of the 9th SS Legion." the skipper replied, introducing Luchens.

"Major Luchens, pleased to meet you. Gather you had a few spots of trouble on your way down. Glad you could make it, only my last consignment never showed up, and I've been laid up here for three weeks now playing nursemaid instead of out sinking allied ships."

"What sort of a ship do you have Captain?" Luchens asked politely.

"I have a flotilla of E Boats between here and Sardinia and the coast of North Africa. We provide an express delivery service, be it your cargo or the entire headquarters of a General's army. Only last week I was highly honoured when I took your famous 9ths' Eagle across to Tunisia with the new General to take command of the legion there. Looking forward to joining them Major?"

Luchens smiled, suitably impressed at the recognition by the captain towards his regimental honours, but was a bit nonplussed at the news of the new general.

"Thank you for delivering our Honours safely Captain, but who is the new commander?"

"General Stummel. But he was amongst four other generals. One of them is to take over the Afrika Corps and push the Tommies clear across the deserts to Persia. We carried one general and his staff in each boat, which means that we can carry two tons of your load per boat."

"When do we leave Captain?"

"Not until I get clearance from naval command. But in the meantime, you and your men are welcome to billet in my barracks." the captain said, and pointed to some low-lying buildings nestled under some tall trees along the sandy shore.

Luchens looked around the jetty and down to the group of buildings.

"But where are your launches Captain? I can't see them anywhere."

The captain laughed and pointed to a half-concealed cove.

"Over there and out of sight from prying eyes, especially from the Tommies own E boat squadrons who've been trying to find us for ages now. They've no chance!" the captain bragged and smiled at the skipper.

"It seems that you've learned a few things or more from the last lot Helmut! Even I could not see your hideaway base." the skipper said, slapping his friend's back gently.

"You were always playing battleships skipper, that's why." came the gleeful reply.

Luchens looked at these two aged mariners and shook his head in wonderment at their obvious delight in each others company.

The skipper turned to Luchens and told him that he was now in good hands and that he could report to his agent accordingly.

"You can use my radio room Major if you wish, but there's somebody arriving soon who will be wanting to see you immediately she arrives. Need I say more?" the captain informed. Luchens paled at the thought of 'her' and wondered why she was plaguing him even at this end of the first terminal.

"Search me Major. We have our controller you have yours. Typical German efficiency dictates duplication in all things, including arse paper." the skipper said sombrely.

"Better bring your barge through the boom defence cordon and lay her alongside the empty jetty I've got for you." the captain advised.

"Are you going with the Captain or coming with me Major?" the skipper asked.

"Yes skipper. I've had enough of you and your barge to last me a lifetime. Better get the boxes transferred over as soon as possible. Once I've met with my controller and had clearance, I'll be off. See you when you get alongside." Luchens said quickly, and walked away with Hartz.

"It looks as if we've got a night on dry land before we return then Sergeant." the skipper opined as Kretshmer and he watched the two officers leave.

"We shall be unloading the cargo soon, but the Major will be there to oversee it. That is just in case his documents do not tally with what's in the boxes. In other words, he will be opening each box in front of his controller, who will verify that he has the right weight come amount. This will take a long time, but if you want to see to your own business ashore skipper, then carry on. Anything untoward then you'll soon know."

"Glad you're on board Sergeant, otherwise I'd have to stay for that useless major to get his fingers and toes together to count more than ten. You'll find us in the Hotel-du-Bay just down the road from here. The proprietor is a friend of mine who acts as my agent for my cargo when I'm away. Maybe if you can arrange time off, come and see us, you would be more than welcome." the skipper replied enthusiastically, gathering his two crewmen and went ashore.

Chapter XI
A Compromise

"**W**elcome Major Lucky!" Wintemann purred, pointing to a seat next to her and enveloped him in a ring of tobacco smoke.

Luchens greeted her with a kiss on her offered hand and sat next to her as prompted.

"What brings you to this neck of the woods, as if I didn't guess?" he asked politely.

"Have a glass of excellent champagne! We will dine shortly, but tell me about your recent trip down here. I gather you have done very well for yourself, and congratulations in exterminating those pirates you came across. Maybe you have now opened the way for more consignments without us following every miserable mile to get here."

"You are kind! But it was really the barge's skipper…" Luchens started to explain, but Wintermann interrupted him.

"Perhaps you emphasise too much on the deeds of the navy, and not enough on your own. As a senior officer in the SS, you really must believe in your own efforts, and especially to repudiate anything that they have done. However, as you've just arrived, take me to lunch and we'll discuss your next move." Wintermann said quietly, but with deadly undertones in her voice that Luchens took specific notice of.

Luchens rose and offered the crook of his arm to escort Wintermann to the Officers dining room, where he met a neatly dressed steward who directed them to a table marked 'reserved', even though the rest of the tables were empty.

"I like it when there's just the two of us, lets hope the cuisine is as good as I've heard it is." she cooed, licking her lips and drank deeply from her ever-full glass of champagne.

The two of them enjoyed their meal and after-dinner wine, but Luchens was still waiting for the real purpose of their meeting, and it wasn't too long before she delivered her bombshell.

"I will inspect each box stowed on board the barge, because I have the suspicion not all is at it should be. There is an amount missing and only you can help me with finding out. Apart from that, I have a special report from a contact that a certain sea Captain is making, shall we say ' a double entry' or at least keeping a separate set of books." she said with candour.

"I have accounted for each consignment, and will verify each box. But please tell me about our friend the sea Captain. You do mean Captain Von Meir, of course?"

"Yes! He's a little man who thinks he can win the war on his own. He's sending shipments home via the Spanish Sahara and via Cadiz, but his figures do not tally.

I have already accounted for those in Cadiz, L'Orient and other places, but our captain seems to have some sort of system that emanates from his special bases in South America.

I have got at least ten sets of cock and balls from them and I'm thirsting for a few more. So tell me Lucky, what is this famous sea captain like?" she said, licking her lips when she mentioned 'balls'.

Luchens shook inwardly at the thought of his last meeting with this vampire, but realised that if it were he that she was after, then he would have been dead by now. He also remembered about the 'Pot people' and perhaps how lucky they were in comparison.

"Come now dear Lucky! You have proven yourself to me how good you are, so relax and tell me all. I need to know before I arrange my next visit." she purred, and gave him a kiss on his forehead as she stood up and went to the lavatory.

When she came back, she found that the captain and a few other naval officers had joined Luchens.

"Good evening Captain!" Wintermann said expansively,

"Your men serve up a good meal, congratulations. Now maybe we can get down to business." she added, but with a change of attitude bordering on anger.

"These are my boat skippers, who will take the major and his cargo over to Tunisia. We offer an express service but we need to refuel at Sardinia for the fast transit, which means that these officers will see that you arrive safely. As for the trip it will take about six hours to my forward base and a further six hours non-stop from there." the captain greeted, as he introduced each boat commander to Luchens and Wintermann.

"Be that as it may Captain, but I'm too suspicious of you navy men to believe it. You may wait here until the Major and I return from visiting another so called sea Captain." Wintermann said with a wave of her hand to dismiss the men, and walked out of the room with Luchens.

"You men play silly games with your toys, in fact all you do is willy wave. As an expert on willy waving, or at least the severance thereof, I can soon tell if a man is for real. Lets go and see this skipper that you keep moaning about."

Luchens caught sight of Wintermann's face in the street lamplight and shuddered, realising that just maybe the skipper was a true German after all, and didn't deserve the attentions of this 'She Devil'. And besides it was the skippers efforts that had finally got him here despite all the odds stacked against him.

The two walked slowly towards the barge, stopping to take in the scenery, before they finally arrived.

"Halt! You will not go any further until you identify yourself!" a loud voice commanded, stopping them suddenly in total surprise.

"It's me, Major Luchens. I am with Agent Wintermann from the Gestapo. Let us through!" Luchens demanded, as he shielding his eyes from the piercing searchlight coming from the barge.

"Stand still and show us your papers! Any false move and you will be shot!" came the directive.

The both of them produced their papers for close inspection by somebody they could not see because of the light, but Luchens recognised the outline of the Sergeant.

"Really Sergeant! Haven't you got enough to do other than disturb Officers of the Reich trying to do their own duty?" he said indignantly.

"You will be quiet. Any sudden moves and you will suffer the consequences." came the same stentorian voice.

"It appears Major Lucky, that this barge is well protected and well drilled. Full marks for your insistence in full security measures. I know now that you have done a good job on board this barge, well done my brave little man." Wintermann whispered patronisingly.

Luchens said nothing, but realised that his turn was to come when it came to handing out the medicine again.

"As you've been recognised you may come aboard." came the invitation, as they walked slowly over the gangway and were escorted down into the crews' cabin.

"So this is where you planned and made your home, dear Lucky! It's a tiny little place for all your work. Where do the barge crew and the men sleep then?" Wintermann asked, snuggling down next to the still warm stove.

"The barge crew share this with me, but the men live up in the cargo space where the boxes are." Luchens lied, moving over to the stove and started to make some coffee for them.

"From what you've told me, the barge skipper is much decorated. If this is so, then why does he sail this thing and not a luxury yacht somewhere?" Wintermann asked, seeing a photo of the skipper in his uniform from a bygone era.

"It appears that he likes to keep in touch with his old comrades, and the only way to do that was by river and this barge. The captain of this E Boat Flotilla is one of his old time warriors, which means that both of them must be doing some good for the Reich, otherwise they would have been shot long before now." Luchens said bitterly.

"Come come now Lucky! They're old and don't understand the needs of the new Fatherland, so unless you have something specific to draw my attention to, then we can leave them alone.

After all, General Gueller is their guarantor behind this, and as Gueller is my Godfather I need not concern myself too much with your complaints."

Kretshmer came down into the cabin and informed Luchens that the skipper was coming aboard and that he was ready for the offloading and inspection.

"Very good Sergeant! Make sure that all the crew and the men are mustered and ready for the inventory." Luchens ordered sharply.

"Hello skipper! The Major and Agent Wintermann are on board waiting for the inventory to begin! Kretshmer announced, as the skipper came over the gangway.

"Thank you Sergeant. This is an unnecessary procedure as all the boxes are there. I was hoping to sail back before daybreak to catch the canal's north-bound convoy." the skipper said philosophically.

"Skipper. My men are starting to unload the boxes. I need you to be on the jetty to witness that each box is as it should be and as it was when it arrived on board." Luchens stated curtly, watching the men move the heavy boxes out of the barge with ease.

The skipper stood humming to himself and looking disinterested in the procedure of counting and examining each box as it was stacked up on the jetty.

This went on for a little while until it was nearly over, before Luchens came over to the skipper and asked him to look at a certain box.

"As you can see skipper. This box is damaged, and to me it looks as if it was tampered with." Luchens said with glee, as he showed Wintermann, then the skipper what he discovered.

"You see these marks on the side? They are greasy finger marks, which means that someone on board has been tampering with it." he said quickly, then ordered Kretshmer to open it up.

Luchens inspected the contents before showing his discovery to Wintermann, and asking the skipper to look for himself.

"It appears that there are two items short from this box, where are they skipper?" Luchens asked sharply.

The skipper looked at the box and shrugging his shoulders denied any knowledge of the missing items, by asking.

"Did you check these last boxes before they were put on board, or were you too interested in contacting your fancy telephone number?"

Luchens went red as a beetroot before he managed to counter the accusation.

"I checked each box as they came on board. It appears that you or your crew have decided that you wanted an advance payment for your services, isn't that right skipper?"

The skipper narrowed his eyes and looked into Luchens ruddy face.

"Don't accuse me of any skulduggery Luchens. The last time we took your cargo was when we took the new engine on board. You were not anywhere to be seen, so as far as I'm concerned it's your pigeon not mine."

Wintermann looked at the box more closely, and saw that the box had been opened roughly but re-sealed neatly again.

"See this? There are two sets of nail holes in the wood. One made from the original, and one where the nails were replaced. To me that means someone has been tampering with the boxes." she said quietly, pointing out her own discovery.

"Sergeant! Arrest the skipper and his crew and bring them over to the cargo bay." Luchens bellowed.

The skipper and his two crewmen were grabbed and bundled unceremoniously down into the cargo bay by the burly soldiers, who then stood guard over them menacingly.

Luchens looked around the cargo hold but could see nothing or nowhere where the two bars of gold could be hidden.

"Right! The skipper had been ashore so I will assume that he has got rid of the evidence. Take them up to the barracks. I will get to the bollocks of all this!" Wintermann said with glee, drawing her large dagger to show them what she intended.

"But Major, the crewmen could not have taken anything otherwise the soldiers would have been disturbed, as they were sleeping on them all the time." Kretshmer protested on the skipper's behalf.

"You were always a soft hearted man, pity I left yours on, Sergeant!" Wintermann said with annoyance, as the crewmen were manhandled out of the cargo bay and onto the jetty.

The crewmen were frog-marched into the base and taken down a set of stairs to what any decent German base must have. A special area designated for torture and murder.

"Right have them stripped!" Wintemann ordered, as the crewmen were dumped onto the cold flagstone floor.

The soldiers ripped off the clothes from the three men, then strapped them spread-eagled out against a wall, as Luchens and Wintermann looked on in amusement.

"I'll start with you." she said, moving slowly over to the cook and started her famous tease and pain method of interrogation.

"Such a young man with such a lovely dick! Unless you tell me where you've hidden the gold you will no longer need it. Pity though, because it's quite good looking." she said gently.

"All you've got to do is look down my blouse at my tits and let me do the rest." she added, opening her blouse and exposing her cleavage to the boy.

She sensed his delight and with expert deftness brought him to an erection, whereupon she masturbated him until he spent his seed over her chest.

"There, that didn't take you long! Did you enjoy the view and your moment of pleasure? " she asked gently wiping herself with a hankie. Then with a sudden change of mood she grabbed hold of his genitals roughly and said

"A typical boy, with no control over your body. That was probably your first time to look at a good pair of tits and get your sap going. But unless you're careful it could be your first and only time to enjoy the pleasures of the flesh, and by the clock on

The Lost Legion

the wall it took you precisely all of 90 seconds. That's how long you've got to tell me what you've done with the Reich's gold! she snarled, as she wiped her hands clean, all over his hairy chest.

"I don't know what you're on about, really I don't!" he gasped in protest.

Luchens was sitting on a chair watching with glee, at the torture methods that he had managed to endure and escape from. "You'd better do what she asks cook, or she'll chop it all off for you!" Luchens said soothingly, as if to coax him to submission.

"But I don't know about what you speak about. Honestly I don't! Skipper tell her I don't know. "he pleaded, and started to whimper.

Wintermann looked at the overhead clock and counted down the seconds to the last, before she went over and sliced the genitals off the cook and stuffed them into his open mouth as he screamed in his last breath.

"One down and two to go! Now who's next?" she said as she wiped her bloody hands on a towel that was handed to her by Luchens.

She turned to the engineer whilst still cleaning her large dagger and said softly,

"Must have this nice and clean for you, don't want you catching some disease, now do we!"

"I don't know what your game is Wintermann, but we are not guilty of your accusations. I have a personal warrant from General Gueller as my guarantor and the safety of my men. Why don't you phone them and verify my claims!" the skipper called out, in hope to save his engineer.

Luchens asked the skipper where the piece of paper was for him to phone up and check his story. The skipper told him it was in his trouser pocket.

Luchens went through the pockets and finding the sealed envelope, opened it and quietly read it. He showed the letter to Wintermann first, before he threw it into the open log fire in the corner, saying.

"What paper? I saw no paper! You have been lying to us all along skipper. Maybe if you give me your contact telephone number, I'll phone them instead."

"The piece of paper you've just destroyed you stupid fucking asshole, was a duplicate. The real one is with Gueller." the skipper said furiously and divulged the contact number.

Luchens went over to the telephone and cut the wire from it, then tried to dial the number.

"See! There's no such number. You've been lying again skipper! Tut tut! For an old wartime hero, you should be more careful with who you deal with. Now perhaps we can dispense with your pretence and get down to the real truth." Luchens said, with content and a smirk on his face.

Wintermann was now tending to the engineer and managed to get some sort of conversation from him.

"But I tell you! That crate must have been damaged when we changed engines. The engine must have smashed into it, and when I noticed it was broken, I simply nailed it back together again. The sergeant was there at the time, he witnessed it all, honest!" the engineer gasped, as Wintermann completed his involuntary ejaculation.

"That sounds very suspicious to me laying the blame on my best sergeant! But to give you the benefit of the doubt I'll only make you a eunuch!" she said, cutting his testicles off and threw them onto the wooden table next to Luchens.

The engineer screamed loudly then fainted as the blood poured from him.

Wintermann removed a safety pin from one of her lapels and pinned the wound up to stop the man from bleeding any further, saying.

"He's got some truth in what he says, but I want the sergeant brought here to verify that statement."

Luchens left the cellar and brought back Kretshmer to explain to Wintermann what happened to the box.

"Yes, that's true. I didn't see the box until it was nailed up again although I was watching all along. Nobody could have spirited away the missing pieces, unless someone used the special hatchway to get at it again afterwards." Kretshmer said at length, then added.

"Come to think of it, the major used the hatchway to get to me and the men, when we were on the lake."

"Yes, he was the last man to go through that hatchway, and probably stood upon the very same box to climb over all the others. Me and my crew don't wear fancy footwear, maybe that's why that strange footprint is marked on it." the skipper said swiftly.

"Is this true Lucky?" Wintermann asked offhandedly, seemingly disinterested in any further interrogation.

"Yes. But I only had time to get the men organised for the lake pirates. Come to think of it, the engineer took too long in shutting the hatch behind me again!" Luchens said in his defence.

"So it seems that it's your word against the skipper, Lucky. But there can only be one to remain alive from this. Sergeant, have the skipper dressed and brought outside." Wintemann said coldly, and then turned to Luchens.

"No wonder I call you Lucky! You have just one bullet to do your duty, do it well lover!"

Luchens marched out behind the struggling skipper and told him to stop just by a wall.

"So this is your final payment Luchens. You really don't give a shit if I, or my crew are innocent, do you! I'll bet you didn't look or search the barge properly in case the missing gold bars had fallen out of the boxes and into the bilges. In which case the engineer was too busy with his engine, and when he discovered that the box was damaged and reported it to the sergeant, all they could have done under the circumstances was to nail the box back up again, totally unaware of the real event. I don't care if you shoot me or not, but if the gold is found in the bilges, what will you do with it?

Wintermann has already written it off, so are you going to keep it for yourself in case of the truth coming out? Are you really Major Luchens or just a double agent trying to feather his-" but the skipper didn't finish.

Luchens shot the skipper in the head and watched the dead body fall to the floor before kicking the lifeless skipper in the crotch, saying.

"You might not have felt that, but I did at the time, you old bastard!"

Kretshmer had hidden himself behind an old water barrel just a little way off, to observe and hear Luchens execute the skipper, and waited until Luchens was almost by him.

As Luchens approached, Kretshmer stood up in front of him and kicked him so hard in the crotch, that Luchens was lifted several inches off his feet, making him fall backwards over a low wall and knocking himself out as he hit the ground.

"That's for the skipper you bastard!" Kretshmer whispered as he moved silently over to see if there was any life in the skipper. He felt a faint trace of a pulse, so plugged the bullet wound with a piece of the skippers shirt and gently lifted him so that he was sitting up against the bullet-riddled wall behind him.

"Live, old man, live." he whispered.

"Tell Gueller and my missus. Get Hartman to take my..." The skipper whispered, before he passed away.

Kretshmer gently laid the body down on the ground and covered him with his own overcoat before standing up and giving him the traditional salute from one serviceman to another.

"I'll see that your body is sent back. Pity I wasn't quick enough to show them what I've just found." he said quietly then gave Luchens another hefty kick as he passed him on his way back to see Wintermann again.

"Luchens shot the skipper, but there was no need, because of this!" Kretshmer said angrily, throwing a heavy bundle of metal wrapped in oily rags onto the table

"This was found in the bilges of the barge. If the skipper and his crew wanted to pilfer from the boxes, they would have taken much more than that. Besides, there was much more missing at the hand-over to the Swiss agent. So how will you account for the skipper's death to General Gueller?" Kretshmer asked, as Luchens came staggering into the room.

"It was you who attacked me! You are dead meat now Sergeant!" he growled.

"On the contrary dear Lucky! Here is the missing gold that you cared not to search for. It will be for you to account for the death of the skipper and his crew, not me. I'm only here to get the merchandise back again." she said sombrely, and picking up the bundle of gold and the gruesome remains of the cook's and the engineer's testicles, left the torture chamber.

"More to the point, what's going to happen to a perfectly good German barge?" Kretshmer queried, as Luchens started to swear and kick the furniture around like a spoilt brat.

"I kept telling the skipper I'd shoot him, but oh no he just didn't listen, did he. It's yours and his fault that I shot him!" Luchens expostulated.

Kretshmer gave a throaty laugh and raised his machine gun at him.

"You are a spineless bastard, with no thoughts of anybody else but yourself. You're used to shooting innocent people for no reason whatsoever, but you should not have shot the skipper. I've asked you a question Luchens! What about the skippers barge? Are you going to shoot and sink that without trace too?"

Luchens looked nervously at Kretshmer and tried to gauge his chances of turning the tables, but decided to appease him and wait for a better chance to get even.

"That Hartman! He's the only one that can handle the barge properly, so he can take over as its new skipper and maybe he'll be able to take it back to the skippers wharf, wherever that is. There, how's that for a compromise, a life for a life, Sergeant!"

"Too late for all that Major, but under the circumstances you've actually made a wise choice this time. If it were up to me,

I'd give you a good kicking then have shot. I'll be watching you more closely from now on. One false move and this gun will give you a severe dose of lead poisoning. So you can take it not as a threat Major, but a solemn promise. Now lets get moving before a search party is out for you again, you first!" Kretshmer snarled, as he pointed to the door with his gun.

"You'll never get away with it Sergeant. I'll have you transferred to the Russian Front before you know it, if in fact you survive getting to our other destination." Luchens said, as he spat at the ground in front of Kretshmer.

"Better make your move a good one Herr Major! Your last one was a total disaster, as you will find out when Gueller gets the word that you shot his best agent. Now move along, we haven't got all night!"

Chapter XII
Something Stinks

The gold was transferred to an antiquated steam ship that looked as if one good wave would sink her, and the only modern thing on it was its crew. A squadron of E boats earmarked to escort this very valuable cargo surrounded her, making her look like mother goose and its chicks.

"All your cargo and your men will embark on the *'El Bronco'* whereas we in the gunboats will ride 'shot gun' as the Yank cowboys would say."

Hartz stated, but looked behind Luchens to see where his friend the skipper was.

"Where's the skipper? I know he can't sail with us, but he was to sign a special paper before I took your shipment and delivery."

Luchens felt very uncomfortable at the mention of special papers and suddenly realised what Kretshmer had said. He tried to bluff it out by offering an excuse, but Hartz saw through what he said.

"Major Luchens! The skipper would not have departed without seeing to the 'small print' on his contract. Now please tell me where he really is!" Hartz demanded sharply.

Luchens turned round and faced Hartz whilst tapping his lapels.

"See these Captain! This means that you do exactly what I say, or is required of you, and without question. You will not speak of that traitor to the Reich; otherwise you will receive the same punishment that he got. Do I make myself clear, Captain?" he snarled ominously.

Hartz sneered and spat into the face of Luchens before striking him.

"You stupid fool of an asshole. We may only be Reservist Forces, but we out-rank you many times over, and if you've harmed the skipper in anyway then you'll face your own firing squad sooner than I can take you over to Africa. We have direct orders from the Chief of Police himself, who has been behind all that the skipper and I have been doing."

"I think you'd better shut your face Captain, as these lapels override any of your orders or whatever you think you must do for whomever your lowly command thinks!" Luchens said drawing his pistol.

"Now unless you get a move on, I will find an officer to take your place, and you will join your erstwhile friend in the ditch where he belongs."

Hartz looked at the much younger man and saw much fear in his eyes, which belied the bluff and arrogance his tongue was spewing forth.

"Major! You're in for a dose of your own medicine sooner than you think. As for me, I don't give a shit who I'm ferrying. The sea and the British Navy are my only foe, not you jumped up pen-pushers who think they know and see all!"

"Well better get your ship moving then Captain. I have a deadline to meet." Luchens said quietly as Hartz turned away to do his duties.

"Before you go Captain, I want no delays or funny strokes pulled on me again like your dead friend. Get me to my second destination safely then you can disappear over the ends of the earth as far as I'm concerned."

Hartz sneered at Luchens as he signalled the squadron of E boats to start up and leave the base.

The E boats skimmed over the waves of the Mediterranean, making light of the occasional wave that lifted their bows up and over into the tops of the next wave, leaving the antiquated steam ship to plough its way through the oncoming seas.

Luchens was thrilled at the breathtaking speed of the boats that ran rings around the mother ship.

"How fast are they going Captain? Faster than any British boat?"

"Only doing about fifteen knots, but watch when they meet a

The Lost Legion

convoy of Britishers who are in our pathway. Then they'll really skim the wave tops at a good thirty knots."

"Is that all? I was on a merchant ship recently that could probably outrun these toys! Luchens bragged, as he remembered his time on board the *Black Rose*.

"Is that so?" Hartz asked sceptically.

"There's no British warship around at the moment can match us. Unless of course one of their mine laying cruisers happens to come our way, then we can look out. But their boats equivalent to ours are much slower because theirs are more heavily armed, and we can outmanoeuvre them at will."

"Whatever. But our own speed certainly makes up for the four knot speed I've been doing on the river and canals, recently."

"Different craft, different waters. They can't carry the load, nor sail as far as this tub can, but even then, we're in and out of a landing area before anybody can take a breath."

"It's good to hear positive talk again Captain. My last skipper was shot as a traitor for his attitude against our leader. Heil Hitler!" Luchens said loudly over the noise of the craft ploughing its way over the waves.

"Maybe he was too old to appreciate the good of the Reich and still harboured the weakness of the old Kaiser!" Hartz said promptly, which pleased Luchens immensely.

"You are a good sailor and a credit to our cause, skipper. I will see to it that you are able to relieve your squadron commander when we arrive, as he is part of the old guard that signed up to the Versailles Treaty which we are re-writing, even as we speak!"

Hartz merely nodded but said no more, as he fought the bucking craft over the wake of one of the other boats as it crossed over in front of them.

"They may be fast, but they still have to be very careful they don't take off and do a loop!" Hartz added, as Luchens grabbed hold of his safety harness more tightly.

"You had better go below Major and get yourself settled for a three day voyage. Our friends will keep watch over us!"

Luchens merely nodded and went below to rest and get rid of his disappointment in not being able to ride on one of the swift launches, that played hide and seek with his grubby smoke enveloped bucket that should really belong to the deep with all the others.

Luchens had got used to the vast open oceans, and found it somehow embracing again compared with the almost walking pace he'd endured on the barge down the rivers and canals.

The voyage across the Mediterranean in the creaking, smoke-stained vessel was benign, and uneventful for Luchens, as it arrived at the port of Tunis.

"Here you are Major. Our friends left us a few hours ago to escort another VIP going back. So consider yourself lucky you arrived in one piece. Better get your men organised whilst I get your cargo ashore. You by the way Major will be in charge of all the cargo, which is 200 boxes." Hartz smiled happily as Luchens appeared to be staggered by the amount in his care.

"But I only brought fifty crates. Where did all the others come from?" Luchens gawped, watching the heavy crates being unloaded onto armoured half-track vehicles.

"I told you that you were only but one small fraction in the delivery of a much bigger load awaiting you to take for delivery. My old friend that you had shot, was responsible for delivering this cargo onto my ship, and your particular load was the last one." Hartz said ominously, glaring at Luchens.

"Nobody tells me anything, and I have been lucky to escape the Merry Eunuch maker so far." Luchens moaned.

"Then you'd better start showing signs of remorse when general Hanschel and Gueller comes to meet us." Hartz said gruffly, making Luchens turn pale and mutter incomprehensible words that only he understood.

"Oh look! There they are Luchens! Isn't this your lucky day to be able to explain what happened to the skipper!" Hartz said as he tormented Luchens and watch him writhe with fear and uncertainty as to what he should do next.

"You had better go down and greet these officers. But a word to the wise Luchens, there is another more powerful than these two, and she should be waiting around somewhere for you!" he added.

"But how did she get over here so quickly Hartz!" Luchens groaned and started to wipe his sweaty forehead.

"One of my boats brought her over yesterday when you were still trying to eat your breakfast!"

"You bastard Hartz! Why didn't you tell me all this was in front of me!" Luchens stuttered as the two generals walked over the ship's gangway.

"What? And spoil a perfectly good day for you! No way Luchens! You murdered a good pal of mine, and one of Gueller's top agents to boot. Suffer it gladly, you fucking idiot!" Hartz said with a growl as the two generals arrived to receive their salute from them.

"Captain Hartz! Good to see you again." Gueller greeted light-heartedly.

"How was your trip Luchens?" Hanschel asked tersely.

Both generals spoke to their own men for a while before they decided that it was time to see the offloading of the cargo.

"Major! Necessity dictates that you will be given a Field Commission to Colonel. For that you will be required to form a special regiment that will guard this cargo and the other two which already landed some days ago." Hanschel started to say, but was interrupted by Hartz.

"You can't be serious about this General! This is the very person who, under the flimsiest and outright mistaken evidence, murdered our skipper!"

"You did what?" Gueller exploded.

"Well it's like this General!" Luchens started to explain, as Gueller drew his pistol and waved it under Luchens nose.

"General Gueller! Be very careful to what you are about to do!" Hanschel advised.

"I want to know why my best agent was killed by this no account pen-pusher. Unless he has a valid reason as to why he should not be taken away and executed, he will meet the same fate!" Gueller said, his face red with anger.

Luchens explained the outline as to what happened but only what he wanted them to hear, and not the truth as to what really happened.

"There you see Gueller! We knew there was a mole in your midst, and he must have been a double agent to survive so long. He's dead now and we've got the right cargo to deliver!"

"Pah! Something stinks, and I'm betting that your man isn't telling the truth!"

"He was met by Frau Wintermann before all this and he is still here. Which to me means that he's in the clear, and all the cargo is here and accounted for, Hans." Hanschel replied in a conciliatory tone.

"Besides. He has to try and account for his own shortfall from the South American and Spanish Sahara operations, which as of now, I believe, runs into several hundred tons."

"Maybe that's why Wintermann's hovering around like a buzzard with several new eunuchs to point to where she had just visited!" Gueller said slowly, as if he was convinced of Luchens' innocence.

"Anyway. As I've said Luchens. Here is your documentation and insignia of promotion to a Colonel.

There is an armoured column to be taken to a special location out in the desert, where you will set up camp and protect them whilst you await further consignments before they are eventually handed over to our Arab friends in the east. In fact you will rejoin your 9th Legion, where their Eagle will be based, which is far to the south of the allied land forces.

There is a new general being sent over to take command of the entire Africa Korps, but your general in command will be separate from his operations, save for supplying reinforcements and supplies on his southern flank." Hanschel said smugly, handing over the symbols of rank.

Luchens looked down at what he was receiving and stuttered his thanks.

"I shall see that I wear these with pride Herr General!" Luchens said finally, giving his standard Nazi salute accompanied by the singing of his Legion's anthem.

Hartz turned away with disgust at this sickly display of Nazism, and went back to his work on board the ship.

"It appears that some of us do not appear to share our Fuhrers dream of a glorious 1000 years Reich!" Hanschel said to Gueller, as Luchens finished his rendition.

"Some of us are still civilians under all this gloss of military badges. After all, I'm still the Reich's Chief of Police whether I'm in uniform or in civvies!"

"Yes Gueller! You have a point, but decorum is still requested when a man gets promoted even to a lowly corporal such as Mein Fuhrer!" Hanschell replied as Luchens put on his new lapel badges to denote his rank.

"Here you are Colonel! Here is your declaration signed by the Fuhrer himself. Earn it with pride and glory. Heil Hitler!" Hanschell said patriotically, which Gueller echoed, although only going through the motions, half-heartedly.

After a further briefing, Luchens was dismissed by the two generals to return to the ship and see to his men.

"Sergeant Kretshmer! Come here this instance!" Luchens commanded sharply, seeing that his men were standing idly by the big pile of boxes.

Luchens looked to see if his order was obeyed and found that nobody had stirred in front of Germanys' newest colonel.

"Sergeant Kretshmer! Come here this instant before I have you shot for insubordination!" Luchens shouted again, but still no answer.

Luchens strode over to the men and harangued them to get into a cohesive formation, more in keeping with a formation of soldiers.

"Where is Sergeant Kretshmer?" Luchens demanded angrily, as he glowered at the impassive men in front of him.

"If you mean Captain Kretshmer, then here I am!" Kretshmer said coldly, arriving right behind Luchens.

Luchens spun round and saw Kretshmer with his machine gun pointing towards him.

"You! A Captain? How? Why?" Luchens stuttered as his anger was replaced by scorn.

"Let's put it this way. You a Colonel? Why? In fact, how?" Kretshmer responded.

Luchens took a long time to regain his composure before he spoke.

"Captain Kretshmer! You will see to it that all these men are to remain guarding these crates until such time as I get suitable transport for us."

"There is no need Luchens!" Kretshmer said with total disdain for the man.

Luchens pulled his pistol out of its holster and pointed to Kretshmer.

"Now look here. I'm the commanding officer around here. You bloody do as you're told right now or I'll shoot you down like a dog." He snarled.

Kretshmer crooked his finger at Luchens and pointed to a waiting half-track, then told Luchens to climb up and see for himself.

Luchens stood up in the driver's seat and looked out all around him.

Kretshmer stood next to him and growled.

"Just look around you Colonel Luchens and tell me what you see?" he asked with a sarcastic emphasis on Luchens rank.

Luchens looked around him for a moment but said nothing.

Kretshmer waited for a moment before pointing out to the vast array of men and war machines that was amassed for as far as the eye could see.

"It is obvious you cannot recognise any of our troops you see before you, which really emphasises that you do not fit the requirements of a military man in charge of a whole regiment, let alone a barge full." Kretshmer said with total disrespect to Luchens, then pointed to the vast array of military might.

"Over there, you've got The Italian Littorio armoured division. Next to them you've got the Italian Trieste motorised division. In front of us you've got the 15th Panzer division, with the 7th Nebelwerfer division. To your right you've got the Deutch Afrika Corps (D.AK.) with an armoured recce battalion. But most importantly, you fucking assshole, you've got the final element of the 9th Army, but in your case, the 9th Eagle, all ready in column and ready to move off. You'd better take this opportunity now to familiarise yourself with your own troops so that when the general asks you about them you'll be able to answer him in a suitable manner despite you being a jumped up pen-pusher."

Luchens looked at each place to where Kretshmer pointed and gasped in amazement at the magnificent sight of such German military might.

"Before you get carried away Colone1, you've only got a column of twenty assorted vehicles plus about two squadrons of panzers at your command. Word has it that we'll enjoy the main van of this army as company for part of the way before we split off to go our own separate way. So you see, there's no need to panic about security around here."

"My order stays the same Kretshmer! Get them loaded immediately and have them positioned in the middle of the convoy. I shall be back soon to move us out!" Luchens responded angrily, then jumped down from the vehicle and walked off with a swagger towards the main command complex that overlooked the harbour.

Luchens walked out of the baking sun and into the cool interior of the sandstone building that was the HQ, and felt the goose bumps rising on his skin, as the difference of temperature started to bite in to his body.

"Major! No, Colonel Lucky! How nice to see you again!

Congratulations on your promotion, a girl can feel secure with a good rank around her!" Wintermann purred, and drinking from a large rimmed glass and blew a smoke ring at him.

"Frau Wintermann! How lovely to see you again, Lenka." he acknowledged, with a nod and clicked his heels.

"You have a special unit with you that I need the use of soon. How long will it take to settle your regiment down in your new camp so you can join me on a special assignment?" she asked swiftly, finishing off her drink.

"I have not had my instructions and final briefing, but as soon as I can dear Lenka!"

"You have a new general in command of the 9th Legion, who carries the 9th Eagle everywhere he goes. General Von Stummell, no less!" she said arrogantly.

"What, the Stummell from the Ardennes campaign?" Luchens asked politely, but was suitably impressed.

"Well, part of him anyway! " she said wickedly, licking her lips, and poured another drink into her large empty glass.

"Care for a drink before we go in and see him, Lucky?" she teased.

"Why not!" Luchens said boldly and took hold of a glass and waited until Wintermann filled it up.

"It's a naughty little wine that was given us as a present from our Italian friends who should be guarding this little patch of sand from the Britishers." she laughed, as he smiled and took his first sip of the sparkling red liquid.

"Ah yes!" Luchens replied, before they walked into a large hall full of books and ornaments.

"Here we are Willy!" she greeted, but giggled at the reference to the general's name as she clung onto Luchens arm.

"Colonel Luchens!" Stummell said politely, taking no notice of the tipsy woman.

"Very pleased to meet you Herr General!" Luchens responded, suitably impressed both with his commander and the surroundings in which they arrived at.

The Lost Legion

"You have a special duty to perform, which I do not envy you. Which is to set up a special camp about 200 kilometres due south from here." Stummell commenced, using a pointer at a large map hung on the wall behind his seat.

"The purpose of your mission is to provide a secure area that will hold a large gold depository, which the Fuhrer will draw from to pay for the Arab oil we are currently in need of. If all goes well, then by this time next year, we shall have pushed the British and their Allies out of North Africa, thus giving us a clear run into those Arab oil states.

Once there we can take as much oil as we want, without any further payments, and once that is done, we can seal off the depository until it's needed to fund future campaigns with our Japanese allies against the Ruskies and the Yanks.

You will have a full regiment of motorised infantry to man the depository, along with a squadron of Panzers. You will also have several artillery batteries, a squadron of various aircraft, and of course a full range of clerks, cooks etc."

"That sounds good to me Herr General, and I've already seen the troops, very impressive too. But what about the logistics involved for all this? Who supplies this depository, you, or do I have to get my own men to bring them in?"

"For the moment, it will be done by the D.A.K. supply division until you have secured your perimeter. From then on, it will be by regular supply runs to and from your base by your own supply units. However, you will be given replacements or re-enforcement's on each depository run, to supplement your own men making the delivery."

"What about security, communications etc?"

"You will be responsible for your own base security, but we have a special telephone link already set up for you which also links up to my command here, and directly to Berlin. That includes your radio communications links too. Should you be contacted directly by the Arabs either by communications or by physical representation by way of a deputation then you will report this immediately. Under no circumstances are you to answer them or even meet them yourselves, as this will be done from Berlin, and under strict directives from the Fuhrer himself or his Deputy."

"How long will I or my men remain on guard of this depot?"

"If the Britishers know what's good for them and pack themselves off this continent, then I expect it will only be a matter of say, six months, maybe one year at the most! But you will have a rotation of guards as the depository also has a Desert Warfare training camp next door to it that will also use your facilities. Do not concern yourself on that score Colonel, as your men will be glad to remain there instead of being sent to the Russian Front!"

"I'm not concerned Herr General! Just trying to get an overall view of the situation."

"Indeed Luchens! There is just one thing else before you go, and that is the suitability of some of your men to help you achieve your duties. Your rank is that of an SS Officer, but you are restricted to Depot duties and will have no hand in promoting or demoting your men at will. That is why I have already promoted at least five NCOs, to an appropriate commission and I intend to promote more as and when I deem necessary. You will be advised to take heed of these officers, whose military expertise will help you achieve your own glory under our Eagle."

Luchens pursed his lips and looked at his feet for a moment before taking the risk of countermanding the general's decision.

"Don't take it too hard Lucky! All you've got to do is make sure nobody runs off with the gold. If they do then you can send for me and we'll sort them out together!" Wintermann said quietly, watching Luchens squirm to gain control of his feelings.

"I suppose you're right Frau!" Luchens conceded, drawing himself ramrod straight and saluted Stummell in the statutory Nazi fashion.

"You'd better get going now Colonel, as this is the start of the sand storm season, and you don't want to dig yourself out from under several feet of stinking sand!"

Luchens nodded his head and left with Wintermann hanging onto his arm.

"Not so much the sand and dust dear Lucky, it's the damn fleas that seem to get into any hiding place. Get a mosquito net and a stout pair of shoes to squidge the scorpions!" she advised as they parted company in the large hallway.

Chapter XIII
Arabs

Luchens gave the order for the armoured column to move off before he stepped inside his mobile headquarters, as it too lurched into motion in the midst of the heavily laden vehicles.

He looked at the survey map and smiled at the irony when he read the words 'By courtesy of HBMS Ordnance Dept'.

"It seems that our maps are well documented. But we have several changes to add to it in order for us to arrive at our given map references, Captain!" Luchens said with glee.

"Yes! The British have been very productive in these parts, thankfully in map making only, Colonel!"

Luchens turned his head to see where the unfamiliar voice came from and saw an officer not known to him.

"Just who the hell are you? Where, in fact how are you involved with my command?" Luchens asked more in surprise than in anger, which was rising rapidly by the second.

"You are in your command vehicle and I'm its senior officer. All you have to do is direct the operations and I will implement them from here. Until we set up our base, that is."

"Yes, Yes, Yes!" Luchens replied impatiently.

"But who are you to take command of a Colonel!"

"I'm Agent Kohls of the 9th Eagle Gestapo Unit. You have probably met my Great Uncle, the skipper off the barge that brought you down to the Med from Nemegan." the fearsome looking man stated, his bulk overshadowing Luchens.

Luchens looked at Kohls and gulped vigorously for a while, trying to catch his breath just like a freshly caught fish.

"Your, your Great Uncle did you say?" he stammered.

"But how are you linked to that traitor?" Luchens managed to say, whilst gaining his composure again.

Kohls looked at Luchens for a moment and with his eyes half shut took out his revolver and pointed it to Luchens.

"So it's true then! You were the one who murdered him!

Give me one good reason why I don't shoot you this instant, just like the stinking cur your kind always turn out to be?"

"Let's put it this way Captain. I'm your Colonel and I'm the Colonel of this regiment. You will be advised that from now on, you take your orders as and when I give them. Failing to do so, then I will have you shot as a traitor too, Gestapo or not." Luchens growled, pointing to his new insignia on his lapels.

"Your badges of rank only means that you're a Colonel of the SS whereas I'm Gestapo just like the eunuch maker that's on the prowl around here. I shall be requiring a full confession from you as to why you murdered a valued member of the 3rd Reich!

But before all that you will tell me what happened to his barge. Where is it now and who is looking after it? That barge is needed for further shipments due for transportation our way."

Luchens gulped and stammering at the reminder of what still could befall him, and tried to bluff his way out of the situation.

"I care nothing for your Great Uncle, nor his favoured position within the Officers Brigade. I have a job to do, and before you say anymore, Fraulein and I are lovers and we've teamed up together to get to the bottom of the pilfering that is affecting our Fuhrer's ability to pay the Arabs for the oil we need to win this petty war. It turns out that your precious Great Uncle was found with his hand in the tills. Also he was spreading treason and sedition with that foul mouth of his. And that he deliberately sabotaged my gold delivery by setting the river pirates onto us, that's why I had to take a full platoon of heavily armed men with me all the way here. So it's for those very reasons he was shot."

Kohls smirked at Luchens, which seemed to goad Luchens into further revelations about his time on the barge, before Kohls stopped him.

"You always were a fucking asshole Luchens. Er sorry, I mean a fucking asshole of a Colonel. You're trip on my Great Uncle's barge was only a decoy, as the real shipment arrived last week. The papers that my Great Uncle carried were not found on his body, nor did he make the phone calls to say that he'd arrived despite all the attention you got from the pirates. This shows that although he did arrive, his death means that somebody in the know is in fact the mole or double-dealer we've been looking for all the time. Your profile and description fits in nicely to our investigations, which means that you'll be sent for in due course to attend a special hearing with the Fuhrer himself."

"You dare to threaten me, Captain? You seem to forget just who promoted me. I am the Colonel of the regiment and earned my spurs in doing so, now get out of my way or I'll have you removed feet first." Luchens shouted, trying to re assert his newly gained promotion.

Kohls looked at Luchens and his badges of office, and decided that his own skin was worth more than the past honours of his now dead Great Uncle. Instead, he spoke further but in a more conciliatory tone of voice

"You are indeed the colonel of a regiment. But I too have a duty to perform, whether you like it or not. Let us agree on that for the benefit of our beloved Fuhrer, and maybe try and co-exist between our separate but dovetailed duties." he said, replacing his machine pistol into its holster

Luchens nodded slowly in agreement, and felt very much relieved when he saw the holster buttoned back up again.

"Glad you approve Captain. Now get on with those duties and let me get on with mine." he snarled, and turned to scan the terrain that was displayed on the map.

It was several hours before Luchens decided he had had enough swaying and lurching in the desert sands, and called for the column to halt for a meal break.

"Kohls! Have the column move into an ever-decreasing circle. This command truck will be in the centre, but make sure the panzers and the other heavy half-tracks are out on the perimeter to stand guard. In fact, get a perimeter guard posted outside that as lookouts. We don't want any intruders or nosey neighbours coming uninvited towards us." Luchens said, drawing a picture of what he wanted onto a piece of scrap paper.

"We have a special routine for the desert storm conditions Colonel! These are contained within the Afrika Corps manual that we must adhere to. Suggest you adopt these, otherwise if we're buried under the sand, then nobody would recognise our formation as traced in the sand when it's gone." Kohls said diplomatically, tossing the manual over to Luchens.
Luchens flicked briefly through the booklet, and threw it back.

"As I've just said Captain! Get the column into the formation I'm ordering you to do. Which incidentally is on page twenty of that ancient book that you gave me. I don't want to see it ever again, as things have moved on since it was printed. And if you don't believe me, circa 1918."

Kohls caught the thrown booklet and looked at the date of issue.

"Maybe First World War, Colonel, but very much up to date considering that this desert existed well before the Pharaoh Kings' time some 5,000 years ago" Kohls sighed before he left the command vehicle.

Luchens growled at the departing man, and at the two other men that were part of his command team, but decided to dismiss the incident with a shrug of his shoulders.

Kohls arrived back to report that the regiment was as ordered, but wanted to know how long the stop was for.

"There is a sand storm brewing up and coming our way. When it's gone, then so do we Captain. In the meantime, you will keep proper communications with HQ. Unless you have something else to disagree with me?" Luchens asked belligerently. Kohls said nothing, and left the cosy interior of the command truck to brave the winds that were starting to whistle noisily around the encircled vehicles, as the sands of the desert were blown around like a snow blizzard.

The vehicle rocked violently for several hours, as the storm blew itself over it then left the half-buried column to continue its devastation on more unsuspecting victims who found themselves in its path.

Luchens felt rough hands shaking him from his slumber and woke up to find Kohls shouting at him.

"Colonel! Wake up! Our column is half buried in the sand! Wake up you bloody idiot!"

Luchens pushed Kohls violently away from him.

"Next time you waken me like that Captain, I'll shoot you like a dog. What have you woken me up for at this ungodly hour?" he snarled checking the time from his watch.

Kohls stood back from Luchens as he rose up from his camp bed, and opened the door for Luchens to see out.

"Our column is digging itself out of the sand and we need to be moving on to our first r/v position where our water and fuel is kept. We have to be there by tonight." Kohls said animatedly.

"Well don't just stand there moaning about it Captain. Get it organised. Have the column ready to move in one hour." Luchens said angrily, looking at the frantic efforts of the soldiers trying to dig their vehicles out from under several tons of sand.

"Come back and report to me when it's done!" he added, dismissing Kohls with a wave of his hand, and laid back down into his little bed.

"Corporal! Bring me some coffee and something to eat!" Luchens roared.

"Would the Colonel like some toast and marmalade with his coffee?" came the response.

"Yes! And plenty of it, I'm starving!"

Luchens decided to get up and ready himself for his meal, but took a look outside his vehicle door to see what was going on. He marvelled at the men digging furiously and shovelling the sand away, to reveal the rest of what was buried under it. He noticed that the weapons were caked in the sand and that some of the men were coughing and spluttering as they were finally released from their sand tombs.

Kohls came back some time later to report that the column

was now ready for moving, but the men needed a little break to have food and water before they did so.

"Give them fifteen minutes Kohls! And I want each soldier to test his weapons, especially those of the heavy machine guns and the panzers too. Can't have sand clogging them up just when we need them, now do we!"

Kohls gave Luchens a look of total surprise, as if to wonder how he knew of this technical detail.

"Don't look too surprised Captain! I know of these things even if you don't. In fact you will instruct each tank and half-track commander to make a canvas cover for their weapons, which will be installed on them before the next sand storm or dust dervishes. That way, our weapons could be used immediately, instead of wasting valuable time in cleaning them out before hand. Good tactics always win the battle, as a famous navy captain told me recently, Kohls. See to it!"

Kohls saluted and returned to the anxious listeners that were gathered around the command vehicle. The 'food' order was received with great cheers from the men, who started to busy themselves with renewed vigour to get their bodies sustained for the next lap of the desert.

The column moved off in concertina fashion, as the column first stretched itself at the front, then compacted itself whilst the rear vehicles caught up.

"Colonel! Our overall advance is only 10kph, but we need at least 15kph if we're to get to our camp in time." Kohls volunteered, pouring over the maps with Luchens.

"It's the prevalent conditions of our terrain that dictates our speed Captain. On top of that, we have to keep our formation so that the Luftwaffe can recognise us. Besides, we have all the time in the world to get to our new designated camp area, so what's the rush?"

"Colonel! Half of this column has just been assigned for other duties on the Eastern front near a place called Benghazi, and here is the signal, and your orders!" Kohls said, handing the signal pad over for Luchens to read.

Luchens read it quickly and started to rant and rave at its implications:

"But the general promised me a full regiment. How am I going to guard all this without at least that amount?"

"We're supposed to set up a depot within the main camp area Colonel! As long as we maintain our own column of tanks, half tracks, and at least a battalion of infantry, then we could just about manage." Kohls said softly and as diplomatically as possible, but it was not enough to assure Luchens.

"When we get to our r/v, get me HQ on the line. I need to speak to them!" Luchens barked, as he read his new set of orders again from the signal pad.

Luchens busied himself with his new orders and other written instructions for hours, before the vehicle door opened up and Kohls stepped inside.

"Captain Kretshmer reports that he's located the hidden well and fuel dump, which is a kilometre up ahead. I have the column already on its rotation, but into two opposing circles." Kohls reported, taking off his dusty goggles and cap.

"Very well Kohls! Get the land cable connected up as soon as possible, and have the men bedded down for the night. We move off at 0600 tomorrow morning!"

Kohls saluted and left, just as Kretshmer entered the vehicle.

"Colonel! There appears to be a whole army of Arabs camped a little way off our secret well. They appear to be the Black Dervishes, but according to one of my men, they're some several hundred kilometres off their own lands." Kretshmer said calmly, as he too removed his goggles and dusty cap.

"Haven't a clue what you're talking about Kretshmer! Come and show me." Luchens replied, angry at seeing Kretshmer again.

Kretshmer took Luchens up the side of a steep sloped sand dune, and indicated that they should lie down and look at them through binoculars.

The Lost Legion

Luchens looked at the several hundred coloured tents sprawled out over the desert, and at the large herd of camels that were corralled at the foot of bust on the other side of their very own sand dune.

Kretshmer tapped Luchens on the arm and pointed to another direction that had many more tents covering the desert.

"These below us are the Black Tribe, hence the colour of their tents. Those over there are the Dophens, their tents are blue. There is another tribe just arriving from the south.

Their colour seems to be turquoise. What is more, another tribe is just arriving from the south. Their colour seems to be amber. I'd say about 1,000 or more in each camp."

Luchens looked more closely at the tents but scoffed at the feebleness of what he saw.

"Pah! What chance have they got against panzers and a full regiment of mechanized infantry, Captain! Not even the entire Polish Cavalry could match just one squadron of Panzers!"

"The thing is, we're restricted to solid ground or light sandy areas on which our engineers have made our roadway. They can come and go on their camels, and out-pace us at will. I've seen such a raiding party in the Sudan, several years ago. I know exactly what these little men are capable of, and so do the British, that's why they left the Arabs alone."

"The British are soft and have no idea of fighting a real mans war, that's why we threw them off of the continent, at Dunkirk. They're no match for us, neither are these filthy wogs." Luchens said arrogantly, as Kretshmer dragged him off the parapet and back down the slope again.

"Be that as it may Colonel! But if we're about to lose half our column by the morning, then we might as well start digging our graves now. On the other hand, if I know what they're here for, let's just give them the gold that belongs to them anyway." Luchens snarled at that suggestion by saying.

"Oh no I won't. I have the Eunuch Maker watching me. I'd rather face these wogs than have my bollocks cut off and stuffed into my mouth."

"You're stuffed either way! Just like you did those poor men off the barge." Kretshmer snarled, shrugging his massive shoulders and walked away.

Luchens walked back to his command vehicle and had his officers gathered inside for him to make some sort of plan.

"We have a secret cache of water, fuel and supplies. They don't know that we've got a consignment of gold. Look at the map! We're on our way to the southwest of them, which takes us away from them. They don't know we're here, nor do they know of our strength. So all in all men, we've got the upper hand and can do as we please, come what may." Luchens concluded.

"A signal from HQ Colonel!" a radio operator announced.

Luchens read the signal to himself then out to the others: *'Expect an Arab League army that should be forming up to the South East of your position. Keep well away and out of sight. You will not engage in any hostilities, save in self-defence. You will arrive at your new base camp by sunset tomorrow. There will be no excuse for failure to do so. By order! Hanschel.'*

The other officers spoke quietly amongst themselves for a moment before Luchens ordered them to be quiet.

"Get the fuel loaded, and the men fed. We will pull out within the hour, but under strict silence. No speaking, whistling, smoking, clanking. Not even the clink of the change in your trouser pockets. Every engine must be muffled, and every axle greased, so that no noise could be heard. Kretshmer, you will provide outriders and form a cordon about 500 metres from us. If you hear any noise, find out where it's coming from and deal with it. Captain Kohls, you will see that all weapons are loaded but safe. I don't want any trigger-happy soldier firing off at some ghost or whatever he thought he saw. Lieutenant Hertzel, you will seal off the secret well and supply dump before rejoining the end of the column. Major Becker, you will form the column in double file and close to the roadway before we move off.

The Lost Legion

Remember that there are mines placed alongside the road, so nobody is to stray off the road for any reason. Any breakdown, then the vehicle in front will tow that vehicle until we're safely out of range, which I estimate is around ten kilometres distance. Any questions?" Luchens asked after a short pause.

"Just one, Colonel! We can destroy these Arab tribes, no problem. But what happens if we get hit by another sand storm?"

"Good question Hertzel. We simply make a double circle as before, but make certain that our heavy armour is outermost and ready for use when we need it." Luchens countered, which satisfied them all. The officers left one by one to go to their duties, as Luchens started to make diagrams and marks on his field map.

"This will show exactly what was what, and who did what!" Luchens muttered to himself as the vehicle finally lurched into motion.

"Bring me something to eat, Corporal! Even the Colonel must eat some time!" he said expansively, feeling pleased with his little plan.

The column snaked its way quietly around and behind the unsuspecting Arabs, and made a peaceful get away long before a sign was reported that the Arabs had finally detected them.

"They must have been gathering to gang up on us as we came along the roadway. But we've tricked them and now they're hopping mad that we've escaped them. They won't travel overnight, so we'll be long gone before they come after us. Once we've got within the main camp area then they'll pull up and leave us be until the next time." Kretshmer said with a grin, as Luchens looked through his binoculars at the distant Arab camp sites.

"Better get a signal through to HQ about this!" Luchens said absentmindedly, and wrote his signal on a pad for the Telegraphist to send.

"Here, send this to HQ and to our new base camp to expect us much sooner than later."

The column roared its way through the darkness until sunlight, before they stopped for a brief respite and for Luchens to get his bearings.

"We've got less than 10 kilometres to go, but the road has been obliterated, and it will seem more like 100 kilometres. I want two half tracks up ahead and in that direction." Luchens said, pointing to the road markings on the map, then out to where the road should be seen.

"Have an engineer on each vehicle to mark or disarm any landmine you come across. We will follow on behind you at 50 metres, and in close formation. I don't want to lose any of the column now, after what we've just come through." Luchens ordered, as the two half-track vehicles roared off in front of the column.

The slow forward pace of the column was starting to prove troublesome for the engines of the panzers and the other heavily armed trucks. That in turn created breakdowns and frayed tempers from the men who tried to cope with it all. This went on all morning until they met a half-track vehicle coming towards them.

Luchens was alerted to this visitor, and was brought forward to meet them..

"I'm looking for Colonel Luchens!" came the request from the stranger.

"Speaking, but who are you?" Luchens asked back at a very dusty uniform that told him it was a general standing up in the front cab of the truck.

"Ah Colonel, you've made good timing. I wasn't expecting you for at least another six hours or so. Gather you met half the Arab legions earlier!"

Luchens saluted the man wearing the regalia of a Generals' uniform but still couldn't recognise the officer.

"It's good to meet up with friendly forces, but who are you Herr General!" He asked diplomatically.

The General laughed and remembered his military etiquette.

"Come now Colonel Luchens, you should make it your business to be able to recognise your own General. I'm General Stummell of the 9th Eagle! And don't you forget it!" he said quickly, ordering his truck to turn round and face the way he had just come from.

"Follow me Colonel. I'll lead you to our secret base camp up in those hills, that's why you couldn't find any more road to follow." he said, and the truck roared off quickly, followed closely by the mile long column of tanks, trucks and various other military transport.

Luchens was standing up in the lead truck as it twisted and turned in a maze of wadis' that led them to the foot of the hilly terrain that stretched out before him.

"Welcome to 'DEATH SANDS VALLEY' proclaimed a notice Luchens passed, before entering into a barbed wired compound.

He climbed out of his vehicle and strode over to meet the general, who was waiting for him.

"This will be your new base area. These hills are like rabbit warrens, and where I have my base area. These wadis' are dry watercourses that never see water, only sand. The winds come up them quite strongly, which funnels any sand through it and out onto the open desert.

That's why you see nothing but bare rocks and stones around the place." Stummell stated, pointing to the various features he'd just described.

"How often does this funnel effect occur General?"

"We had one the other day which started the season for them. But the real big ones are due any time now, and will last for up to a week. That's the time for everybody to take cover, or they'll be buried alive if caught out in the open beyond the Wadis.

These winds can shift several fifty-foot high sand dunes into oblivion. My reckoning is that the next big sandstorm will come in about two weeks time, and will siphon at least one million tons of sand through these valleys and blow it clear across the desert and dump it some 1000 kilometres away to the west. At least we only get the winds, but anybody in the way gets the sand, thank goodness."

"Thank you for your assurances General." Luchens said gratefully.

"Not at all Colonel! My Adjutant will show you where and to get your men billeted and where your camp will be organised. Call on me tomorrow morning, as I will give you a guided tour of the entire area. Any problems speak to the adjutant. My quarters are over there in that thing, which outwardly, looks like an old cave, but in fact it's a very comfortable one, with all mod cons. See you at 0900 Colonel!"

"Very good General!" Luchens responded, saluting the departing man.

Chapter XIV
Delicate

Luchens walked into his new accommodation, which was a maze of corridors and rooms were carved out of the sandstone hills.

"It looks very familiar to the work done by a Navy engineer I happen to know, Major Sturmer." Luchens observed, as the adjutant showed him the extensive underground workings.

"Perhaps Colonel. But an obscure French archaeologist discovered these caves only five years ago. Nobody knew of his discovery until we rescued him from the Arabs recently, and he brought us here to see it. He met with an unfortunate accident causing his demise, which incidentally happens quite frequently around here. But here are your quarters, which are next to a large cavern where your depository will be set up."

"What about my men and my military hardware?"

"Your men and their equipment are housed in similar arrangements as you, but on the other side of the wadi. There is a fully equipped radio room next to your quarters, and you have a central service corridor to use to get down to the General's command post. Here is a diagram of your camp and its amenities. I suggest that you get it duplicated for the benefit of your officers and men. One wrong turn and you'll get lost, Colonel!"

Luchens took the map and stuffed it into his pocket and followed Sturmer closely into a surprisingly brightly lit cave.

"As you can see Colonel, all mod cons. Hot and cold water; lighting at the flick of the switch; lots of fresh air. You even have a fully operational central heating system to counteract the cool temperatures, especially under all those metres of sand above you."

Luchens shivered slightly as he felt the coolness on his skin, which was bliss to him and a great relief from the baking heat of the deserts.

"This will do me nicely Major! Before you go, kindly send one of your orderlies to take me to see the General at 0900 tomorrow morning!" Luchens asked, as Sturmer was leaving.

"Very well Colonel! In fact I have an orderly assigned to attend you, his name is Private Blucher. Be gentle with him, he's such a delicate creature."

"Not for me thank you Major. Send me someone more, versatile, if you like." Luchens replied swiftly.

"Oh but he is very versatile! Someone who will not tell any secrets that you might share with him, in your moments of loneliness, Colonel." Sturmer said, giving a knowing wink to Luchens, before shutting himself out of the room.

"Private Blucher! Come out wherever you are!" Luchens shouted.

He heard soft footfalls on the sandy floor and saw a shadowy white figure coming towards him, before it spoke in soft lisping words.

"You called, Herr Colonel?"

Luchens looked at the slender youth and was surprised at how young and delicate looking he really was.

"How the hell did you get in this mans' army? Get your arse and the rest of your cock-sucking body out of my quarters, I've no truck with such goings on. Go on, get out!" Luchens screamed, kicking the private up his backside, propelling him into the main door of the room, which was opening at the time.

The private almost knocked Kohls over who had entered the room, but Kohls managed to catch the crying youth and steadied him.

"Colonel! That is no way to treat your manservant. If you don't want him, I'll swap you with the one I've got. Mine is, shall we say, over-ripe for me." Kohls said quietly, nodding to the youth.

"You go over to my quarters and bring back my man over here, and stop your crying, dear boy!"

Luchens almost retched at the sight of this homosexual behaviour, and was glad to see an elderly Sergeant come into the room.

"This is Sergeant Kramsfeld. Now we both should be very happy!" Kohls said, leaving the room with his arm around the still sobbing youth.

"Kramsfeld! Get my effects unpacked and provide me with some food within one hour from now!" Luchens snapped, and strode angrily over to a large map that was hung up on one of the walls, and studied it until the sergeant came back.

"Your food Colonel!" Kramsfeld announced, placing a large silver tray full of piping hot food onto a table in the middle of the room.

Luchens looked at the food and smiled at the extras that the sergeant was also laying out for him. Looks good Kramsfeld. But where did you get this very excellent bottle of wine from!" he asked, holding the bottle reverently.

"We have our own wine cellars out here Colonel. Nothing but the best of everything apparently, due to the fact that most of us are here for the duration of the hostilities on this continent, certainly."

"Oh? But according to your Military profile, you're a South African Dutchman! How come you're down in these caves dishing up my food and not fighting the British?"

"We're called Boers, and it's a long story Colonel. But for now, my primary role here is as a Tracker and Guide. I go out with search parties and bring in those units who get lost or are on the wrong end of a pasting from the wogs or the fuzzies. From what I gather, you may have encountered a few of them during your march down here."

Luchens laughed at the understatement of the 'few', and started to eat his meal with gusto, with Kramsfeld fussing around him throughout.

"Thank you Kramsfeld, that was the best meal I've had for a long time. The cooks should be pleased." Luchens said expansively, draining the last drop from the wine bottle into his glass.

"Thank you Colonel! It was nothing. Just desert chicken in a special sauce!" Kramsfeld said with a slight smile as he cleared away the meal debris.

"Anything else before I leave Colonel?" he asked politely.

"Yes! I need you to explain this map on the wall. But first, I need to take a shower, or a bath. So come back in about thirty minutes!" Luchens replied civilly, as Kramsfeld left with the tray.

Kramsfeld returned and explained the map to Luchens in great detail, then reminded Luchens that it was time for his other duties, concerning the consignment that he had spent weeks bringing to the camp.

"I have a good Captain taking charge of all that Kramsfeld! But I suppose you're right, after all he was a Sergeant just like you once. Is it light up top still?"

"Yes Colonel. Four hours of daylight left before we go black. So if you have any surface inspections or whatever, now is the time to do it. Nobody is allowed on top after dark. If anybody, that includes you Colonel, is found up there during that time they will be shot on sight."

"Is that so! Then we'd better get on with it. You will escort me at all times, and make any notes that I may need taking down. Any problem with that Sergeant?" Luchens asked coldly, and waited to gauge the response.

Kramsfeld nodded slowly before saluting in army style.

"No problem Colonel!"

"Well don't just stand there, let's go!" Luchens prompted, following the very large and burly man out of the room.

Luchens inspected the soldiers' billets and found that they were Spartan but functional. Then saw that the trucks and all the other military hardware were stowed properly. During all this time, he had Kretshmer report on everything and anything he wanted to know, but really was trying to belittle him in front of his new sergeant.

Kretshmer knew what Luchens was trying to do, and was always at least two moves ahead of him. He even smiled at Kramsfeld, who was looking impassively at everything taking place.

"He's the Eunuch Maker's lover, watch your step Sergeant!" Kretshmer whispered, as Luchens was busy looking at something a little distance away.

"Yes Captain! I've met his type before. He's no chance in the survival stakes out here, but thanks for the warning!" Kramsfeld whispered back before Luchens returned again.

"Right then Captain! The last thing is the shipment. Have you got it deposited and accounted for?"

Kretshmer indicated to where they were to go, and all three marched across the hot windswept bedrock of the Desert Mountains.

Luchens entered the labyrinth of tunnels that led to the underground vaults.

"Almost like the pyramids, Sergeant!" Luchens said, as they finally entered the large chamber.

"Each consignment has its own coding, and its own place in the rows of boxes. For instance, DJ1 to DJ20 is the amount of Dutch Jew gold boxes; BJ1 – BJ10 is the Belgian Jews, and so on. All except for this row, which apparently was here before we arrived. That has the emblem of what looks like a rose alongside its date identification numbering. But all our boxes are accounted for as per the manifesto sheet we had made on our way here Colonel. And for your interest, that includes the double nailed one." Kretshmer added sarcastically, but drew no response from Luchens.

"Indeed Captain! That will be all for today. There will be a special meeting with the General tomorrow morning at 0900. See that all officers attend." Luchens said, returning Kretshmers' salute, then left with Kramsfeld at his side.

"This way Colonel. This is your short cut to your quarters. Incidentally, the General's office and HQ is on the other side of the cavern. But you can only get there by way of the main tunnel that runs above this one. Its complicated at first, but you'll get used to it, then you'll start swearing about the amount of tunnel detours you've got to make just to go 100 metres underground, yet only about fifty feet when above it." Kramfelt apologised, shutting yet another tunnel door, before opening the one in front of them and finally entering Luchens quarters.

"It's dark up top now Colonel, which means that the camp zone will be in 'total black-out state' until sun up again. I repeat my warning to you. Nobody, not even you Colonel, is allowed up on top, only the general and our special patrols and guards. They kill first then ask questions afterwards." Kramsfeld said ominously, then added

"Unless you wish to dine alone, I will call for you to escort you to the officers mess to dine there. They have a good selection of drinks, tobacco and even a cinema show every other night."

"That sounds fun Kramsfeld. In about an hour, yes?"

"Yes Colonel. But in relaxed mess dress." Kramsfeld nodded, leaving Luchens to his own devices.

Luchens enjoyed his evening in the officers' mess and retired to his room to enjoy his first night in a proper bed, since leaving the naval patrol harbour in France.

He was woken up by the rattle of crockery as the smell of rich coffee filled his nostrils.

"Time for breakfast Colonel! You have one hour to meet with the officers before the General arrives!" Kramsfeld said quietly and placed the breakfast tray on the table.

"Morning Kramsfeld! I have to say that was the best sleep I've ever had in over two months. Last night's party was a good one too, but I didn't watch the film." Luchens greeted affably.

"Indeed Colonel! You nearly outshone the Adjutant, which would have been a first. I'll lay your uniform out for you before I leave for my own meal."

"Don't forget to come back for me. You're my official minder from now on!"

"As you wish Colonel!" Kramsfeld said diplomatically, and left the room.

The meeting with the general was full of surprises for Luchens and his officers, who were given a special conducted tour of the camp zone, and its special natural phenomena.

"The wadi system is valley-like and akin to a snake, with the landing strip as its belly. The wind comes up from the desert, and by the time it twists and turns and comes out the other end of the valley, it's a horizontal tornado of some force.

The reason why the rocks are so clean is because the wind blasts them with the particles of sand as it flows through the funnel, hence the curved shape on the sides of the valley that is almost a tunnel in effect. The bends are of special interest, because that's where all our tunnel and emergency shelters are. The storm season is nearly upon us. The one we had a few days ago was only a *hisser*. We expect the next one as a *moaner* followed by several *howlers*. Each *hisser* can turn into a *moaner* at any time or even into a full *howler* within thirty minutes. Which means that anybody hearing the *hisser* and is caught out in the open, must get the hell out of there and into one of the 'bends' with dugout shelters. The winds can flow through at over 200 kph making the sand particles like armour piercing bullets. That half-buried tank you saw down the valley in fact isn't half buried. It was cut in two by the last *howler* we had. The crew couldn't get into one of the bend shelters in time when the sand blast came through, and the poor four man crew was never found again."

"If the wind can shift several thousands of tons of sand, does that account for the escarpment we came over to arrive here General?" Kretshmer asked simply, earning a disapproving look from Luchens.

"Yes Captain. And the reason why our road has been obliterated for several kilometres to the north. In fact, half that escarpment will probably not be there when the howlers have finished their act this year. Incidentally, our secret water and fuel storage dumps which you used to get here, are the remains of valleys just like this one, but much smaller.

We had to dig out the bodies of the troops that perished there, and that's why we've moved everything down to the very gates of the wind tunnel so as not to be caught out again. Also it's a great place for a secret gold depository that nobody would dare approach, especially during the windy seasons."

"How is it that the coastal towns and villages are not affected by these storms, General?"

"I'm no weatherman nor geologist, but my educated guess would be that this valley and others like it along the mountain range always manage to divert the sand storms directly east or west, and they expire naturally over the vast distances they cover. We're in the middle with the Moroccan coast about 2,000 kilometres to the west, and the Suez at roughly another 2,000 kilometres to the east.

We have hard rock under us, but there's a lot of shifting sands all around us, until you reach the salt pans of Egypt where you meet the quick-sands before arriving at the Nile and onto the Red Sea." the general explained, pointing across the expanses of the map.

After a brief halt for lunch, the meeting went on well into the afternoon, with the general detailing the duties of Luchens and his half regiment.

When it was over Sturmer had the officers stand up, and led an impromptu rendition of the 9th Eagle's battle song, which the general was well pleased with.

"Thank you gentlemen! It is good to hear such music from such a fine legion to which I'm proud to command. Keep the Legion spirit going and good luck!" he said, saluting his officers and left the briefing room.

Chapter XV
Flaps and Ziffers

Over the next few days, Luchens and his troops got fully acclimatised and into their desert routine, before he decided to venture back out into the desert wilderness again.

"Here, here, here and here, are where we shall be setting up temporary bases and shelters!" Luchens stated, pointing to the large wall map of the entire North Africa.

"If you notice, I have given specific route co-ordinates, and all emanate out from this base like the points of a star. Each one will have its own codename, and will be replenished by each outward movement of troops, so that on the return trip they will have fresh supplies when they need it." Luchens explained, and then waded into company duties and which officer would be responsible for them. The briefing lasted quite some time before he finished and sent his officers away to conduct their new tasks.

Kretshmer had his company engaged in defensive manoeuvres against sandstorms and enemy attacks. During that time, he devised a system of protecting his men and vehicles, which he demonstrated to the General.

"I am suitably impressed Captain, but the real test and effectiveness of your system will need live action. Let's hope that it's up to the imminent storm seasons." the General sighed and returned the salutes before being driven away in his staff car.

Kretshmer and a platoon were on the move down through the valley towards the airstrip, when he detected an eerie silence and felt uneasy.

He silenced the men and told them to listen very carefully, but after a little while the consensus of opinion was, nobody could hear anything.

"That's just it men! Silence." Kretshmer whispered and held his breath for a moment.

"Something's not quite right, better get ourselves underground and to safety!" the platoon Sergeant whispered but was hushed by Kretshmer.

"Look at the sands on the landing strip, it's starting to move slowly towards us! Do you hear the faint hissing noise? Once that gets loud then we'd better be elsewhere!" he said, as the sands started to creep slowly at first around their feet, then speeded up as did the hissing noise.

The platoon ran flat out towards the underground aircraft hangars as the hissing noise got louder and louder, and managed to shut the heavy iron doors before they heard a low moan. The moan got louder and louder to an almost deafening pitch and kept that way for several hours. The men discovered that the entire mountain seemed to vibrate with the noises, and also found it was useless trying to shout at each other over the noise.

This phenomena gave Kretshmer the idea of inventing hand gestures and signs for times like this, and wrote it all down whilst the sandstorm raged outside.

As the noise was ear bashing, so was the deafening silence in the storm's aftermath.

Kretshmer led his men outside again and carried on with his interrupted work around the camp, until the platoon Sergeant signalled for him to come and see what he had found.

"Who is it Sergeant? Was he one of our men or what?"

"The ID tag says it's a Private Bluker, and it looks as if he's been buried up to his neck!" came the reply.

Kretshmer investigated the immediate area around the head sticking up out of the sand, and found that it was only the head and nothing buried underneath it.

"Better get it wrapped up and take it to the M.O, but lets see if there are any more casualties in the valley, Sergeant." He said with a shrug of his shoulders.

The men combed the entire length of the valley but only found one or two wrecked vehicles that were also caught in the maelstrom. But what surprised everybody was that a large V had been carved through the escarpment that fronted the camp.

"It's as if the wind must be made of solid steel to carve out such a dent, Captain."

"Yes Sergeant, the next storm will probably complete the job. Still, look on the bright side. It saves us driving over it because it's making a pass through it for us." Kretshmer replied philosophically, and indicated to his men to follow him.

They trudged over the sand dunes, getting almost buried up to their knees in the yielding sands, before Kretshmer decided to take his men back, as a useless exercise on how to travel across soft sands.

It was during the evening in the officers' mess when another *moaner* was at its height, that Kretshmer sought out Luchens. Not by choice, but by duty and what he had to say.

"Well Kretshmer! Speak up, the Sergeant here won't bite you!" Luchens gloated as he saw Kramsfeld tower over Kretshmer when he came near.

"I have an idea that you'd probably not appreciate Colonel, but one that Kramsfeld would. So you had better listen up!" Kretshmer snarled. There was no love lost between these two, and Kretshmer did not hide his disgust or disdain for Luchens. The feelings were mutual, but because of the circumstances and fates of war, both men were inextricably bound together by a superior force neither of them had the power to overcome.

Kretshmer showed his drawings and plans, first to Kramsfeld then Luchens almost as an afterthought.

"Well Sergeant! You're the expert, what does all this mean!" Luchens asked petulantly.

"The tracks on our half-track vehicles are half the width of a panzer. These new ones I have in mind are twice the width of them. The theory is that because of the wider tracks, the weight of the vehicle can be spread much more, and help the vehicle to move more easily over the soft sands.

We can have special sleighs made so that the container

platform can be pulled over the sands just as if it was snow.

The lead vehicle can be modified to have a tank engine and tow two maybe three of these containers. That way we can cut down on the vehicles and men required to travel across the desert.

It won't take long to get them made, and we can try them out when we make the next consignment run. If the outward stores drop cannot be handled by this means, then we'd have to revert back to the full convoy of half-tracks again." Kramsfeld explained carefully.

Little did the trio know, but the *moaner* had stopped and the general who was standing nearby was listening to them.

"It appears Kretshmer, you are more than a gallant soldier. I will give you permission to build a full working set of these, and we'll test them down below the airfield. You have two days to produce this, and its protective screening that you also suggested." the General beamed, as Kretshmer, who in turn, smiled at Kramsfeld.

"You can have my Sergeant to help you Kretshmer. That way I can keep my eye on you!" Luchens whispered aside, as the General walked away from them.

Kretshmer dutifully nodded to Luchens remark, and asked Kramsfeld to join him in the vehicle workshop.

"Keep an eye on my inventions Sergeant! I don't want no fool Captain getting too big for his boots and deciding to usurp my ideas again!" Luchens shouted at the two departing men, as the other officers looked around curiously at the disturbance.

Kretshmer had his company working flat out making the sleigh containers, and special protection shields, whilst he, Kramsfeld and other mechanics toiled in making the new vehicle. They worked all night until Kretshmer decided that they were ready for a maiden test run.

Both he and Kramsfeld sat in the new vehicle that looked just like a four-wheeled paddle-ship, and started up two powerful engines, which coughed and spluttered before finding their full throat and roared into life as the ungainly monster sat throbbing and vibrating on its chassis.

There was a loud but tired cheer from the men as the vehicle started to *flap-flap-flap* noisily as it moved over the solid rock until it met the sand where the sound got changed to *ziff-ziff-ziff!*

Kretshmer steered the vehicle in a tight circle then raced it down part of the valley before turning back to the workshop again.

"It can do 40 kph but I need to have a loaded container or something to tow, to see how it handles, Sergeant! Get a half-track hitched onto it and we'll see it for real, but I need you to ride the half-track in case of an emergency. Just put it into neutral and keep it headed behind me."

Kramsfeld nodded excitedly then ordered a half-track to be shackled onto the tow-bar and signalled to Kretshmer that he was ready.

With a puff of smoke, the test vehicle moved off again pulling the half-track with ease. Again Kretshmer raced the vehicle down the valley, and finally returned to the workshop, feeling pleased with himself.

"Sergeant, it pulled with ease, but I want to test it out on some virgin sand to see how deep my tracks are compared with a normal track, and that of the sleigh!"

By now most of the men had filtered off to their quarters to sleep off the arduous night. But Kretshmer, Kramsfeld and one other mechanic were still in heightened euphoric mood, which kept them going until all the important tests were completed, and the snags almost ironed out, before they too went to get some rest.

The test vehicle pulled two sleighs, and a half-track that had its engine running in a slow reverse gear, which proved no problem for the vehicle but it kept breaking the tow-bars.

"The strain of the reversing half-track is the problem Captain! But we could always put a tow-bar on the front as well as a backup, then steer the vehicle just like what a steam train would do.

Our depth of track depends on the weight of the tow, but nowhere near what a panzer let alone a half-track would make. The sleigh tracks are almost the same depth as the tow-vehicle, which leaves the engine consumption and cooling problem." Kretshmer stated, after they had finished all their Major tests.

"We have a special filter for the engines, and we can have it air cooled by installing an ordinary electric cooling fan that has its own battery!" the mechanic said sleepily, as the sun rose rapidly over the sands to create yet another baking hot day.

"Right then, men! That's it for now. Have it cleaned and ready for the general's inspection at about 1600 hours. Get yourselves off to bed, and see me at 1500 hours, that's all!" Kretshmer said gently as he smiled and returned the salutes from the departing Sergeant and the mechanic, before he took one last look at his creation and left for his own bed.

"Its 1500 hours Captain!" Kramsfeld said softly, placing a tray of food at the bottom of Kretshmers bed.

Kretshmer woke with a start, but went automatically for his weapon, which Kramsfeld took away out of reach.

"There's no need to shoot me Captain. We have a very important meeting in one hour, but the colonel wishes to speak to you before the General arrives."

"Oh it's you Kramsfeld. Why does the colonel wish to see me? Is there something I am supposed to have done or not done?"

"No Captain. The colonel ordered that I should give him the low down on the test vehicle just in case the general asked too many awkward questions. But I told him a few items that will ensure you get the glory and not that idiot colonel of ours!"
Kretshmer looked at the deadpan face of the Sergeant, and smiled slowly at him.

"You don't like our Colonel then, I take it Sergeant! It is good to appreciate who is what, and who does what in the regiment.

That way you will know right from wrong or not, whichever the case may be.

The men have done a good nights work, especially you and the mechanic. I shall see that your labours are well rewarded when I have the second surprise revealed to the colonel and in front of the general." Kretshmer chuckled as he rose naked from his bed to go and have a quick shower, and added:

"I'll take food when I've had my shower, Sergeant. Tell the colonel I shall be there in about thirty minutes."

Kramsfeld merely nodded and left, shutting the door behind him.

Kretshmer had his meal and dressed impeccably to meet the General, relishing the mind games Luchens always tried to play.

"Kretshmer! I hear you have a very poor report to give me on that junk of metal you took all night to work on. Tell me exactly what the problem is, maybe I can help in some small way. A fresh mind always helps, according to the sea Captain I met recently."

Kretshmer related exactly what Kramsfeld had said, and even embellished a few technical ones.

"All in all, it doesn't work due to this so called flap-board and what you really need is a *ziffer* valve. How do you propose to overcome this?"

"If I can make this new ziffer valve, then the boffins in Berlin would be able to mass produce it for all our vehicles out here in the desert!" Kretshmer said slowly, trying desperately hard not to smile let alone laugh aloud at the colonel being taken in.

"Oh well! That's for the general to decide. As for me, you had a whole company of men up all night in the workshops instead of on perimeter guard. I'll see you after you have made a fool of yourself in front of the general. Maybe you'll get demoted back to Sergeant again where you belong!" Luchens said nonchalantly, brushing his fingernails across his crisp white shirt.

Both officers marched off to see the general with Kramsfeld leading the way, and arrived in time as the general pulled up in his open-top staff car.

The regular troops saluted whilst Kohls, Luchens and others likeminded gave the Nazi arm waving salute, which the General returned with a wave of his little gold baton, his symbol of rank and office.

"Captain Kretshmer, come! Show me this wonder machine of yours!" the General commanded.

Kretshmer nodded to Kramsfeld and managed to whisper aside to him to get the mechanic there too.

"All organised, Herr Captain! We have a little surprise for the colonel too!" Kramsfeld whispered back, and led the way for the officers, with Luchens and Kohls mincing their way along behind the general's retinue.

"Here it is General!" Kretshmer said proudly, nodding to the mechanic, who unveiled a large and impressively well-polished engine for the General and everyone to see.

Everybody was taken by surprise at this powerful and handsome machine, all except Luchens, who wormed his way to the front to stand next to the general.

"She is a wonderful, expensive but totally useless toy General." Luchens rasped, as the general turned to look at him.

"Oh Colonel! It looks all right to me!" he replied, and then turned to Kretshmer.

"Does this thing work? If it does can I have a ride on it?"

"No it doesn't! There is a problem with its flapboard, and needs a ziffer valve!" Luchens said as he looked down his nose with disdain at Kretshmer.

The general turned to Luchens and glowered at him.

"So you have an intimate knowledge of engines Colonel. And here's me thinking you were just a pen pusher. Do tell me more!"

Luchens went pale and started to stammer out some excuse, but his voice tailed off into silence just as a loud roar and a small whiff of smoke that came from the two powerful engines.

"Come this way General. Meet the mechanic who helped Sergeant Kramsfeld and myself, to test this beast out. Its basically two half-tracks joined together with double the track gears to handle the wider track plates. The bright red lettering on the front is what we've called it, as you will find out." Kretshmer announced,

The Lost Legion

as the general returned the soldiers salutes, before climbing up into the spacious driver's cab of the vehicle.

Kretshmer eased the throttle of the engine as it flapped its way out of the garage.

"Here that flapping sound General? It's because of the extra wide tracks. Wait until we hit soft sand, then tell me what you hear!" Kretshmer invited, looking over his shoulders and saw Luchens holding on to a roll bar for dear life, and his two helpers laughing at him.

Flap-flap-flap went the sound of the tracks for a few more minutes before it changed to *ziff-ziff-ziff*.

The general looked at Kretshmer and started to laugh.

"There Luchens! There's your ziffer valve. It works a treat!" he said with great delight.

Luchens merely scowled and mouthed some verbal abuse at everybody as the vehicle went effortlessly over the soft sand.

"This is where I'll stop General. I have a panzer and a half-track follow me in a parallel course so you can see the difference in the track marks." Kretshmer said, switching off the engine and waited for the other two vehicles to pull up alongside it.

The general climbed down off the test vehicle and examined its tracks then compared it with the marks of the others.

"Hardly a dent! If the Britishers do see these tracks they will think we've got some Super Tigers or heavy artillery coming up to face them. I'm very impressed Captain Kretshmer." the general said, then burst out laughing as Luchens finally stumbled onto the sand to see the marks for himself.

"Looking for the flapboard Colonel? Maybe the zi*ffer* valve works too well for your liking!"

"You have a second demonstration to observe with this ZIFFER machine General. Please come this way and I'll show you!" Kretshmer said as the general was gaining his composure again from his fit of laughter at the expense of Luchens.

A half-track had towed one of the sleighs out which was hitched onto the Ziffer, and made to drive around in a circle for the general to witness.

"See the tracks! Just like a snow sleigh. The Ziffer can tow up to four of these, or even tow two half-tracks or a panzer with their engines in reverse!" Kretshmer said proudly.

The general looked at the circling machine and was very impressed with what he saw.

"You, Captain, may have just solved our transport problems, but how is it for fuel?"

"It can run on its own at 20 mph and per gallon. But under full load, it does only 10mph. Obviously, the slower the more mileage, General! But it can handle steep gradients and although I intend to take one out on my first patrol, I reckon I can cover a range of about 200 kilometres before refuelling. It also has standard armour plating of 50mm, and two drive shafts because of its independent front and rear drive to get up those steep slopes."

The general listened to the technical details described by Kretshmer until he was finished.

"But that's incredible Captain. It's just the type of vehicle we need in a desert warfare situation. Maybe you'd care to forward your drawings and other details to my ADC later today, in time for me to catch my plane to go and attend the Field Marshal's special operations meeting." he stated with amazement and in total awe of the vehicle in front of him. He turned to Luchens and with a withering look commanded him to step forward.

"I have four regimental colonels at this base, but you are the one that wears the donkey outfit. You Colonel, are a total jackass! You will not take your leave as requested. Instead, you personally, will prepare a full report on today's events, to include your own comments and recommendations. Subject to weather conditions, my plane leaves in two hours, so you'd best get away and get it done.

As you, as somebody with an apparently recent knowledge of all things mechanical, I want every technical detail and drawing collected and handed to me personally when I leave. Do you understand?"

Luchens was writhing under the public dressing down and humiliation the general was giving him, but it did not prevent him from looking irately at Kretshmer.

He merely nodded and saluted before rushing away in such a hurry, he almost tripped over one of the extended track plates on the Ziffer. This made the general burst out laughing, and call Luchens a few more choice names, which the other officers laughed at for fear of being singled out as well.

"Captain Kretshmer! You will make three more of these machines and their sleighs, then take them eastward for your first heavy consignment for the depository. I want a thorough test on these machines before we have them branded a success and before you present it and yourself to our Fuhrer in Berlin.

As for other consignments and your regimental duties, you'd better get your instructions from that asshole of a colonel of yours. Keep well Captain!" the General concluded, and waved his little white baton before leaving in his staff car.

"Well Captain! It looks as if we just might earn ourselves a couple of weeks in Berlin if all goes well." the mechanic surmised.

"The general has assigned you to my command, so you'll be coming with me Kramsfeld, never mind your so called 'private minder' duties. You will be needed to act as guide every time I go out on missions, as I'll be the principle retriever of the shipments. As for you, engineer! You will be responsible for the safe keeping of our design copyrights, in case some useless colonel, no names mentioned, tries to usurp our ticket to easy street once we've won this war against the Britishers." Kretshmer said softly, smiling after the rapidly disappearing colonel and his mincing partner, Kohls.

Chapter XVI
Hissers and Moaners

The camp became a hive of activity in creating several of these *Ziffers*, but this was made more difficult by the constant threat of danger from the storm cauldron that they occupied.

Before long, each man recognised the deadly unseen telltale signs of the imminent dangers they faced, as he went about his daily business out in the open. Those who ignored or did not take heed of these signs, always fell victim of the deadly forces of nature that the valley let out into the world of man.

This awareness helped Kretshmer and his men find ways to combat the driving walls of sand, as they made their regular replenishment trips to and from the 'safety zones' and even help figure out a way to survive a full blown storm out in the desert.

It was when returning from a Moroccan consignment trip, that a strategy so successful it would become the standard adopted by the rest of the Africa Korps, and even borrowed sneakily by their enemies that were devised.

"Sand squall coming our way about fifteen kilometres ahead Colonel!" Kramsfeld shouted from the lead vehicle.

"The *hisser* should be on us in about five minutes! Form a spiral, make sure the guns are covered and pointing outwards!" Kretshmer ordered, as the lead vehicle turned, with the others following in behind in an ever-decreasing circle until all the vehicles were formed into a tight ball.

"Get those side flaps down on the outer vehicles, and the tarpaulins over from the inner vehicles. Get the supply sleigh into the middle and rig the radio mast. Make sure the tarpaulins are interlocked and tight." Kretshmer ordered, hastened by the verbal prompting of Luchens, who was on his first proper consignment retrieval patrol with his men.

"Come on you lot! We've got less than five minutes to get under cover. Any man caught out knows its certain death, so shift it!"

Luchens shouted and goaded the men to move faster than they seemed to be doing.

The outer vehicles had wooden shields dropped down on the outside of the vehicle wall, to prevent the sand from coming under them. The next ring of vehicles had large tarpaulins unreeled from them to form a large circular tent that was propped up by the telescopic radio mast and looked just like the big top from a circus.

The supply sleigh had the stove and several days of provisions to last the sixty men until the winds blew over. This was also one of Kretshmer's inventions, along with the Ziffers and sleighs that transported the several tons of gold over the huge empty wastes of the desert. Empty except for the sandstorms and the occasional army of marauding Arab bandits. It was the three heavily armed platoons of men and vehicles that kept those marauders at bay, and the protective covers kept the sand away.

The hissing sound turned slowly into a low moan, then into a deafening one until it finally reached a crescendo the men dubbed a *howler*, the most fearsome of all sand storms, which nobody could ever survive from unless well prepared for it.

Luchens kept within the confines of the supply truck and close by the radio, whilst Kretshmer and his NCOs were sleeping, quite comfortably enough with the men.

Apart from keeping a watch on the tarpaulin roof, which needed an upward poke here and there to remove the sand that was collecting on it, nothing could be done except to wait it out. The spiral shape created enabled the men to creep around the inner vehicle circle to the outer ones to make sure they were okay.

It took three days for the *howler* to blow itself away, before the men could dig themselves out of the sandcastle that had formed around them.

"The system works well for a multi-vehicle convoy such as this one, but what about say just the minimum of two Ziffers and their sleighs Captain!" Luchens asked with annoyance, at having to brush some of the sand that fell off the roof tarpaulin onto him.

"Just the same Colonel, but in a smaller, singular circle. Pretty much like the Cowboys fighting the Indians in the films, that's all." Kretshmer said, helping a soldier hitch up the supply sleigh to its parent Ziffer.

Luchens climbed onto his vantage point above his command Ziffer and looked around the now empty desert.

"Radioman, call HQ and tell them that we've been held up three days by a *howler* and we're about one day's drive from the codename of our next safety zone." Luchens barked.

"Captain! Get the convoy rolling. I don't expect any trouble coming from our east where we're pushing the Britishers off the deserts, but get your weapons tested in case we run into trouble of the Arab kind. They have the habit of turning up out of the blue, or black or amber, depending on their tribe colours."

Kretshmer had the NCOs clean and test the heavy calibre machine guns that were mounted on each side of the Ziffers, and sleighs. Then had the men clean and check their various weapons before he was satisfied that the retrieval mission was as safe and armed as possible.

The day wore on as the vehicles ziffed and swished their way over the freshly piled sand dunes that looked identical for as far as the eye even through Luchens binoculars could see, yet nothing could be seen to relieve the eye.

"Look Sergeant! There's a plane coming our way!" the lookout shouted anxiously.

Kramsfeld looked up to the oncoming plane and ordered his men to stand by to open fire.

Before long, the plane swooped down low and circled the column, before it waggled its wings and left from whence it came. "That was a close one Kretshmer! For one moment I thought it was a recce spitfire that has been plaguing our long-range patrols. But what would a H190 bomber be doing down this far in the deserts. We're too far south for enemy engagements!" he opined.

"It's one of our Search and Rescue aircraft, perhaps looking for us after three days without word, Colonel!" Kramsfeld stated.

Luchens nodded as if to accept the reasoning before shouting and berating the radio operator for not getting his signal off in time.

"You could have saved that patrol, you stupid moron! Unless you perform your duties better than that, I'll have you sent to the Russian Front!"

Kretshmer and Kramsfeld left Luchens to his ranting and ravings, and leapfrogged over the close column of vehicles to check on them.

"Sergeant! Move your vehicle up to swap over the lead from Corporal Lutz. Tell him to drop in behind the supply wagons. We have about three hours before we reach our next safety zone and checkpoint.

Some of the Arabs are starting to become wise to our camps and might just be watching us, so tell your crew to keep their eyes peeled for any movement. Any trouble, start forming the defensive circle."

The convoy arrived at their safety zone and managed to form their protective circle before the next *howler* arrived to dump several hundred tons of sand over them again.

During the storm Luchens took time to brief his men on the latest news he received by special coded signal, which was welcomed with much joy and merriment, despite the *howler* trying to find them out and destroy them.

"When we get back to our depository, no doubt there will be big changes in the camp Colonel?" Kretshmer asked.

"Now that the British and their allies have been pushed way back beyond Tripoli again, it means that we can relax from any of their attentions. But it might mean that we will have to lift and shift if the Eagle goes. Then maybe not, and the 9th Legion will remain to guard over the amassed wealth the Fatherland has collected from the conquered lands. That's all I can tell you for now Captain. When we get back, then I'll be able to give you a correct update."

Luchens replied with a shrug of his shoulders, and dismissed Kretshmer with a wave of his hand before settling down to yet another plate of re-hydrated food.

The storm only lasted a day, but when the men came to dig themselves out, they found the place was eerily silent and looked like a moonscape, everybody stopped to wonder at the strange sight. There were large rocks and small boulders everywhere, but almost no sand, except around their camp.

"If we have to traverse this section then we'll be heard for kilometres Colonel! We're only twelve hours from here to camp, so I suggest that we double back about a mile and get back onto the sand, to skirt around this bare patch." Kramsfeld suggested.

"I've already thought about that thank you very much Sergeant! We've got a heavy load this time, and I don't think the sleighs can carry it over these rocks. We'd better get the men to start laying a path of sand to cushion the tracks as we go. I've already ordered a column of half-tracks to come and help us, which with luck, should be arriving soon. Best keep our defensive formation until they arrive!" Luchens replied sharply.

"Then I'd better get the weapons at the ready, as there's a dust cloud coming towards us and its not a *howler* either!" Kretshmer responded, quickly rounding the men up and got them into action mode again.

"It's probably our relief column, so don't panic!" Luchens said aloud but the alarm in his voice fooled nobody.

"Lutz, get your range finder on them and let me know who it is! 'B' Platoon Sergeant, you will take a machine gun and four men over to that pile of boulders on our right flank, and the same over to the left flank. Keep an eye on me for your recall back to the defence circle. The rest of your platoon along with C Platoon will disperse around the defensive circle, but stay out of sight, and be ready to engage on my command. 'A' platoon Sergeant! Position your battery of mortars to cover the large gaps in the boulders front and rear of the camp. Fire on my order or when corporal Lutz's range gets to 1500 metres. You will also provide an ammo supply team. 'D' platoon Sergeant, man all the heavy machine guns on the sleighs. The rest of you just get on with your normal duties and act nonchalant and unconcerned. Sergeant Kramsfeld, you and I will be with the colonel, but you will act as my interpreter as the Colonel is fluent in Arab tongue, and might just get shot whilst my back is turned. " Kretshmer ordered quickly.

The camp was quickly turned into a hive of activity, quietly and calmly getting themselves ready for imminent action against this so far unseen enemy.

"I can see different colours in the dust cloud. Range 6000 metres!" Lutz called down from his vantage point on top of a large boulder.

"Must be Arabs from different tribes then." Kretshmer stated, as he and Kramsfeld also looked out towards the object with their binoculars.

"In that case, and judging by the dust they're kicking up, there must be at least 500 of them and moving pretty rapidly too." Kramsfeld said.

"Maybe they don't know we're here, and we could sneak away around these large boulders without them ever seeing us!" Luchens said after a little while.

"One move and we'd be spotted, let alone heard. Besides, their scouts have probably reported our presence long before we arrived on camp and before the storm overtook us." Kramsfeld advised.

"In which case, we'd better remain dug in at this camp site, and move off when they've gone, or are all dead!" Luchens replied coolly, taking out his pistol and checked it for bullets.

"I can see four different colours clearly now, with about 500 or so in each colour, and in their separate columns. There's a second and much bigger bunch way behind this lot, but seem to be moving much slower. Range 3.5 kilometres!"

"What's the range of the second bunch Lutz?" Luchens asked aloud.

"A further 3 kilometres Colonel!"

"Shout 'MARK' when they get a range of 1500 metres, then at the range of 800. Once done, get yourself back here Lutz rather sharpish!" Kretshmer shouted, as everybody could hear quite plainly the noise made by the oncoming Arabs and their camels.

"Mortars! Two weapons to set a pattern of shrapnel shells, using a range of 3,000 metres, then set a decrease roll of shrapnel down to 800 metres at one-minute intervals. Commence firing when ready. Remaining four mortars will open fire on the 1500 mark. Heavy machine gunners will use connecting arcs of fire at the 800 metres mark. Light machine guns at 500 metres and the rest of you at will under that. Those of you in hiding will commence firing when I give the command. Make sure you have your water bottles full and plenty of ammo. Any casualties will remain at their post until the medic gets to them!" Kretshmer shouted out then made sure that everybody had heard him by asking randomly around the camp. Once he was satisfied, he and Kramsfeld armed themselves with a machine gun and several hand grenades, and even took time to show Luchens how to shoot his machine gun.

"Your pistol is for the dying enemy, Colonel. But make sure you keep one bullet for yourself if we are overrun. They don't take any prisoners especially after you've shot at them." Kramsfeld explained.

"They might only be on a peaceful migration to a different part of the desert. They are nomads after all and I should hate to be the one to upset the Arab League!" Luchens complained, breaking a fingernail trying to operate the safety catch on his machine gun.

Kramsfeld sighed and shook his head in disgust, then moved off with Kretshmer to make a last inspection of the defences.

"Unless they've got modern weapons, it'll be a piece of cake. Our only problem will be those high boulders to our left. We'll have to get our best shots over that side to cover it, and the sooner the better, Captain!" Kramsfeld said, after carefully looking around the camp with his binoculars.

"We have sixty men that can take on several hundred enemy soldiers, and certainly a few hundred more Arabs wouldn't make much difference, Sergeant. We also have a good supply of water and ammo that the Arabs don't. So unless they give up and go home, all that remains of them that is, then they'll all die out here without any water, and none will be going home after that."

"Something puzzles me Captain! If they're just on a migration march, why the rush and the firing of their weapons as they come?"

"Perhaps its because they know our Colonel can speak their language of gold, and can't wait until their next gold shipment is due to them. Little do they realise that most of this is theirs anyway, so killing us to get it would really throw the proverbial camel dung into the fan." Kretshmer chuckled softly, as the noise of the oncoming menace got much nearer and a lot louder.

"Mark on 1500 metres!" Lutz shouted twice, which was the signal for the mortars to lob their destruction towards the hordes of men and animals.

Kretshmer and Kramsfeld observed the initial bursts of shrapnel over the heads of the Arabs, which seemed to crush them into pulp and down onto the now bloody sands.

The Arabs still came rushing on, firing their weapons as they rode their horses and camels towards their next unforeseen wall of death.

"Mark on 800!" Lutz screamed out over the noise of battle.

The *ratta-tatta-tatta* of the heavy machine guns literally chopped men and animals into little pieces as the lighter machine guns joined in.

The rear of the Arab columns stopped and retreated before they too got caught in the murderous cross fire. Within minutes, only the carpet of dead flesh was to be seen as guns fell silent, and only the thud of the mortars were heard, as they kept up their rain of steel over the fleeing marauders.

"Kramsfeld! Come out there with me to find out who they were. We have to get hard evidence of these people, just in case they accuse us of starting another Arab war." Luchens ordered, climbing down off his Ziffer and made his way out to the carpet of body parts.

"I wouldn't do that Colonel…" Kretshmer started to say, as several bullets whizzed past him and spent themselves at the feet of Luchens.

Luchens went completely white then turned and ran back into the safety of the defence circle, with bullets flying after him. Kretshmer nodded to Kramsfeld and said.

"It's just as we thought! We've got snipers up on that rocky outcrop. Get the mortars to use H.E. to blast them and any large boulder away. In the meantime, get our best shots onto them and return fire. Keep the hidden men out of sight, as they'll be our reserves the Arabs don't know we've got."

"I reckon the same Captain! Once nightfall comes, we can set up a booby trap system as our outer perimeter. Just in case some of them decide to come visiting without an invitation." Kramsfeld said with a grin.

"That first bunch we chopped up was only an advance guard. The second bunch must be their main army, but who the hell sent them out here after us?"

"Those are my thoughts too Captain. I think we'd better ask the Colonel and get on the radio to report all this."

Both men went over to Luchens control Ziffer, and put their questions and observations to him.

"It seems that someone has double-crossed our Arab friends to the tune of some 200 tons of gold, or 95 million Deutch Marks if you like. Our last delivery was found to be gold-painted iron ingots, and we've got to examine all of it, including this lot when we get back. Maybe that's why they're out hunting for us and their gold."

"200 tons! That's roughly in the region of 8,000 ingots, and you just sit there on your arse drinking coffee! I wonder what our skipper would have said, especially when you shot him for your mistake over just two lousy bars. He couldn't have been the double agent you painted him to be, so just who is it Luchens?" Kretshmer snarled.

The Lost Legion

Luchens stood up out of his seat and shouted.

"I'll find out who it is, and when I do, he or she will join all the other traitors. You are getting dangerously close to becoming one, with that big mouth of yours Kretshmer. So better watch your step, or Kohls will have you long before Frau Wintermann gets her hands on you."

"Come on Sergeant, lets' get out of this stinking cesspit. We've got a real mans' job to do." Kretshmer sighed, as he turned his back on Luchens, and started to walk out of the confines of the control cabin.

Kretshmer heard the scrape of metal on leather, and dropped to one knee, turned and levelled his machine gun at Luchens just as Luchens had his pistol half drawn out of its holster

Luchens mouth dropped open in surprise at the speed in which Kretshmer moved, as he looked down the barrel of not one but two machine gun barrels.

Kretshmer went up to Luchens and thumped him so hard that Luchens staggered into then over a chair and landing in a heap in the corner of the truck.

"That's the sort of tricks we proper soldiers expect from you spineless and cowardly murderers of innocent people. You try that once more Luchens and you'll end up with a more holy vest than the Pope wears." Kretshmer whispered ominously, and kicked the luger pistol out of Luchens hand, making him squeal with pain.

"C'mon Sergeant. We've got other more important things to do than sort out the trash around here." Kretshmer snarled, leading the way along the defence circle, trying to get their eyes accustomed to the darkness.

"We'll have some food before we organise our reception party, Sergeant. Come, I have a good stock of British Bully beef, much better than the liverwurst, the cook keeps palming onto us."

"Sounds good Captain. Maybe we can have a glass of wine when we come back to finish it off, yes?"

"Yes, but we'll have to keep a close eye on our Colonel.

Get one of your men to keep a watch on him. We've enough enemies to fight in front of us let alone these so called friendly troops."

"I wonder if Tommy suffers the same affliction we do with the likes of Luchens?"

"Not Tommy. He's strictly all fair play and up front. "*It's not cricket old boy*", I believe their expression is." Kramsfeld said in a posh English accent, which made Kretshmer grin and nod his approval

They enjoyed their brief meal before they got a handful of volunteers to go out with them and lay the booby traps and other nasty surprises. Once they had done so, and on their way back, they managed to get a few macabre souvenirs from the now stinking mess of flesh and bones in their way.

The snipers had stopped their firing and everything seemed to go very quiet for a long time, but the soldiers could see the glow of the Arab camp fires over the distant dunes, to remind them trouble would still to be found in the morning.

The extreme heat of the day was soon replaced by the bitter cold of night, as the moon cast its cold silvery beams across the desert.

"First raid should start about two or three in the morning. The Arabs will also come and take their dead away and clear the place up for another day of slaughter. Ours they hope!" Kramsfeld whispered as he and Kretshmer peered out from one of the sleigh troop carriers.

"Yes! 'B' platoon Sergeant put a couple of listening devices around the place, so we will hear what is what as they move in. Mind you, those little sand traps will be just as effective as a trip wired grenade. Was that your idea Sergeant?"

"It took me no more than five minutes to gather up several snakes from the dead bodies, so all I did was to give them a little home for a while until their next live bait comes along." Kramsfeld chuckled at the ruse he explained about.

"In that case, we're in for a few fireworks as well as a few 'snake' charmers running away." Kretshmer finished saying, as there was a howl of pain from their right, followed by another to their left. Soon there were howls everywhere, enough for the entire camp to be alert and stood to ready for action.

"Sergeant, go tell the men to get ready for unarmed combat. Nobody is to fire a weapon, especially the Colonel!" Kretshmer whispered, taking out his commando knife and a long piece of wire.

The howls of pain and surprised voices of the Arabs were soon accompanied by explosions all around the camp, lasting for a little while before it all went quiet again.

Kramsfeld arrived back alongside Kretshmer again after completing his mission.

"Phase two will begin in about another two hours, once they've taken their dead away. So we can relax until then Captain! I've already told the platoon Sergeants what to expect, and have the reserve team on guard to give the others a break."

"Good thinking Sergeant! What's the Colonel doing, or need I ask?"

"Curled up in his bunk pouting over your thumping, or sleeping like a baby, even through the pyrotechnic display earlier."

"Maybe he's already counting out the ingots, to save us the bother when we get back. If he weren't an SS Officer I'd have had him shot long before now. Him and his arse bandit Kohls!"

"Now he's another odd fish! Ever since I gave him the remains of his bum boy, he's been locked away in his little caboose, threatening to get even with the devil himself. He's got the entire camp wired up with his secret listening devices."

"You mean like the ones we had planted out there?"

"Yes! It means that some of us can talk freely in the camp again, without Kohls arriving in the place unannounced and demanding to know what was said only a few moments ago. We've got a special game going, which is driving Kohls absolutely nuts, if that were ever possible."

"Shhh!" Kretshmer whispered, pointing to a large boulder some metres in front of them.

Both men looked through their binoculars to get a better look, and saw several Arabs trying to creep up on the camp.

"Keep watching those in front of us, I'll keep my eye on those to our right. I've got a special wire hooked up to me, to alert the other platoon commanders. If they get past this second or even the third one, only if they're lucky, then the platoons will be ready with their hand weapons." Kramsfeld whispered in Kretshmer's ear, who had responded by nodding his head.

Once again the eerie silence was shattered by several piercing screams of terror or small explosions followed by moans and groans of the injured.

Kretshmer smiled at the antics of the men he saw in his binoculars, and watched the would-be attackers retreat once more to lick their wounds and calm their fear-stricken friends.

"We still have the 3rd ring Captain! But after that lot I don't think they'll try anything more tonight. Tomorrow will be their revenge and face-saving attacks, as tonight we've surely dented their religious faith and fighting ability somewhat."

"What made them run away in terror Sergeant?"

"Severed hands that have snakes wrapped around them. Once the snakes detect a movement and move to attack, the limbs move with them. This gives the appearance of ghostly hands crawling across the desert as if to get them, if you like. One of our volunteers had learned of that trick several years ago, somewhere out in the Congo I think. The thing is it's a strict taboo and looked upon as the devil's work by most niggers and Arabs."

"I know that trick too! In that case Sergeant, if they think we're the devil's men, they might just leave us in peace and find some other poor sod to pester!"

"That would be just up the colonel's avenue that would. But we mere soldiers must battle on no matter what, Captain!"

"We'll give them another two hours to regroup, if they don't, then we can stand down and get some shut-eye before it gets light again. Have the reserve men relieved just before dawn and breakfast over with before we stand to. I'll get that lazy bastard of a colonel up before I kip for a while."

The rest of the night proved peaceful, as Kretshmer and Kramsfeld finally got their turn to have some food and most of all some well-earned rest.

Chapter XVII
Hello Again

The sun was climbing rapidly up into the sky to start yet another scorching day, as the soldiers prepared themselves for a repeat performance by the Arabs.

"Captain! Its time you were seeing to your duties!" Luchens shouted, and went to kick Kretshmer.

Kretshmer had in fact already been woken up by Lutz and was taking a moment to gather his thoughts when a shadow appeared over him. He grabbed the foot of his attacker and wrenched it in such a way that he threw the owner into the air to land a few feet away from him.

Luchens gave a gasp of surprise then a whimper when he landed on his arse in the sand.

"You stupid ass! I could have easily put a bullet in you. Don't ever come creeping up on me again, Colonel or no Colonel! I would have thought you'd have learned your lesson by now. Next time I will kill you, you fucking asshole." Kretshmer snarled, standing up slowly and putting his helmet on.

Luchens gasped and moaned about this undignified treatment yet again from Kretshmer, but Kretshmer merely walked off and went over to take charge of the troops again.

Kretshmer looked out from the safety of his Ziffer and was truly amazed at the completely cleared battlefield. Not a single scrap of evidence was to be seen where several hundred men and animals were slaughtered only the day before.

"See what I mean Captain! If you look over there, where we saw their campfires, you will see nothing. They've gone away, probably waiting for some other poor sod to come along and murder."

"We'll wait until about 1000 hours before we strike camp and go home. Go and tell the Colonel. So much for his relief column Sergeant!"

Kramsfeld nodded and called out orders to various soldiers as he made his way over to inform the still pouting Luchens.

The Lost Legion

"The general promised me a relief column, Sergeant! But after our success from yesterday, it won't be needed after all. When we move off, do so with all possible speed."

"The safety zone is being sealed off again Colonel, and the new radio beacon is working well! Let's hope we get a little rest before we go off on our travels again."

"For you maybe Sergeant! But as Colonel of the regiment, I must be available at all times for the Field Marshal and his staff!" Luchens bragged.

"That comes with the badge of office Colonel. I'm glad I'm only a Sergeant! Still you can't say that your very first 'Desert retrieval mission' was uneventful. You've managed to save the company from an army of Arabs and saved the gold all by yourself. You'll end up a general before long, you watch!" Kramsfeld said cheerfully, leaving to do his other duties.

Luchens merely watched the large frame of the Sergeant leave his little control cabin before he allowed himself to be cheerful too.

"Captain! It's now 1000 hours, let's be off home and get into a nice cool bath. I fancy a decent meal before we settle down to do our other work. Maybe we could take in a movie before that though!" Luchens said in a strangely affable mood, which took Kretshmer by surprise.

"Yes Colonel! It would be nice to sleep in a decent bed again. This trip from Morocco has been one hold up after another. Still, our next one is to the fabulous Nile, and the Valley of the Kings. When we go there we get paid to do so, unlike those rich tourists who pay through their nose just to ride a camel."

"I'd like to be on that trip, but I fear I'll be needed elsewhere, judging by the successes we've had up north recently. Anyway, more on that when we get back, as I gather there's a lot more to it than I've been told over the radio."

"Whatever it is, we'll soon know Colonel. Let's get this show back on the move." Kretshmer concluded as he left.

"Decamp and get the lead trucks rolling!" Kretshmer shouted to the waiting soldiers.

Kretshmer moved the column of vehicles out of the safety zone and back onto the soft sand where their progress was much easier and faster.

It took them a few hours less to arrive even though they had a much bigger load in tow. They were greeted by the general, who feted their arrival as conquering heroes, even though some of the men were only doing a menial job no self-respecting soldier would even volunteer for.

"You and your men can rest up for a while Colonel, before you embark on your next trip. There is one thing you should know, and that is we've pushed the British right back and have retaken Tobruk.

Our Field Marshal is looking to drive them out of Cairo by the middle of the year, which means that the Ziffer machines and sleighs will be produced in great quantities to out-manoeuvre the allies from Egypt and the Persian Gulf by Christmas."

"If that's the case, then we won't be hauling consignments eastward any more. Merely containing them here with the Legion?"

"Yes in part, Colonel. You will continue to run the depository, and be ready to accept other valuable items from the continent as well, irrespective of the military efforts.

The reason I'm telling you this, is that I have been called to support our efforts here in the south. The idea being it is that the British doesn't know that our entire Legion is down here. So, we will advance east and outmanoeuvre them from behind. This is to co-incide with a pincer movement along the coast as a double diversionary tactic. But once they've discovered that our presence coming up from the south is of significant strength, they would be forced to deploy most of their artillery, infantry and tanks to stop us.

In reality we'll be sending almost the entire Afrika Corps right down the middle of the expected lightly guarded throats of the Allies, to go all the way through and capture Cairo and the Suez

Canal before they know it. Good plan don't you think Colonel?" Luchens looked at the large wall map and studied all the coloured flags and arrows before he offered his opinion.

"There is one item you've forgotten General. A unit of the Arab League army set us upon, as in my last retrieval mission report. If they were to arrive before you made your timed pincer move, then you'll probably get severely delayed if not decimated in your attempt to fulfil your manoeuvres."

"Ah yes! Glad you mentioned that. The Arab League has been assigned to you, as your own particular problem Colonel. You really must insist on being an honest paymaster. The Fuhrer is absolutely livid about all this gold being missing, that's why you were promoted to Colonel and given a full regiment at your disposal to see everything is done in traditional German fashion. Efficiently and effectively!"

Luchens felt quite betrayed at the general, for lumping all this responsibility on him. In fact he felt quite chilled at the thought of being hauled in front of his beloved Fuhrer, to be branded a common traitor by him.

"As you say General. That's my new mission in this war, and I intend doing it in the best traditional German way which I am already aware of." Luchens replied, but found that the general was talking to someone else, and got dismissed from his presence.

It took a full week for the examination and evaluation of the depository, before Luchens was satisfied and sent off his report to Hanschel:

"'*It appears that the missing consignments stem from two sources. One of which concerns the special operations carried out in Cadiz. The other one I have my suspicions about but need further proof. Request written authority to expedite that matter.*' *Colonel Luchen. SS 9th Eagle HQ.*"

The signal came through the following day, much to Luchens delight.

He sent for all his officers and senior NCOs and briefed them on exactly what was to happen.

"Kretshmer, you leave in two days time, for the Morocco base with three full columns of Ziffer machines. Before you leave, you will be given your final instructions concerning map co-ordinates and other details such as what radio frequency to use. You Major Becker will stay behind and guard the depository. The rest of you officers will take your lead from Captain Kretshmer. That is all!" Luchens said offhandedly and left the briefing room to the sudden outburst of noise from the men.

Kretshmer and Kramsfeld formed the triple column, consisting of 300 fully armed men, several half-tracks and a whole squadron of Ziffers and their sleighs per column.

During that time, Luchens and his regiment was visited by Hanschel who had strong words to say to him. He managed to side step the flak he was given until his second visitor turned up.

"Hello Lucky! Aren't you pleased to see little me?" Wintermann purred, as she snuggled up to him.

"Hello again! Fancy seeing you here!" Luchens said guardedly.

"I'm here for you to escort me to see our sea Captain. He's been very naughty especially in dealing with the depository accounts. We'll have dinner and discuss it over a nice bottle of wine, what does my Lucky lover say to that!"

Luchens felt a bit embarrassed at this show of affection in front of the General.

"At least it's nice to find someone else who thinks our Captain is bent as a donkey's hind leg. Yes, that would be a good start, mind you there's always a nice sherry in Cadiz if you care for it Frau!" Luchens said smoothly and diplomatically.

"Forget Cadiz! Some of them are dead and the rest are but little boys now, since I caught up with them. My supply of trophy jars are almost full, but I do have a score to settle with the sea Captain, which has been put off by my Step Father until I get the proof we need." Wintermann said languidly, as she lit another cigarette that was sticking out of an over-long holder.

"I got this to remind me of you lover boy!" she said coyly, as she sucked on the stem of the holder, then added.

"But really, it's all to do with the taste."

"The only way we can nail the Captain is for our normal retrieval mission to be carried out. Then after the pick-up is completed, the commander will signal the amount he received, for us to check against the original manifesto. If they don't tally, then we know he's being helping himself, and for quite some time too." Luchens declared, which was quickly agreed upon by Wintermann.

"Right that's settled then! Lets get a party going, I feel like celebrating for a change!" She said, linking her arm into Luchens and walked into the officers' mess for their meal.

Chapter XVIII
No Fear

Kretshmer left early with most of the regiment, whilst Luchens and Wintermann were completing their inspections of the depository.

It took Kretshmer over seven days to reach his destination and to report back as instructed.

"Only 250 boxes, which tallies at 50 tons, Colonel!"

"What? You took enough equipment for at least three times that amount. You should have at least 400 boxes to bring back. Leave a half column there, then make your way back, and I'll see you when I come back."

"But you should be there at base camp when I arrive Colonel, what has changed?"

"From what you have reported, I will be flying out to the base with Frau Wintermann to find out where the rest of the consignment went to. All you have to do is get safely back into base camp and await my return before you surrender the consignment to the depository."

"That is acceptable to me Colonel, but keep radio contact with me at all times in case."

"We have a full 24 hour listening watch over you Captain, so don't worry. Just get the consignment here a.s.a.p. Any slip ups and you'll be joining the barge skipper. OUT!" Luchens snapped as he concluded the radio link abruptly and switched off the radio to prevent further contact.

"Frau, lets pack and go off to see our favourite sea Captain. He's been to sea for quite a while now, so he'll be a bit on the salty side if you get my drift!" Luchens said wickedly with a wink towards Wintermann.

"Yes, your drift agrees with me! But a bit of salt and pepper does a girl's complexion good sometimes." she replied, and giggled and hung onto Luchens arm and left the radio control room.

The Lost Legion

Luchens and Wintermann climbed into their light aircraft, and flew west to the secret naval base in the Spanish Sahara. They were off to see Germany's most dashing, yet allegedly, most corrupt sea Captain.

Meanwhile Kretshmer ordered his split columns and troops out of the naval base and made their slow but steady way back across the thousand kilometres of desert from whence they came.

When they moved between the first two safety camps, they caught a glimpse of Arabs in the distance who seemed to shadow them, whilst the deserts only hissed at them. Occasionally there were sand dervishes that danced around them, but everybody knew there would be one last big storm to come their way to end the stormy season.

It was the main talking point for the men who were doing their duties almost robotically and without thought.

"The men have no fear of the enemy or the bands of marauders following us. It's the next big blow that has them jittery Captain." Kramsfeld stated quietly as both men looked around with their binoculars.

"Yes Sergeant, I sense that too! Let's hope we reach our next safety base camp soon. The radio beacon sounds loud and clear, so we've only got about another half a day at this speed to reach it!"

"I don't care so much about that as our defence circle works a treat. My concern is the lack of communications from the Colonel, even though he's such an asshole."

"Our Colonel might be a grade one asshole of the first water, but at least he's a stickler for punctuality and radio contacts. I'm expecting him to call me soon, when we reach our next camp."

A *hisser* started up just as the convoy arrived at the safety camp, which heightened the men's awareness to the dangers about to befall them.

"Get the convoy into double circle around the supply camp." Kretshmer shouted at the same time, using the hand signals, which were acted upon with alacrity by his vehicle commanders.

Soon the convoy had circled itself tight into its cocoon and braced itself for the oncoming storms.

"This place gives me the creeps! The first time we ever camped here, there was nothing but large sand dunes everywhere. Yet last time, there was no sand only boulders and bare rocks everywhere." the 'B' platoon Sergeant complained.

"Let's hope the storm puts some of the sand back, as the sleigh runners are getting too worn to move over bare rocks." Lutz commented, tuning the wireless set into their listening frequency.

"That's it Lutz! Listen out for the Colonel's signal, but get in touch with the general to let him know where we are." Kretshmer said appreciatively.

"We've made good time to get here Captain, a full day in fact. Let's hope the general's operator is listening out for us." Kramsfeld stated.

"Yes Sergeant! Tell the men to adopt the defensive circle routine, before settling down. Get the cooks to rustle up a good meal for us, as I feel it's going to be a long wait before this storm is finished. Make sure the platoon sergeants and the vehicle commanders know that I intend staying here until we get further instructions." Kretshmer said evenly to his trusted Sergeant.

The men tucked themselves into their first decent meal as the storm became more violent around them.

The hissing sound got louder then turned into a low moan which also grew louder and louder as the hours went by, until finally the wind literally lived up to its name, by blowing so loud in an ear shattering howl that sounded like millions of banshees.

The men had their special helmets on to protect their ears, which Kretshmer demanded they wore, because without it meant total deafness or even insanity as the noise would affect their nerves too.

All night the storm raged around the cocoon of man and his machines, before it finally abated as the sun managed to escape the black shroud of sand that fell down upon the land.

"Column commanders, and platoon sergeants. Get your men out and check the damage. Sergeant Kramsfeld, 'B' and 'F' platoon sergeants come with me to make a recce of the camp on the outside. Corporal Lutz, try and make contact with the general. Better still, our colonel. Somebody must know we're still here."

The column commanders acknowledged their orders and hurried out of the command vehicle to get the men active again after a night of comparative leisure.

Kretshmer and the three sergeants dug their way through the wall of sand to emerge out into the open desert, and started to scan the area with their binoculars.

They all climbed on top of the highest point, which was a large rock about half a mile away from the camp.

"The storm has shifted the sand back over the rocks and boulders again, and by the looks of it, in drifts up to about ten feet high, Captain." 'F' platoon sergeant observed.

"From what I can deduce Captain, the sand has been dumped into an almond shaped mound around us, and over to our right where there was another bald area of rocks. And if I remember correctly, there were several sand dunes between us and the Arab camps to our left, but there's none now just a large flat piece of bedrock, enough to land the entire Luftwaffe on." Kramsfeld stated.

Kretshmer just grunted at their observations as his attention was diverted to the campsite.

"We are in the eye of the storm at the moment, which means that the back-end of the storm will be hitting us again with just as much force as before. By the look of our camp, we'll have to raise the outer shields and put them over the top to replace the shredded tarpaulins from the roof. When we get back, salvage the tarpaulins and wrap them around our weapons and vehicle engines, just in case we have the Arab League of army after us again." Kretshmer announced.

"But won't the sand breach our outer defences Captain!" 'F' platoon sergeant asked with a deep frown on his face.

"The sand that's already around the base of our vehicles is solid and stable. We have almost three complete circles, which will act as redoubts to protect us in the middle, all we've got to worry about is stopping the sand coming over the top and swamping our central arena and the supply base. In the meantime, we'd better start digging ourselves out before the storm does come back."

"From what you've said Captain, I suggest that we concentrate on creating our next wall of defence on the weather edge of our camp. We can create an exit point on the leeward side, so that if we do get buried we have an escape route out the back door, so to speak." Kramsfeld said quietly as he too looked over the half-covered cocoon of men and machines.

"That sounds about right Sergeant. Lets get down and get started, as I fear we're about to be engulfed again pretty soon, judging by that cloud of dust over there." Kretshmer said, pointing to a distant sand dune beyond the black headstones of the rocky area they were in.

"That's no storm Captain, we've got company!" the 'F' platoon Sergeant said, lowering his binoculars.

"Visitors coming from that direction?" Kretshmer asked in puzzlement, before he looked at the area with his own binoculars for a moment.

"It's a military convoy! Better get ourselves into battle stations, as we did last time we were here, Sergeant!" He stated flatly, as all three men climbed down off their vantage point.

When they arrived to get organised, Lutz called out to Kretshmer from the command cabin telling him he had a strong radio contact.

"It's from one of the general's radio transmitters coming from a DF bearing. I make it East South East of here Captain." Lutz announced hastily.

"Yes Lutz you're right. There is a large body of men and vehicles coming our way, but why is what I would like to know. Have you contacted the Colonel yet?"

"Not even a dot from them Captain. I happen to know they have a very powerful transmitter and I've spoken to them several times recently whilst on base camp. So its not their equipment that's at fault."

"Very well Lutz. Listen to the radio traffic from this oncoming force and let me know who they are."

"Each supply station has its own special and secret radio beacon complete with its own call sign and frequency. So if it's our mob, Captain, they'll let me know they've picked it up and make their way to us."

"That's very reassuring to know Lutz, well done." Kretshmer replied, suitably impressed with the corporal's knowledge and expertise.

"Sergeant Kramsfeld!" Kretshmer shouted.

Kramsfeld arrived breathlessly and covered in sweat.

"Sergeant we've got visitors arriving soon, which are from our own forces. Get the men into defence circle weapon positions just in case they are in disguise. Nobody can assault us from the front or sides and the only weak area is the back door. So put a sleigh across the back door and have two heavy machine guns manned and ready to protect it. When you've done that, report back to me at my command vehicle."

Kramsfeld nodded and doubled away to carry out the orders.

"Captain! I have just picked up a voice transmission and it sounds like my pal from the 9th Legion's HQ Company. Do you want me to answer it?" Lutz called out to Kretshmer who was standing on top of his Ziffer vehicle watching at the dust cloud getting nearer.

"Well done Lutz! Answer him by telling him to r/v at the beacon co-ordinates. But that's all in case other ears are listening in too."

"Column commanders and platoon sergeants!" Kretshmer commanded. Which was the signal for them all to attend him right away.

"Listen up men! We have a large body of our own troops descending upon us, which means there's bound to be some brass hats amongst them. Get yourselves and your men smartened up and at your defensive posts and ready to receive them. We have about two hours before we meet them face to face, so get to it." Kretshmer announced, then dismissed them to do what was ordered.

The camp was ready in no time, and Kretshmer looked through his binoculars to see a half-track race towards them. He noticed a small pennant on the bonnet of the vehicle, which denoted that there was a senior officer on board.

"Sergeant! It looks like our general's flag, what do you make of it?" he asked quietly.

Kramsfeld looked at the oncoming vehicle and agreed with him.

"If that's him he's going the wrong way! He should be going east!" Kretshmer said softly.

"We'll soon know, Captain!" Kramsfeld said philosophically. Stummell arrived at the camp and was made to stop for the back door to be opened before his vehicle crawled its way into the inner sanctum of the circle.

The general looked slowly around at the fully armed men then towards Kretshmer before he descended from his vehicle.

"What an impressive sight Colonel! It appears that you're planning and ideas have done you proud!" the general said, returning the obligatory salute from Kretshmer and his other officers.

"General Stummell! What brings you to this neck of the woods, so to speak?" Kretshmer asked, ushering the general into his cramped command cabin.

Stummell was still looking all around him, and was very impressed with what he saw, but emphasised his opening statement.

"Colonel? But I'm only a Captain, General. My colonel is still in the Spanish Sahara naval base and won't be back for at least a week." Kretshmer replied.

Stummell turned to Kretshmer and giving him a small black box, told him to open it, which he did and was surprised by its contents.

"Your colonel and his tart have somehow disappeared somewhere and cannot be found. It is therefore incumbent of me to ensure continuity of rank and to see that each regiment has its own commanding colonel to operate it. As you've been the nominated, in fact, the chosen one by the Fuhrer himself, you are now the new colonel of your regiment." Stummell announced with a big smile, as Kretshmer looked at the badge of office and at the General in total bemusement.

"But you could have given this to me when we arrived back at base General. Why are you coming west instead of east?"

"Since you've been away, we've had a right pasting by the Britishers and their Allies. It appears that they knew all about us here in the south. So in order to regroup and concentrate our efforts in the Western desert, my Legion has been ordered out of that base camp, and I've had to blow it up in case the enemy got hold of it. Your depository is still intact, as are the rest of your regiment, and I've left a company of my men there to strengthen it a bit. The only gold there now will be this consignment, as special Arab army units have shipped the rest south and east. Here are your secret and special map co ordinates, for you to reach to complete this consignment, in case your erstwhile Colonel turns up out of the blue."

"If I'm the Colonel, then what of my other officers and senior NCOs'. Sergeant Kramsfeld and Corporal Lutz in particular?"

"Ah yes. Your officers will move up one rank, but Sergeant Kramsfeld and corporal who?" Stummell asked in jest.

Kramsfeld was standing ramrod straight next to Kretshmer, when Stummell offered him a similar black box.

"You Kramsfeld have shown your genius in the field of battle, which your colonel here had correctly identified. You are now the second in command of the regiment as its only Major. All the men who took part in the Arab conflict last time you were here have been promoted one rank upwards.

In fact the entire regiment has been awarded the special commendation medal, as recommended by our top Field Marshal, just before he left for Berlin last week!" Stummell stated, and pinned the award onto the wall map hanging up in the cramped command cabin.

"There! I've pinned it exactly where you earned it."

For a few moments Kretshmer and Kramsfeld said nothing, as they basked in the praise and glory of their sudden meteoric rise in rank.

"You forget that I was a colonel many years ago!" Kretshmer started to say but was cut short by Stummell.

"Indeed you were. In fact I had your records traced and found that you had been cashiered out of the forces due to lack of foresight in your interpretation to your orders. That however is history and what we are talking about now, which is the main reason why I'm here!"

"I was wondering about that, Herr General."

Stummell went to the door of the command cabin and signalled to his driver, who carried a long black object over his shoulders and gave it to the General.

"This is the 9th Eagle, and the standard of the 9th Legion. I want it to be draped over the boxes of gold you will be depositing, and kept safe until I return. My legion is with me and is about to be committed to battle against the Allied advance and broke through our defences only a few hundred kilometres to the northwest of here.

I cannot risk it being lost or surrendered which is why I sought you out. My Eagle and my General-ship was given to me by the Fuhrer himself way back in 1936. But according to the historical archives, the Eagle and its legion was in existence against the Roman armies. Because of its now infamous name, it has to have a full Colonel and 100 men to guard it against capture or surrender. You are now its Colonel, and I give you 100 of my best men to complete its transfer. Will you do this for me Colonel?"

The Lost Legion

Kretshmer and Kramsfeld looked at the solid gold icon and at the vibrantly coloured silken standard then at the pleading face of Stummell.

"This I promise General. I will deposit the gold and spread the standard over it like a shroud. Your Eagle will be placed on the topmost box with two machine guns facing outwards to signify its protection." Kretshmer said sombrely, taking hold of the Eagle standard and Kramsfeld the Legion's colours.

"It is good that I found you Colonel. I can now go to war without fear of ignominy if my eagle should fall. You have made me very happy."

"But if you leave now General, what are my orders apart from looking after the 9th Eagle?" Kretshmer asked in bewilderment.

"You are to stay here until you hear from Luchens, or at least for a few more days. I hope to be back shortly once we've thrashed the allies again, but in case I don't then you have your special map references to go to and complete your assignment. If you arrive there alone, then you will call general Gueller in Berlin to get further instructions. However, if things do not go well for us, then you'll probably be instructed to join the Field Marshal at wherever he is up north. Anyway, its all in your sealed orders in this brief case." the general said, handing the black leather briefcase to him.

Kretshmer looked at Kramsfeld and knew that a superior officer, in passing his burden of obligations to him had just used the both of them.

"I must leave you now Colonel! I'll send you the 'colour guard' when I reach my own troops." the General said and waved his little baton at them as his salute.

"No General! It's not necessary to give me those men. Besides, I have no provisions for them, only enough for my own."

"If that's the way you want it Colonel, then so shall it be. Must dash, there's a war going on up north you know." Stummell shouted from his vehicle, as it spun round and roared out of the camp.

Kretshmer and Kramsfeld climbed onto the top of their Ziffer vehicle and watched the General return back to his command.

As they watched the army of men disappear over the distant sand dunes, Kretshmer heard the faint whispering of the sands again.

"Hope they get away in time Sergeant. I mean Major!" Kretshmer said with a smile, suddenly remembered their instant promotions.

"They couldn't have timed it better Colonel!" Kramsfeld replied with his own wide grin.

"I feel like as if we've been left holding the baby. But where the hell is Luchens, I wonder."

"Well, he won't be arriving here until this *hisser* is played out, Colonel. We'd better get ourselves battened down again I think!"

"I have a very funny feeling about all this Major. Get the men out and follow me down to the supply dump. There is something we must do, which you'll appreciate."

Kramsfeld leapt down and gathered the men around Kretshmer for him to tell them what was to be done.

He had the men dig out the supply cave to make it much larger, then unloading all the boxes of gold from the sleighs, and had them placed neatly into it.

"Major. Get three senior NCOs' to form an escort, and bring the Eagle and the standard down here too. I also want two machine guns mounted on their tripods, just as we promised the General."

The 9th Eagle and the Legion standard was ceremoniously ensconced in the cave, with the two machine guns on guard and looking threatening to any person who entered the cave.

"Seal that part of the supply cave off in such a way that no prying eyes will spot it, Major. Then get the men fed and back to defence circle duties again." Kretshmer ordered, walking slowly away from the scene.

It was only a few hours after the men had eaten their meal and settled down when the *howler* hit them again. But this time it was much fiercer than had been know before, and such that even the special earmuffs the men wore were almost ineffectual.

Kretshmer and Kramsfeld were in the command cabin trying to work out their new orders under the dim light. Lutz was in the corner struggling to listen to the radio, but only hearing the *howler* outside and the static from the radio.

"Only static now Colonel. I must switch off the radio to conserve my battery." Lutz said after a short while.

Kretshmer merely nodded, threw his dividers onto the map and sat down on his little bunk.

"It appears that we'll be going nowhere if we can't dig ourselves out of this sandcastle of ours, Sergeant!" he said absent-mindedly to Kramsfeld.

"Yes Captain! We've been duped by our own kind and that's what I don't like about all this."

Before Kretshmer had time to answer, there was a knock on the door and a column commander appeared.

"Colonel. Our second defensive screen has been breached and our roof is starting to lower onto us. I have several props to keep it up, but not enough to be effective." he said in a state of panic.

"We'd better go and look Major! " Kretshmer said quickly, leaping into action and raced out into the covered compound.

Kretshmer looked around the camp and deciding that it was getting too dangerous for the men to remain there, so he ordered them to climb into their respective vehicles. But he got the men to remove as much food and water as possible from the cavern and share it amongst them, then had the cavern sealed off.

Lutz had the command cabin packed with food, water and a spare battery before Kretshmer and Kramsfeld returned to lock themselves into their little world too.

"It's just turned midnight, so maybe this storm will only last until morning. Let's hope we can dig ourselves out from under here afterwards!" Lutz said quietly as he sat beside his radio.

"You know something Colonel! When I first met you on base,

I knew I had met you somewhere before, but I couldn't remember where. When you spoke to the general about your past life, I realised when and where it was. I was with the Central African Rifles when you arrived as part of a special survey team and needed my men to guide you up the Congo, in 1932. If I remember correctly you were a Major then."

"Yes Major! I remember that too. You saved a lot of my men from the Gmombo tribes at the cost of most of yours. To this very day I couldn't figure out why."

"Simple dear Colonel. I only had conscripts who couldn't hit a barn door with their rifles, whereas the natives could strike you down at a 100 metres with their spears."

The two officers talked and reminisced for a while before they too succumbed to sleep, and joined the snoring Lutz in his slumbers.

Part Two

Chapter I
Flying

Several years later, three friends were enjoying an evening cocktail on the veranda of their sumptuous hotel overlooking the sweeping panorama of the famous Gateway to the Mediterranean Sea, guarded by a honeycombed rock that is Gibraltar.

In the 16th century, the rock was originally a hideout and the principal port for the gold digging cutthroat Spanish pirates who exacted a terrible price from each ship moving though the narrow straits between Spain and North Africa.

This piece of real estate at the very entrance of the open spaces of the Mediterranean Sea was taken easily from the fortified Spanish troops who heavily outnumbered the hundred British soldiers that were the forerunner of the modern British Marine Commandos of today.

It became a Crown possession that has been fiercely defended since then, as its people became more and more ardent 'British' citizens, and wishes to remain so even though it has its own independence in the form of Local Government.

To get back to these friends, blissfully unaware of the future, as they contemplated their prospects of getting back to sea again and where the story begins once more.

"Now that the ship is in the hands of your friend McPhee for at least another two weeks, it looks as if we might be moved on from here to join some other ship coming through." Sinclair said philosophically.

"We might just be able to stay here until she is fixed then arrive home in time for Whitsun. But if the strike goes on, we'll be stuck here without pay and no means to get home again." Larter offered.

"Let's look on the bright side! We've got free lodgings here until we get moved out, so we might as well stay and enjoy ourselves 'til then." John suggested.

"Gib is just a rock with plenty of rabbit stalls, and plenty of duty-free boozers*.

But what about something a little more oomph! Maybe we can get across the causeway and into La Linea or even Algiceras and have a crack at the local nightlife. Even take a trip across to Tangiers and get a hump somewhere apart from a camel." Sinclair said crudely, which made the other two laughs.

"Our best bet is to hang-tight and see what the Shipping Agent has to offer, that way our contracts are covered!" John said cautiously, which drew banter from the other two, but concluded the brief conversation as they decided to leave their room and look for a table in the hotel dining room.

They were tucking into their meals and enjoying themselves when the subject of their earlier conversation walked up to them.

"3rd Engineer Grey! Just the very man." The short but stocky man commenced.

"In fact all three of you, which means that I only need to find two more."

"Shipping Agent Armfield! What can we do for you?" John asked amiably, taking a drink from his wine glass, and then remembered his manners.

"Care to join us in a glass? " John offered.

"No thanks all the same." Armfield said politely then produced a large brown envelope and pulled out several documents from it.

"It appears that the Seaman strike is now official, which leaves several ships stranded in whatever port they are presently in. Unfortunately for you and the crew of your ship that's currently undergoing repairs, each one of you can be sent to other ships without breaking the strike rules. And for that the company has

---

* An old Naval expression for presents or gifts.

given me the documentation to send you three to join the *Cardigan Bay* now loading up in Tunis and bound for the UK. But if you should miss it then all three of you will join the *Orchard lea,* bound for Hong Kong, but stuck in Alexandria." Armfield said smugly, but was cut short by Larter.

"Now just hold on a minute! We cannot go anywhere during this strike, and especially to abandon our own ship. That would be tantamount to tearing up our contracts for that ship, which also means that we'd be under no guarantees of any payment or insurance cover whilst we're either in transit to join or in fact board any of those ships. Which one is it anyway?"

"Unfortunately you are right in what you say, but you've got to pay for your present surroundings for a start!" Armfield stated, sweeping his arm around the dining room.

"If we get off at Tunis and find the ship already sailed, just how do we get to Alexandria?" John asked pointedly.

"You will just have to contact the local shipping agent and organise yourselves from there."

"In other words, if we're out in the desert on our own, and all our ships are on strike, just how do we get some 2000 kilometres across the desert to the second ship? Come on now Armfield, just whose pecker are you trying to pull?" Larter asked angrily.

Sinclair was starting to get angry at the stuffed shirt attitude of Armfield looking ominously at him, which Armfield noticed and tried to defend himself.

"Now there's no need to take it out on me, I didn't call for the strike, neither did Lord Belverley and his friends who will be arriving here shortly to sort things out."

"What are they doing coming down there, and on what?" Larter asked with surprise, and then answered his own question.

"Don't tell me they've got the old *Brooklea* out of mothballs and it's on its way, surely not?"

Armfield merely nodded then started to hand out passports, visas, letters and other documents to the three, saying.

"It's all there gentlemen. On board instructions and who will be there to see you. Travel documents, visas, and of course a special payment to cover any expenses until you get there. Any questions?"

"That's all very well Agent Armfield, but when do we leave?" Sinclair asked grimly, quaffing the last of his wine.

"Tomorrow morning, 0900 hours, it's in your travel instructions. Any problems contact your nearest agent. Failing that, phone me on that number I've given you. Good luck gentlemen, I'll see myself out!" Armfield concluded, and sauntered away from the bombshell he had just dropped on the friends.

All three thumbed quickly through their own set of orders and came to the same conclusion.

"Once more into the breach dear friends!" Larter said, beckoning a waiter and ordered something a little more becoming.

"A magnum of champagne for me and my friends, and three King Edwards if you would. Put it on our bill, Senor!"

The following morning was a hazy one, as the friends climbed into the rickety old taxi that took then down to the sea front for the start of their journey.

John looked over the giant Sunderland flying boat that had the blue insignia of Britain's flagship of aviation, B.O.A.C.

"When I read 'clipper service' I thought it was a sailing ship, swab the decks and all that! I hadn't realized it was a dirty great flying boat!" Sinclair said, patting the side of the plane before climbing into it.

"I wonder if we get a parachute or a life jacket on these things!" John quipped, as a pretty stewardess helped him into the cabin.

"I flew on a Walrus last year, good fun too!" Larter added, and smiled at the same pretty stewardess. "But you're too pretty even to be a lady walrus!"

The large aircraft was soon moving through the water with great speed, then lifted itself gracefully out of the water and was airborne.

The Lost Legion

* * *

John looked out of his porthole to see the wing sweep up and over the 'Rock' as the flying boat circled around to its course, before it started to head its way eastward.

"This is your Captain speaking. Welcome to BOAC's Clipper Service. You may smoke now. A meal or light refreshments will be served soon on the lower deck. This is our scheduled service to Beyrouth, calling at, Oran, Algiers, Tunis, Tripoli, Bengazi, Alexandria, Cairo then Beyrouth." Came a posh English accent seemingly out of nowhere.

Larter and Sinclair started to relax and remove their seatbelts as John sat bewitched watching the blue sea below them sparkle in the morning sunlight. He marvelled at the white trails that were left behind the ships making their way in the water, but saw no land for him to look down on.

"C'mon John, lets get down to the buffet deck, you'll be able to see the African coast on the other side." Larter chuckled, and tapped John's shoulder showing him the way.

"I've never flown before Bruce, and am very curious about those engines above our wings. Must get to speak to the engineer if there's such a person on these things." John replied, and followed his friends down a set of winding steps and into the seemingly spacious belly of the giant seaplane.

They were the first passengers to arrive in the buffet area and grabbed the best seats as other passengers followed them down. Soon the duty-free drinks and cigarettes were being consumed before the announcement came by the same plummy voice ordering everybody to take to their seats again prior to landing in Oran.

"C'mon lads. It's closing time until we take off again!" Larter quipped as all three downed their fresh drinks and left.

The same welcome and announcement was made each time they left one stop and arrived at the next.

"Like musical chairs Bruce! But I'll be glad to get off this flying coffin and onto a decent boat that just stays in the water." John commented as they rejoined their table down in the buffet area.

"Just enjoy the hospitality when you can John. I can't remember seeing any prettier stewardesses anywhere on our ships." Sinclair said, smiling at his thirsty flying companions.

The flying boat bumped its way through the waters again as it landed in its sea landing strip and taxied to arrive alongside a pontoon-landing jetty, where the three friends and a few other fellow travellers stepped out of it and onto the bobbing jetty.

John took out a hankie and mopped his brow and felt the instant heat of the deserts on his face.

"Funny how cool the sea air keeps you. The land is stifling hot, I fancy!" he opined.

"Come on lads, the shuttle coach is waiting to take us to the arrival gate for customs and the like." Larter said quickly, as they walked to the awaiting bus with their baggage.

"Judging by the look of this place, there's still a war on. Where's the ship? Did you see it as we landed John?" Sinclair asked as he scratching his head in puzzlement.

All three looked around the harbour that still bore signs of the destruction of war, and saw no ship, but witnessed the giant flying boat take off again just as the bus arrived at the 'Air terminal'.

"Well there goes our only way out of here lads. Can anybody ride camel?" Larter asked with dismay, as all three looked at the disappearing seaplane.

They went through the customs checkout, which took seemingly for ages, before they walked out of the building officially 'Free to make their way into the country'.

"Well here we are again!" Larter said, spotting a building that he seemed to recognize.

"Look! There's where we'll meet our agent." He announced, pointing to a building that was right across the harbour on the opposite side to where they stood.

"We walk or what Bruce?" Sinclair asked sarcastically.

"No! We jump into that taxi over there. Let's hope he takes

English money!" John replied, and walked swiftly over to the battered vehicle.

All three climbed into the bemused taxi drivers vehicle, who was trying to speak 'Pidgin English' before Larter managed to get some sense out of him by speaking Arabic.

"Well Bruce! You've kept that in the dark. Where did you pick that up?" John asked full of intrigue.

"I spent several weeks in Alexandria waiting for my ship to be repaired, but it's no big deal." Larter said quietly, looking out the taxi window at the passing scenery.

They arrived at the shipping office only to find a notice on the door telling callers to come back later in the week.

"Better pay the taxi man before he has his tribe onto us. We'll stay here until he arrives. In fact we'll break down the door and camp here until he does arrive." Sinclair announced, shoulder charging the office door open.

"There, now we've arrived, and its up to the company to help us out!" he said, and threw his bag onto the agent's desk.

They looked around the office and started to make themselves at home when a phone rang.

Larter answered in Arabic then put the phone back down again.

"That was some female asking where her husband was. It appears that her husband is our absent agent, who's taken the day off and is accused of absconding with some floozy that works here." Larter said, chuckled at what he was saying.

"If that's the case, then he just might bring her back here for a quick one before going home." Sinclair said slowly.

"Yes! We can give him a nice surprise when he arrives. Now wouldn't that be fun." John said, switching on to Sinclair's thinking.

The three got their surprise trap ready and waited for the unsuspecting and wayward agent to arrive, which was not too long.

"Here we are my little poppet. We've got the entire office at our disposal!" the agent was saying, leading the half-drunk female into the building.

"Surprise surprise!" the three friends shouted and appeared from behind various pieces of furniture in time to rescue the woman from the groping hands of the agent.

"What? What? Who the hell are you lot? What are you doing in this office? Don't you know I'm the chief Agent for several shipping companies?" the agent stammered, trying to overcome his shock, and seeing that his female companion had ran out of the door screaming to get her revenge on him for all this.

"Now look what you've done! You've chased your next leg-over away!" Sinclair said slowly, pushing his face into the face of the weedy, slovenly dressed man.

"By the looks of it, you've been playing away and that is not in keeping with duties as an agent and the husband of a poor lonely wife at home! Now is it Hamil?" Larter said, mimicking the woman on the phone.

The agent went white and began to stammer again as he reached into a cupboard and pulled out a hidden bottle of scotch.

"How did you get in here? I will have you arrested and rot in the local jail if you don't leave." he said and drank heavily from the bottle.

John was looking through some ledgers and paper work that was on the desk, and came across the entry for the *Carmarthen Bay*.

"It appears that the ship we were supposed to join, the *Carmarthen Bay*, left here last night. Why didn't you report this to Gibraltar?" John asked quietly and ominously, showing the other two the log entry.

"I was going to, only my wife was bad and I had to take her to the doctors!" the agent said in a whimpering voice.

"She was so bad you decided to help yourself to another woman's body! Don't give me that crap!" Sinclair said, as he grabbed the agent by his collars and lifted him up off the floor, almost choking him.

"P. P. put me down! I don't know who the hell you lot are, but I'm reporting this to the Harbour Master who's a close friend of mine." the agent said indignantly, with his feet dangling several inches above the floor.

Sinclair threw the man across the room and neatly into a large revolving chair, which spun the agent around so fast that he fell out of it and lay dazed upon the wooden floor.

"Why didn't you report the *Carmarthen Bay's* sailing last night? We could have stayed on our plane and got off at Alexandria, rather than find ourselves marooned in this God forsaken hole." John asked striving to maintain his own temper.

"If you got off at the wrong stop then that's not my fault. Anyway, as the ship has left its up to you to sort out your own travel arrangements, not me. " The agent replied angrily, getting up off the floor and grabbed the handset of a wall mounted telephone.

"That is your job, and the main reason why you're here. To help out our travel arrangements so that we can make our next ship, which is supposed to be in Alexandria." John said tersely, but was more interested in what Larter was reading.

The agent swiftly dialled a number and spoke rapidly in Arabic to whomever was on the other end, before slamming down the receiver again and looking smug.

"I've just phoned the police. They'll be here any minute now, to take you lousy filthy pigs away. You'll be charged with trespass, theft and burglary amongst other things I can tell them!" he said with a sneer, before trying to smooth down his rumpled suit.

Larter looked at some more ledgers and made a few mental arithmetic calculations before he spoke.

"It seems that he's been very busy running a scam against the shipping companies, to the tune of about £500 a month. Look!" he said, pointing to what he had discovered.

The other two looked at the ledger entries and came to the same conclusion.

"He's right enough! Now that the police are on the way, maybe they'll be interested in a Grand Larceny case against all the shipping companies.

Each company spends thousands of pounds using this port facility, and instead of the local people getting the full benefit, just who has been helping himself? Why it's none other than shipping agent Boukir!" Larter said with a big smile.

"Maybe his wife will also be interested in what we witnessed here this afternoon. I believe they castrate the married men and stone the other poor women to death!" John added before Larter spoke in Arabic to the agent, but mimicked his wife's voice and told him what she had said over the phone.

The agent went completely white as a sheet again and sat down in a chair with a thump.

"All right! I'll get you your travel papers and get you to Alexandria, but don't tell my wife what you saw!" he pleaded.

"Ha! Listen to that! All he's concerned with, is his missus finding out he's been playing out of turn, never mind the scam against the shipping companies!" Sinclair said in disbelief.

"We'll just take the ledgers with us and hand them over to Mr Burford or Belverley when we get back. We have him by the curlies as far as his wife is concerned, so we can travel in style maybe. At least we'll have a police escort to the airport or wherever we will be using." John said eventually, as he had had enough of the agent wheedling and pleading for his life.

"Yes that's it! I get you on the next transport. It's the Trans African Express, and leaves here in about one hour. I'll get your tickets, here's some money to travel with. Anything but don't tell my wife!" the agent wailed and started to weep, as he opened a wall safe and threw wads of money their way.

"I can't put up with this any more. Let's get from here and onto that train." John said with exasperation but took all the wads of money and stuffed them into his holdall whilst Sinclair grabbed hold of the agent and literally carried him out of the office.

A jeep arrived in a swirl of dust and an armed police Officer stepped out from it, asking what the trouble was.

Larter spoke in Arabic to the officer, but was told in perfect English by the officer that he should speak in English instead. Once he done so and introduced his two friends then outlined the problem,

The Lost Legion

the officer merely nodded and promptly arrested the agent, handcuffing him and slinging him into the back of the jeep.

"If you care to hang on to something, I'll get you to the station in time. The Station Master is a good friend of mine, and I'll only take a moment to radio him to expect you. You'll get your documentation sorted out on the train." The officer stated with a grin.

"That's kind of you officer. How long will it take for us to reach Alexandria, only we've just missed one ship and don't want to miss the next?" John asked politely as the officer finished his radio contact with the stationmaster.

"All being well, about five days. But as this is the windy season, add another two to make sure. Last time I did that trip was during the war. But we got delayed for a while in Tobruk, due to the Jerries wanting to take it over as the new management!" The officer said, driving the jeep away down the very bumpy road.

It took nearly half an hour of bone jerking and nerve jangling experiences for the jeep to slide to a halt alongside the entrance to the railway station.

"Here you are gentlemen. Sorry about the rough ride and all that, but you've got one beautiful Pullman train to ride on for the next few days. Enjoy your trip! I'll see to Boukir and his double-dealings don't you worry. The customs & taxmen have been on his trail for some time now, and you have just given us the breakthrough we've been looking for. No doubt your shipping line will be grateful to you when we tell them and show them the ledgers you found." The officer said, and saluted the three men, before they waved back and left to board the train.

John walked to the front of the train and looked at the magnificent steam engine, breathing out its steam quietly at the head of several luxury railway carriages with large ornate wooden signs on them proclaiming that it was the African equivalent to the Orient express.

It was dubbed as the 'Arabian Express' from Casablanca to Cairo.

'A Duchess 4-8-2 steam loco, but why the funny shaped funnel? There's no coal in the tender, so it must be converted to burning fuel oil.' he mused, looking at the eye-catching large four drive wheels on his side of the engine that dwarfed him. His thoughts were interrupted by the shouts of his two friends who urged him to get on board and join them.

"Welcome aboard the Arabian Express gentlemen! I have a double sleeper cabin for you if you just follow me." A uniformed train guard who greeted the friends as they all climbed up into a carriage.

The friends followed the man along the corridor of the carriage until they arrived at their allocated compartment.

"You have a compartment that sleeps four, with an en-suite washroom facility. The water is rationed to one hour during the morning and one in the evening.

All meals or light refreshments will be taken in the dining car, and will be free. But other expenses such as drinks in our well stocked bar, will be debited to your compartment number, which will be paid in full by you before you arrive at your destination. This train has a number of prominent and important people on board, therefore you will be advised to dress for dinner and maintain proper gentlemanly conduct whilst on board. In the meantime, kindly let me see your passports and travel documents!" The guard informed them in passable English.

All three produced their passports and travel visas as requested and got on with settling themselves into their cabin whilst the guard got busy with his paper work.

"Engineer Grey! You are the senior of the three therefore you will be responsible for your party. All your papers are in order, so here is your 'On board train token' to use when you dine or take refreshments. Just show them to the steward, who will note your compartment number etc. Anything else will be by negotiation."

The guard said, handing each of them a neatly printed company card with their name and cabin number scrawled onto it.

"Thank you, guard. When does the bar open?" Sinclair asked.

"Just as soon as we leave, in about twenty minutes. The train is now full, so if you intend getting a drink, now is the best time to get one." Was the reply, as the guard held out his hand expecting a mandatory remuneration.

"See you when we get back! You haven't earned your gratuity yet!" Larter said, barging past the obese man.

John just nodded at the man as he locked the cabin door after him, and followed his friends down the long train into the saloon carriage.

As they walked swiftly along the side corridors and through several carriages, the splendour and opulence of the décor became more and more rich until they finally arrived into a large ornate open-plan carriage, with plush carpets and overhead fans that rotated slowly to keep the passengers cool.

As on the flying boat they were one of the first to arrive, and grabbed a table near the bar. The heavy crimson coloured curtains and crisp white chair backs to their rich brown leather seats made everything seem so royal and forbidding.

There was a grand piano on a raised dais at the other end, and a well stocked bar behind them, which made them almost stare at the decadence of what was really just a train.

"Talk about luxury! Remind me to tell the guard not to go to so much trouble next time!" Sinclair smiled, as a pretty Arab woman dressed in a flowing white and gold garment, came to their table.

"Sorry gentlemen, but this table is reserved. Please vacate your seats and leave the buffet!" she said politely in perfect English, and with a nice smile.

John looked for the 'reserved' notice on the table, but couldn't find one.

"Yes it is reserved, but only for those who get here first!" he said evenly.

"No! Most of the train including this carriage is exclusively reserved for Sheik-Allah-Sheik and his retinue." She said firmly, then asked what carriage they were residing in.

John showed his train visa to the girl, who glanced at it before handing it back to him.

"You are only in 2nd class carriages, which have their own bar at the end of the train. You should have turned right instead of left to come here. You had better leave now before the Sheik arrives. Goodbye gentlemen." She concluded crisply, and pointed them towards the door they had just entered.

"I see! We died in the thousands to protect your countries from the evil Nazis, yet we're not good enough to ride on your trains, is that it?" Sinclair asked angrily, as several large, beefy men approached them with large curved daggers in their hands.

"Effendi! You do not question our Hostess. You will leave now before we force you. We do not allow scum into the Sheiks private apartment."

"Excuse me pal! This is public transport for any passenger to use. Unless you put that pen knife away I'll shove it up your hairy arse!" Sinclair said menacingly, as the men started to approach with even more menace.

"Be quiet Andy! We're obviously not wanted, so lets just get out now while the going is good." John said quietly, standing up and ushering his two friends out of the carriage.

The three of them walked back along the train until they came to the very last carriage, which although clean and tidy, gave the appearance of being well worn and had seen better days.

They looked around the sparsely decorated and furnished carriage but cheered up when they saw that the bar was better stocked and with the just the right selection than the other one.

Larter walked down to the end of the carriage and looked out through the windowed door.

"At least we've got a veranda section out the back, to watch the world go by." He said, coming back to his two friends who were sitting on high stools next to the bar.

"The saloon will do us fine Bruce, so here's your drink and grab yourself a pew like us." John invited, and handed Larter his drink.

After a couple more drinks, John asked the Arab barman about the train and why they were not allowed beyond their carriage, and many other incidental questions that was on his mind. Whereas Larter and Sinclair sat drinking quietly beside him, occasionally offering their own questions, just to keep the conversation going.

The barman managed to escape John's incessant questions when a large group of people filed into the bar and took possession of what empty chairs and tables there were.

"It's party time lads!" Sinclair said, nodding and smiled at a pretty woman sitting down, facing them.

"Be careful they're not the Sheiks spies or whatever!" John chuckled, as a smartly dressed man wearing a military style jacket and sporting a pencil thin moustache, came and stood next to them.

The man spoke in a posh English accent as he ordered several drinks that were taken over to the tables by some of the other men.

"Try and remember all that after a few bevies!" Larter said pleasantly to the man, as if to break the ice.

"What! Oh yes indeed! But no need to, old boy! Got it written down for the wallah to stick to, eh what!" the man said jovially, twiddling with his moustache, before offering his card over to the barman. Once the barman had taken the details and totted up the price the man left the bar and joined his friends.

As the evening wore on, and after their evening meal had been served, the friends were still ensconced at the bar minding their own business, when a few from the large crowd came over and started to chat to them.

Before long, the three friends were invited to join the rest of the group and party late into the night.

"So you all belong to the Triple Coronet line, and are familiar with my good friend Lord Belverley? Mind you, its not very often he sends his officers by land, unless he intends to meet them somewhere!" the moustachioed man said jovially.

"We were supposed to join a tanker in Tunis, but now we're on our way to Alexandria to join another of the line." Larter volunteered.

"Well, you'll be meeting up with him, probably when we get to Benghazi. But we have a special expedition to see to, before we meet up with him." another man said in well-spoken English, but with a strong German accent.

"Let's hope you are successful." John said pleasantly, watching Larter sit next to one of the elegantly dressed women and talk to her.

"If we get to meet Lord Belverley, then who shall I say asked?" John prompted.

"My apologies for not introducing you to everybody." A middle aged man said evenly, and went around the group, naming everybody, including a large rotund man in his late fifties who spoke in a broad Geordie accent.

"Why aye man! You're looking at the king of the scrap merchant dealers in the whole of the UK, you know! Albert Catchpole by name!" he said, then went on to complete the introduction.

"Our friend Ernie Hartman here, is a retired German Army Officer and our friend over there is a leading British Archaeologist, Mr Fahey. Your man with the monocle is a retired RAF pilot, and the ladies are our researchers and travelling companions. All except Lady Farrington who your pal is talking to, she has a private interest of her own in this expedition. That tall skeleton of a man over there is Werner from the German and in company with Moorhouse from the British War Graves Commission; the Brigadier is from the Foreign Office whom you've already met. He's in charge of this expedition on behalf of the walking sheet at the front of the train."

"Sheik-Allah-Sheik you must mean. But you seem to be a mix of professions to be embarking on this expedition. I can understand archaeology, and have a slight interest in past military campaigns,

The Lost Legion

but what is a scrap merchant doing out here?" John asked politely.

"Simple man! Thanks to the war, there are literally millions of tons of scrap metal lying around in the desert, just waiting to be salvaged. Happen of course, you discover them when the storms have done their bit. Mind you, I've got to dispose of the ruddy piles of bones and mines around some of it, but at least it keeps the thieving Arabs from nicking any of it when my back is turned. I've already sent several train loads back along this track enough to fill at least three ships." The Geordie explained, and then continued his monologue in between several slurps of his drink.

"Each of us has a special reason why we're on this mission, especially the jumped-up Library assistant, Sheik ruddy Allah flippin-Sheik. He happens to have even more of an interest than just digging up rotten bones in the desert. But don't ask him unless you want to get your throat cut." Catchpole said off handedly as he drank from his ever-full glass.

"Yes! We met some of his minders." Sinclair joined in.

"They not only look ugly but they smell like a thousand camels!"

"Whatever! But don't turn your backs to them, or you'll end up with several knives shoved into them. They'd even sell their grannies to the lowest bidder, just to make a few shekels."

"Thanks for the warning Albert, but there's no real need to do so, as we're only on passage to Alexandria and not part of your project!" John replied.

"Just as long as you don't look at the walking sheet, and mind to 'kiss his arse' every time he passes you, you'll be okay. As for me, he owes me a few favours ever since I saved his brother from an unexploded mine that the stupid bugger went and trod on.

I didn't tell them that it was a dud, but what the hell. I get the first pickings of any scrap metal and other war debris that we come across."

"What about the personal effects, or valuables found? Who gets to keep them Albert?" Sinclair asked quietly, and looked at his Fathers silver lighter.

"Any personal effects are handed over to Werner or Moorhouse, for onward processing. Anything else found goes to Fahey; all the rest is at the discretion of the Brigadier and the Sheik. But I get the scrap metal, be it phosphor bronze, gold plated instruments, nickel silver, mercury or whatever."

"Sounds a good investment on a good scam then Albert, but what happens to the real finds such as army paymaster boxes, or even a buried tomb of a Pharaoh?" John asked innocently.

"Shhh! Nobody is to know about that! We're going to an area that our German friend wishes to explore. Talk about King Solomon and his ruddy mines!" Catchpole said, evading the question.

"Whatever it is, I feel sure you'll get your percentage of it. But that is not our concern, as we're only on this train due to some mix up with our local shipping agent in Tunis." John said at length.

"Do you mean that conniving, thieving bastard Boukir? When I catch up with him, I'll have his balls on a plate!" Catchpole replied vehemently, which drew the attention of Larter.

"Yes, that's him! How do you know him then Albert?"

"Simple. He charged me for shipping 5,000 tons of scrap, when it was only 4,500. Then charged the shipping company 5,500 tons. I have my own mobile weighing machine to tally the loads and all my records and receipts are kept in my Gibraltar office. Among that scrap were some boxes of pig iron that I had found, which alerted the Sheik and our German friend for some reason. Mind you, I managed to retrieve and keep those boxes for myself, but I won't go into detail about them!" Catchpole said, tapping the side of his nose with his forefinger, before adding.

"Sufficient to say, the contents of just one of those boxes set me up in the scrap metal business for life now."

"As long as you get to spend it all on me, that's all that matters my dear!" Lady Farrington said huskily, and unceremoniously plonked herself onto his lap and ruffled his balding head.

'This is going to be a long night and I'm ready for my bunk' John thought, stifling a yawn and made excuses to leave.

"We'll be along later John. Get us an early call before we arrive in Kalfa." Larter said as John left the carriage.

Chapter II
Start Digging

The train stopped in the cool of the early dawn and blew its last puff of steam, before it stood waiting to be fed and watered by the station workers.

This was a time for the passengers who were awake, to get off the train and stretch their legs by walking the short distance to the little collection of adobe buildings that represented a Major civilisation centre, laughingly called the oasis town of Kalfa.

"C'mon lads, we've arrived at Kalfa. Lets see what this desert town has to offer!" John enthused, and prompted his two friends to rise up from their bunk.

"You don't half pick your timing John! What time is it?" Sinclair asked, bleary eyed, scratching himself and yawned.

"Just gone six thirty. The steward will be here any time now to give us our early breakfast. C'mon, shake a leg and get with it." John replied.

Larter groaned and moaned about how it was too soon to get up after only just arriving back into the compartment.

Larter and Sinclair stumbled around trying to get washed and dressed as John answered the door to get their 'room service'.

"Here you are! Buttered rolls and coffee, just as I like them." John chirped.

The three friends devoured their breakfast and decided to explore the station and surrounding buildings.

John went over to the steam engine and had a good look at it whilst posing several questions to the fairly good English speaking train driver. His curiosity about the strange funnel was that it had to bend and point in an opposite direction to the windstorms.

"To stop the wind blown sand from entering the furnace." the engine driver revealed, demonstrating the rotating funnel.

"Then what about all these wooden panels doing on top of the train, driver?" Sinclair asked lazily, trying to show some interest.

Again the man explained the reason, but declined to show them, stating that they only got used in emergencies.

"Well that's that then! Let's go and get a date somewhere." Larter said chuckling to himself about the phrase he used, walking down the platform with his two friends.

"A date? Listen to him John! He was almost eaten alive by that Farrington woman, especially after Fatty Arbuckle, or Catchpole whatever his name is, had flaked out on the dining car deck." Sinclair said in mock amazement.

"Now don't be jealous just because your piece mustered her supper all over you, then shit herself when you both tried to get her cleaned up." Larter chuckled.

"Now, now, gentlemen! You've got the wrong type of date on your minds." John said with a smile when he realised what 'date' Larter was on about, and watched as the other two exchange some good-natured banter.

They had just reached the little town when one of the expedition researchers met them.

"We had better get back to the train gentlemen, or we'll get stranded. Look!" the balding ex-soldier said, pointing to the sand that was starting to swirl around their feet.

"What's up?" John asked, but saw nothing except a few little swirls of sand around them.

"The last time I was here was during the Desert War, I learned an awful lot about the place. What you see are *swirlers*, but if you start hearing a whispering noise then you'd better get under cover rather sharpish, as there's a sand storm about to come your way."

As if to emphasise the man's words, all four of them heard a faint whispering noise that started to get louder and turn into a hissing noise.

"Better get back on the double, or we'll get caught in it!" John said quickly, which prompted them to almost run back to their train.

"Get on board quickly, before I get the shutters down!" their steward shouted to them, standing on the roof trying with much difficulty to slide the large wooden panels off it.

"Let's give him a hand!" Sinclair shouted over the hissing noise, for all three of them to climb onto the carriage roof and commenced sliding the boards down. They made their way right along the carriages, meeting other stewards on top doing the same.

When the job was done, the stewards and the three friends climbed off the roof and sealed off the carriage doors as they made their way back down the train.

The whole train was protected from the stinging sands as the boards turned it into a long cocoon shape, whereby nobody could get in or out of it until the boards were removed again.

The hissing sound turned slowly into a low moan for a while before it turned into a loud one, which buffeted the whole length of the train.

John and the other two made their way to the saloon and found that all the expeditionary people were sitting talking and looking over a large map that was spread out on one of the dining tables.

"So you made it after all! Better take a seat and relax as this storm will take some time to go away." Catchpole said, greeting them.

"Gather you three were up on the roof! Good show men! Without those boards, we'd be incarcerated in sandcastles!" the Brigadier said cheerfully, twiddling with his moustache again.

The three friends sat down with a drink and were quiet, while the expedition team were talking through their objectives and other salient points that had to be undertaken.

It wasn't long before they were intrigued by what was going on and requested if they could enjoy the privilege of sitting in on their plans.

"Why yes! As we told you yesterday each one of us has an expertise on certain aspects of the expedition. But as you three have trades that we do not, and we see the need for them, perhaps it would be a good idea." The Brigadier announced, beckoning them to the table.

The Lost Legion

"Ernie here has produced several maps of the entire North Africa, that have details of their former secret roads, fuel and supply dumps. The extent of their mine fields, and map references of certain units that were sent here to oppose the Allies. For instance, this large waffle patterned piece of land represents the main battlefields, and is approx 1000 kilometres deep and over 400 kilometres long. We are here on the southerly part of the railway, which the British constructed and the Germans improved on to get their heavy weapons transported. It runs into the desert here where we are now, for about 100 miles before bending back up towards the coast. And from there, it takes a long coastal route until it reaches Cairo. The triangle signs are Divisional HQ's, the stars denote individual regiments, and the circles are supply dumps we need to find in order to complete part of our tasks." He explained at length.

"Yes! I've found several hundred tons of scrap south of that line which wasn't there a few months before when I flew over it for a look see. Judging by the remains, it was nearly all-German stuff.

I have the theory that there are some years with very strong windstorms that can bury or uncover large tracts of land. The last big one was last year and the one before that was about ten years ago, which was a real lulu. Anyway the point is, why do we find it all gone one day and something else appears as if by magic, further back from where the storm started." Catchpole opined.

"Yes! I go along with that. Three years ago, I was flying my Shackleton from Aden to Gibraltar via the desert airspace, when a storm blew me off course and forced me to land on what I thought was sand. But in fact was a solid sheet of rock that stretched for miles not even mentioned on my flight charts. When I eventually took off again, I passed over some dunes that had a funny shape to them, so I flew around them and took some pictures. And here they are!" the RAF man said, producing a pack of aerial photographs.

"See? One's like a large diamond shape and the smaller one close to it is like a circle." he said triumphantly.

"Judging by the diamond shape, it's probably two small but nearby pyramids that got covered over, which the Sheik wants us to uncover and see. But the circular one has us intrigued as we reckon it has to be some unit that we have no record of, which shows it tried to protect itself from the sandstorms. We all did it, much like the Cowboys who formed a circle with their wagons to protect themselves from the Indians!" the Brigadier concluded.

"If that is not one of yours Brigadier, then it must be one of ours. In fact I'm hoping to trace my old unit, last known to be south of the battle ground and heading east." Hartman said, pointing to the map.

John listened to the explanations and immediately thought of how he witnessed the *Brooklea* getting covered in sand some hundreds of kilometres out to sea, but decided to cast them from his mind.

"It looks as if you've got it all worked out Brigadier, but why do you want us?" John asked politely.

"Mr Sinclair here is a navigator who will help us locate these areas, as compasses are of no use in this part of the world. Our own wireless operator took sick before leaving, so as Mr Larter here is a Radio Officer, he is needed to operate our radios that we've got on the train. And as you are an Engineering Officer with expert knowledge of all types of engines and machinery, you will be needed to service any of our complicated machinery."

"But we've got a ship waiting for us in Alexandria. Besides, Lords Belverley and Invergarron would go mad if he found that three of his officers were found dodging around in a sea of sand as opposed to water."

"Come now Grey! My friend Belverley will appreciate what you three will have done, as he is in on this expedition anyway."

John looked at his two friends quickly, sensing that they had been set up. But the Brigadier also sensed something was going wrong.

"Remember me telling you that you'll be meeting up with Belverley even before you reach your ship? Well, to be honest,

The Lost Legion

he missed our train and will be coming down on the next one. But as we're late due to this storm, we'll be pressing on without him."

"So that's the scam! Three ships officers waylaid to some desert digs instead of helping to keep the sea lanes full of much needed provisions for the people back home!" Sinclair sneered.

"Don't be like that Mr Sinclair! If all goes well, you'll be back on your ship long before anybody misses you!" Fahey said quietly, which seemed to abate the rising anger in the friends.

"Well, as long as we meet up with Belverley and he is already in the know, what have we got to lose." John said philosophically to his two friends, who nodded in acceptance to their newly acquired change of plans.

"Good, that's settled then. And now that the storm has now gone away, we can dig ourselves out of this sand trap and get moving. I have a train-load of scrap and a couple of flatbed wagons with our transport and digger equipment on it, which should be arriving soon." Catchpole announced, as he searched for and found a locker that contained several shovels.

"Here! Grab one each and start digging!" he said, handing the men one each.

John looked around the carriage and spotted a square hatchway under a table and one on the ceiling, which he pointed to.

"Andy, Bruce, if we get up there and force our way upward, maybe we can start digging from the other side. You lot can get under the train and dig from underneath, by the doorway." He suggested.

"What are we waiting for then!" Sinclair said, putting a chair onto a table and climbed up to shove the hatchway outwards from the ceiling. He struggled and pushed for a while, before sand cascaded down from the hole as he broke clear.

The other two followed closely behind him and climbed out onto the roof of the train.

"It looks like a long piece of string! We're buried up to about window height on one side and only up to axle deep on the other."

Larter observed, as the three of them slid down the side of the train and onto the sand.

They dug an area by a doorway before finally being able to open it. They were greeted by the women folk who were laughing and crying with relief.

"Now don't you go peeing your knickers again my girl!" Sinclair said to a petite brunette, who rushed up to him and smothered him in kisses.

"That's for being brave! " she said after a little while.

"Somebody gets all the ruddy luck!" Larter said, grinning at Sinclair.

"My new date for the day, again." Sinclair grinned back, standing there and enjoying the attentions of the woman.

John left them all to complete the dig out to go forward and see the train driver, who was glum faced as he sat and looked at his cold engine.

"What's up driver? Shut her down and can't get started?" John asked breezily.

"Hello! Yes, something like that. Only there's sand down the funnel because it got broken off, and the fuel sprayers are all clogged up. The oil must have got contaminated too!" The driver said miserably.

"You get an oil filter and drain some of it off into a bucket. Then go and find the funnel, it can't be very far. I'll see to your fuel sprayers. Have you checked your condensers?"

"Yes, they're all right. Because of them we don't need as much water, but I managed to get a full water tank anyway. Although only half of my fuel."

"That's half the battle then!" John said quietly, starting to work on retrieving the fuel sprayers from the large furnace and started to clean them.

Once he got them spraying correctly and installed again, he fixed the funnel back onto the top of the engine, whilst the driver was filtering all the fuel into empty oil drums.

The Lost Legion

"When we've got it all out, we'll give the tank a blast of steam to clean it out. Just put the oil suction pipe into one of the oil barrels for now for the pump to work off!"

John opened the fuel valve and ignited the spray of oil with a burning rag, and waited for a while before the heat in the water tank was sufficient to create the life-giving steam to the engine.

"Right then driver. Attach that heavy piece of hose to the end of the nozzle and stick the other end into the fuel tank. We'll give a thirty second blast before we open the fuel cocks."

He had to give several blasts of steam before large muddy globules of oil came oozing out of the discharge oil pipe. Once he was satisfied it was clean enough with no more slimy mud coming from the fuel tank, they pumped the fuel out of the oil drums and back into the tank again along with the rest of the fresh fuel that was needed.

He checked the engine controls and levers over quickly for any other defects, but found no more.

"There you are driver, it's as good as new!" John announced, wiping his hands on a damp rag before handing it over to the man to use.

The driver was grinning from ear to ear and very pleased that he had his engine back. He shook John's hand so hard that John almost fell out of the engine cab.

"Thank you very much! I knew you must have known about engines by the damn awkward questions you forced me to answer."

"That's how I learned to become a Ship's engineer. Steam engines are the same all over the world, driver. But you're welcome!" John concluded, climbing down from the engine cab. He looked at his watch and was surprised to find he'd spent two hours, which seemed to have flown past.

"Must be getting better at steam engines then, especially the double condenser ones." he muttered to himself but didn't see his two friends that he had just passed.

"Still talking to himself Bruce! All this sand must have gone to his head!" Sinclair said loudly for John to hear him.

"Yeah! Shame innit!" Larter replied with a grin.

"Hello you two. I've just spent two hours in instant, steam engine revision exercises. Funny how time flies when you're enjoying yourself!" John said disarmingly, and smiled at his two friends.

"Come on John! We've just got time to have a wash, pack, then have dinner before the other train arrives." Larter announced, as they walked down the length of the train and into their cabin to wash and pack their things.

The heavily laden goods train arrived alongside the sleek express train and stopped with the sound of tortured squeals of metal on metal. There was lots of steam spouting out of almost every conceivable hole from the engine and looked like hundreds of kettles all boiling at once.

"It looks as if you've got another patient, John!" Larter chuckled, noticing John watching with great interest towards this much bigger and more ancient steam monster.

"It'll do for another couple of days. But must tell the engineer to lower his pressure, or it will blow up on him." John said absentmindedly, and then smiled as he saw his two friends grinning at him.

"Give him an engine and we can just go home, for all the company he gives us!" Sinclair pouted, then smiled again at John, handing him a fresh cigarette.

"Let's hope they don't find steamers in the middle of the desert John! There's not enough coal let alone water!" he teased.

John shrugged his shoulders and finished his after meal cigarette, when all three were asked to help out unloading the trucks from the other train.

"No thank you Mr Catchpole! We don't do unloading of trains. But let's know when you're ready to move off and we'll join you then!" Larter replied, much to the chagrin of Catchpole.

"Go ask the Arabs." Sinclair suggested.

"Sheik-bloody-Sheik and his mob have already left to join their tribe." Catchpole said with disappointment, watching the three friends leave him.

"We'll be cleaning his boots next!" Larter concluded as they sauntered off.

Chapter III
Little Windmills

The small convoy of jeeps and lorries made their way southwards at a steady pace stopping only for a meal break, but circled the vehicles for protection against any sudden sand squall.

The trucks had the same boards around them as the train, and a heavy tarpaulin was hung over the trucks to form a tent for the people to shelter under.

Larter had his radio unpacked from his jeep and placed under the shelter, with the aerial poking through to give the tent more height and support.

"According to the Tripoli Weather centre, we're in for a few days rain before the first heavy storms hit us." Larter stated, reading through his signal and handed it to the Brigadier.

"Heavy storms! But what did you call that yesterday on the train?" A female archaeologist asked sharply.

"That is what I call a wake up call. Our mob dubbed it a whistling dervish." the little ex-soldier replied.

"Our lot had a special sequence to observe, and it went from hissing right through to a *moaner* then onto a full *howler*. Moaners and the special *Howlers* don't discriminate between friend or foe, as this is where they live." Hartman remarked, which started a small discussion on the similar difficulties between the opposing armies, that both had to endure.

The night was a peaceful one as the expeditionary team got themselves prepared for another day out on the road, which Hartman informed them was built by special units of the German Engineers just before the war broke out in Africa.

"Not a bad effort, but glad you boys did that Ernie! We'd still be several hours behind, instead of where we are now, half-way towards our objective." Catchpole said affably.

"Not all of us were Jew murderers, despite the accusations. I was a bargeman for a while until I rejoined my regiment." Hartman replied, but nodded in recognition to the compliment.

"Just for you to know, we always knew and respected your regular troops that we came up against, that's why we were lenient with you. The black or brown shirt brigades got no mercy from us and dare I say were much loathed by your mobs too." the ex-soldier said softly and with genuine concern to Hartman.

"Yes, you Tommies always played fair, even if some of our troops didn't." Hartman agreed, for the conversation to tail off into silence.

The expedition had decamped and started out again just as a heavy rain squall dumped itself on them, causing the convoy to pick its way slowly along the track

Sinclair was in the lead jeep as the driver, with Fahey, the Brigadier and Hartman. The second jeep carried John, Catchpole, the RAF pilot with the ex soldier driving.

Larter was in the radio jeep, along with Werner and Moorhouse as the driver. There was a truck for all the other researchers, with three more lorries behind that, loaded up with their equipment and supplies. They had to stay in single file on the hard road surface, as flash floods raged down each side of it.

"Maybe if we stay here, we might find a few things worth salvaging!" Catchpole ventured, as they waited under the canvas covering of their lorry.

"Trust you to think of something like that!" the ex-pilot moaned.

"On second thoughts, better keep moving in case the road gets washed away. I've seen an entire column get washed away off what was supposed to be a solid roadway." Catchpole responded.

"We'll have to wait until Andy gets to us, otherwise we wait here." John responded quietly.

They waited for almost an hour before Sinclair shoved his head through the canvas doorway of the jeep.

"Mr Catchpole, John! We don't think we'll be safe on this section of road, so tell the other vehicles to get tied together like a daisy chain. We intend moving off as one until we're clear of this flash flood area. Mr Catchpole, according to the Brigadier, it's the old convoy routine of fifteen paces and at five mph. Come and let me know when all is ready, John!" he said breathlessly as the rain drummed loudly on his foul weather gear.

"Mr Catchpole, you know what the Brigadier is on about so you go and tell the others whilst I tie us up. See you later Andy!" John responded, and leapt out of the jeep.

Catchpole came back almost half an hour later to tell John that the rest of the convoy was ready and fully instructed on what to do.

John leapt back out into the pouring rain and ran forward to the leading jeep.

"All set Andy! Mr Catchpole has instructed all the drivers on what to do."

"Thanks John. You've got about five seconds to get back into your jeep before we move off. See you later!" Sinclair replied.

John managed to get back into his jeep in time for it to move off, and only seconds after that the third vehicle moved off. And so the slow snake-like convoy moved through the rain for several hours before the rain ran out of water.

Every time the lead vehicle stopped, so did the others in quick succession for fear of bumping into one another.

Again Sinclair appeared through the canvas doorway and informed John that the Brigadier had decided it was time to set up camp for the night, and that the vehicles were to form their circle again.

This started the hive of activity again, with everybody helping out and settling down for a more cheerful night to dry themselves off and have a hot meal.

The Brigadier gathered everyone around for a conflab.

"We have reached a safe area of good ground but we're surrounded by boggy areas and the flash floods. The target site is about another four hours drive away, so lets get ourselves a good night's sleep. We decamp at dawn, weather permitting. Any questions?" he announced.

"What happened to the walking sheet, Sheik flippin' Sheik? If we'd copped that rainstorm and kept us from moving, how the hell would he get here to help us?" Catchpole asked with annoyance.

The Lost Legion

"Our Arab friends will have their own problems getting to the area. But as it's their backyard so to speak, then I dare say they're already there waiting for us." The Brigadier answered, and as there were no more questions, the meeting broke up and prepared for supper.

The morning proved to be bright and cheerful and everybody was amazed as the once dull and drab desert was turning into a picturesque garden, right in front of their very eyes.

"It's amazing what a drop of water can do even in the desert." A female researcher said, as she kneeled down and studied the miraculous growth of wild flowers all around her.

"I remember one night when our unit was in the trenches near Tobruk, it bucketed down, so we decided to use our ponchos as a shield and bury ourselves under the sand for shelter. The following morning, my mate who was in the same trench as me, stood up from the sand after the rains had gone. We found that there were flowers growing on the top of his helmet, as if he'd planted them on purpose!" the ex-soldier bragged.

The anecdote tickled some of the team who laughed at the idea, but received a chorus of scorn and disbelief from the rest of them.

Once everybody had a hot drink and some food, the convoy moved off again for their final lap to the site.

But only an hour into the drive the lead vehicle stopped again and Hartman come running back to tell every driver to form a tight circle as quick as they could. The whispering sands emphasised his urgent words, prompting a swift but neat action to form their protection screen again.

"Here we are again campers! Anybody for an ice cream? Lady Farrington asked spiritedly, as the wind built up its crescendo into the deadly *howler* that Hartman had described.

The expeditionary team was warm and comfortable under their little mushroom tent and merely lazed away the hours as the winds howled around them. One of the women researchers had made little earplugs for everybody, which reduced the howl in their ears down to a low moan.

One of the diesel generators that provided them with their lighting and other electrical amenities stopped working, for John to be thankful for the distraction and spent some of the time repairing it.

During that dimly lit-time, most of the team decided to retire early or wrote up their reports and notes.

There was a little cheer when the lights were finally restored, with the usual comment about somebody lending John the coin to put into the meter.

"Yet again you have proved me right to bring you along, Grey. That goes for your two friends too. I shall be telling Belverley and Invergarron when I see them next." The Brigadier said quietly.

"That's down to you Brigadier, but there's no real need. I only did what any other engineer would have done, given the same circumstances." John replied modestly.

"Fancy a drink John?" Sinclair asked, arriving alongside him.

"No drinking allowed whilst on expedition!" The Brigadier said as he rebuked Sinclair.

"Sod you and your expedition. We are ships' officers who should not even be here. Any complaints see your pal Belverley. C'mon John!" Sinclair said angrily into the abashed Brigadier's face.

The Brigadier looked hard at Sinclair and started to twiddle with his moustache.

"Well, not too many as we'll need everybody fit and ready to move off when the storm subsides." He said, going away in a temper, muttering and swearing under his breath.

"You really shouldn't upset the Brigadier like that Andy. We could have had one without him knowing." Larter said, also arriving to make up the threesome.

* * *

The Lost Legion

The friends found a cosy little place under one of the lorries and had themselves a little drink to while away the night. They spoke about their trip so far and wondered what all this was leading to and if the strike was over and why were they not on their ship again.

For another full day the wild wind shouted at them as it dumped tons of sand all over the camp, but the occupants kept calm and got on with their experiments, tests and report filling. The atmosphere was getting a bit heavy with a myriad of smells. But everybody was concerned about the uneasy sense of suffocation, and decided to meet up to decide what should be done about their dilemma.

"If we make a couple of wind scoops and put them on top of a couple of wagons we should be able to vent off some of it. Just like the funnel on the train." John suggested.

"That will get rid of the heavy atmosphere, but we need air to breathe." The ex-pilot replied.

"We can set up a small ventilation system based on little windmills. If we put a double canvas screen across a small opening to windward it will act as a filter for the sand, yet allow the wind to come through the pores. A little windmill onto another one on the leeward side will pump out the bad air thus completing the ventilation." John answered back, holding up a small diagram to show everybody the principle on how it was going to work.

One of the female researchers came over and looked at the diagram and announced that she would sew the canvas screen. The ex pilot said he could make the windmill just like his aircraft propellers. Catchpole said he would make the funnels for the windmills. In the end everybody was helping out to solve the common problem.

Before long the ventilation system was working perfectly and everybody began to feel better again.

The Brigadier came over to thank John again by offering him a bottle of scotch.

"Here. Have one on all of us, but don't get blotto. I need a good man like yourself to keep command of the troops." He said gratefully.

John accepted it gracefully and even offered the Brigadier a glass of it, but he declined the offer saying that as the Brigadier, he had to stay on top of things.

Chapter IV
Pile of Bones

It was early the following morning and everybody seemed to have woken up at the same time, remarked at the complete and eerie silence.

"The storm must have blown away, a female researcher whispered, and took off her ear plugs.

This was the sign for everybody else to do the same, although John wasn't wearing any as he was used to constant loud noises anyway.

Nobody spoke for several minutes as if to savour the silence until somebody suggested that they start digging themselves out.

"Judging by our canvas roof, there can't be much sand above us, so we might as well go up instead of out sideways. Just like the train." John suggested.

As John was the first out through the hole in the roof, he helped the others through it until everybody was standing by him.

The sight was awesome to each person as they gazed round first at their buried camp then at the vast open areas of desert.

"It appears that we camped behind some sand covered rocks, and that the wind has levelled all the sand dunes in front of us to fill in all the hollows behind us. " The ex pilot volunteered.

"And how! It has proved my theory too. According to my count, there's the best part of 200 vehicles over there!" Catchpole said excitedly, removing his binoculars from his eyes and pointed.

The Brigadier and the two War Graves men looked through their own binoculars at the site and decided that they had to go and investigate sooner than later.

The decision to do so made Catchpole dance with glee.

"I'm rich! I'm rich!" he gloated, dancing a jig in the sand.

John was the only person not looking the same way, as his own attention was drawn to a group of vehicles behind them that was half-buried in the sand.

"Brigadier, if I remember correctly, the map said there was a strange round shape close to a diamond shape. Could these be what made those shapes?" John asked slowly, and pointed to what he had spotted.

"By jove, I think he's right!" the ex pilot said, pulling out his wad of photographs from his tunic.

Catchpole came over to see the new site, only to rub his hands together and started to gloat again.

"I must be having all my birthdays in one go. I claim the lot in the name of Catchpole Enterprises." He said expansively.

"Not before we have excavated the site and discovered what and who they were!" Fahey said ominously, which served to burst the euphoric bubble of Catchpole.

Hartman, Werner and Moorhouse were quietly discussing the sites between them when Sinclair suggested that instead of acting like the 'Kings of the castle', they should get down amongst it all and start the dig.

"There just might be another storm to cover it over again, so I suggest we'd better dig ourselves out of this one first Andy." John said philosophically, making Catchpole urge the rest of them to hurry up and do so, as he was eager to get in among all that scrap metal.

Over the next two days, the team started a systematic search and dig of the site, uncovering fresh artefacts by the spade full, and skeletons by the score.

"Ernie! This site is about a mile square, and although we've uncovered several units, each one belonging to your lot, have you any idea as to who they might be? I wonder how did such a large force get themselves buried like this?" the Brigadier asked in puzzlement.

"We have to locate a HQ command vehicle to tell us. But from the formation, it looks as if they were caught napping and unprepared. Look, all the vehicles are in a protective diamond formation with a cordon of tanks around them, but still in advancing columns." Hartman said, and showed them a diagram of the site.

The Lost Legion

"So much for Pharaoh's pyramids or whatever! Sheik-flippin-Sheik will be pleased when he finds out, I don't think." Catchpole said with a smirk.

"Judging by such a force, I'd say it would be at least a brigade. They are too far south to have any effect on the outcome of the battle at El Alamein. Fortunately for us we managed to get wind of it, but such a force might have been sent out and used to cut off our rear supply lines or make for a surprise attack on Cairo. Now that would really have upset the apple cart!" the Brigadier whistled, as Hartman nodded in agreement to that very plausible fact.

"I've found a smaller diamond shape consisting of four light tanks and four half-tracks that have surrounded a large vehicle, probably the command vehicle you're looking for." Sinclair announced, arriving into the site 'office' area.

Hartman jumped to his feet and asked Sinclair to lead the way, as some of the others followed behind them.

Sinclair slid open a large side door of the vehicle and looked inside, but had to step backwards due to the stench.

Hartman and the Brigadier looked inside and were dumbstruck by what they saw.

"Well Ernie! Here's the moment of truth. It looks as if our friends stuck to their posts even after death, including that General over there. As the senior officer on parade, I will take charge of his sword and baton as a belated gesture of accepting his surrender." The Brigadier announced, seizing the valuable prizes and stuffed them into a large bag.

Hartman darted inside and examined the tunics of the dead men whilst the Brigadier was in his element, and peering at the tactical maps and other erstwhile sensitive military secrets that were displayed all around the cabin.

"This is it, this is it! We've found it! We have bloody well found it!" Hartman said jubilantly, first in German then in English, which made others come inside the vehicle to see what was going on.

"What have we found Ernie? Apart from a dirty great pile of bones that is?" the Brigadier asked breathless with the excitement of it all.

"We've found The Lost Legion! That was General Stummell, commander of the now infamous 9th Legion. It has its history dating back to the Roman times, but during the war it was enshrined as the Death Head Dragoons, which all subsequent SS Regiments adopted as their symbol of death before surrender. If you take out his baton from your bag, you'll find it's solid gold and has the 9ths inscription on it. His officers' ring is also of the 9th because it has the regimental crest and motto on it, and of pure gold. Even his sword is pure gold with the names of all previous commanding officers on it, his being the last to be inscribed. This is the one everybody denied existed, and would not listen to me that it did. Here is bloody well General Stummell in his own bloody command vehicle. The ring of trucks around this vehicle must be the Guard of honour that protects the regimental standard and the 9th EAGLE. This special guard consists of 100 veteran soldiers whose sole purpose is to stand guard over the 9ths Eagle. Each one should be wearing a solid gold medallion to identify them from the other troops. We've found the General and the Lost Legion; all I've got to do now is find the lost Eagle to prove myself in front of all the doubters and historians. To do that Brigadier, I demand that you hand back to me, the Generals baton and his sword, to make the positive identification and so on. Anyway, it is not yours to claim but me, as the only survivor of such a legion." Hartman explained.

The Brigadier twiddled his moustache again and declared that the find was of importance to the victorious army, but ceded to the forceful demands of Hartman, and handed the precious artefacts over to him.

"I have to get one of the archivists to record all this and take as many details as possible. If the researchers find the Paymaster wagon, they should be able to find the names of each person in the legion, from the ordinary private right up to the General.

The Lost Legion

I want to have as much material evidence as possible, but to make everything tally up, I really need the German 9th Eagle to be able to take it back home and put to rest." Hartman added, wrapping the items reverently in Stummel's sand encrusted tunic jacket, and tucked it under his arm.

"We'll search the area thoroughly and chronicle each important artefact. There are bound to be other important items of note. These maps and other military items for a start, so don't worry about it Brigadier." Fahey announced, noticing the annoyance on the Brigadiers face at having to hand back such valuable prize items.

The two War Graves men were busy collecting up all the personal effects such as wallets, photographs, and ID tags and putting them into crates. The coins and other items such as rings, watches and other jewellery got piled into more boxes. Fahey and the other archaeologists had dug a large trench and were placing the bones of the dead into it, whilst Catchpole was busy marking up and recording all the different metals he found.

Larter was fiddling with the radios in the command vehicle whilst John and Sinclair were nosing around and generally helping the ex-soldier and others to uncover more and more machines. The ex-pilot was busy photographing everything in sight.

During their fourth day, they were surprised to see a large horde of Arabs race towards them, only to set up camp just a little way off the site.

Catchpole said that it was a bunch of Arab troublemakers and for them all to look out. Several well-armed men riding camels came rushing into the camp and pointed their rifles at the Brigadier and anybody else that was there.

"Stand still effendi! Bow to Sheik-Allah-Sheik!" one burly man demanded in pidgin English, as a snow-white horse came trotting into the camp that was mounted by a golden robed man.

"Good afternoon Allah!" the Brigadier said calmly, as the Arab dismounted and walked over to the group.

"Brigadier, it appears that you have found our pyramids, now we want our gold." The Sheik announced.

"There's nothing here but scrap metal and a large pile of bones, Sheik me lad." Catchpole answered slowly.

"We have been waiting ten years for Allah to deliver our inheritance that the filthy Germans promised us. I demand to speak to the commander of this useless army. Maybe he'll tell me where it is before I cut him to pieces." The Sheik snarled.

"My name is Major Hartman and this was my wartime unit. This is an armed column equipped for war, and did not carry anything else but weapons of war." Hartman said quietly, but was told to shut up in no uncertain terms by the Sheik.

"When I want you filthy pigs to speak to me I will command it. Until then shut your camel shit breath and take me to the commander."

"There's nothing here but piles of bones, as the man said." Fahey re-iterated an earlier comment, but was hit across his arm by the Sheik's riding crop.

John and his two friends were standing by the entrance of the command vehicle and beckoned the Sheik over.

"If you're so Allah almighty then come and speak to the man you think has your inheritance. Mind you he's not very talkative today." Sinclair shouted aloud as the Sheik almost ran over to them.

As he stepped inside John counted up to three before they heard a large shout followed by a tirade of swearing.

"He's calling the General several nasty names and is throwing his bones everywhere." Larter interpreted for them and started to chuckle as the Sheik came storming out of the vehicle.

"Well Sheik! Did you speak with him? I bet he didn't have the guts to speak back, yes?" John asked softly, which infuriated the Sheik even more.

"You will stop playing games with me or I will have you all shot. Where is my gold?" he demanded angrily.

"It's like this Sheik. We've finished doing what we came for, so you and your lads are free to search the place for yourself.

The Lost Legion

Any gold or other such commodities you can keep, but we're off just as soon as we've buried all the bones." Fahey said with an air of composure, which seemed to calm the Sheik down to a simmering rage.

"I will give you four hours to do so before I send you away. If you're not gone by then you will all get shot and buried with the rest of this filth." The Sheik hissed, striding over to his waiting horse and galloped away with his band of cut-throats.

"He knows that I own the scrap metal, but he wants to get his hands on this flippin gold he's on about. So we'd better do as he says. What do you know that we don't Ernie?" Catchpole asked, scratching his balding head.

"I was part of a special unit whose sole existence was to transport boxes of gold from Germany and deliver it to the Arabs in the Sudan, Ethiopia and other such countries. But I got separated from my unit before they were apparently assigned to the 9th Legion. None of my original unit is amongst all this lot, so I suggest that they must have got separated from it too. If my unit is not here, then there's no gold, simple as that. Not even the Eagle is here, which suggests something else must have happened, not even mentioned in the daily report log kept by the General's ADC." Hartman explained, which struck a chord with the Brigadier.

"He's right. I found nothing among the dispatches or other details to record such a secondment. Look, I have the legion's manpower and vehicle strength document, including the names of all the officers under his command. I too would have demanded such a document to be kept, but to be destroyed in the event of imminent capture. It seems as if the storm overpowered them not us." Fahey said, holding out the documents for others to inspect.

"I remember a Major Luchens, who was promoted to a Colonel. Is there any mention of him and what's his name, er, Kretshmer. Yes that's it, Sergeant Kretshmer. I believe he got promoted back to a Captain or whatever, but please look again to see those names.

The Eagle has got to be here somewhere, unless it was left behind at the special depository wherever that might be." Hartman asked glumly.

Fahey looked through the list of names until he came upon the entry for Luchens.

"He's right! It says that a Colonel Luchens was one of the four Colonels within the brigade. His regiment was the special unit in charge of the gold shipments."

"If he's with this lot his ID tag and that of Kretshmer's should be amongst the others in that sack. If it's not, then it means that he and his regiment were out on another mission. Now we're getting somewhere." Hartman said enthusiastically.

After a thorough search through the personal effects bags, nothing was found that would point to those men.

Hartman was not to be daunted the second time, and asked to see the wall charts and other despatch records that were also found in the brigade admin vehicle.

Again the search found nothing, which seemed to blunt Hartman's resolve.

"Oh well, at least I've got the regimental records and the proof I needed to back up my claim of being part of the 9th Eagle, even though the eagle itself is nowhere to be found." Hartman concluded.

"Then again Hartman, if this special regiment was, shall we say detached, then I wonder if that circle of half-buried vehicles over there has anything to do with it?" John asked, pointing out to the smaller mound.

"Oh yes! We forgot about that lot. We'll let the Arabs take over this place whilst we look over that one." Catchpole suggested, which everybody agreed to.

After a brief military funeral to bury all the dead in a mass grave, the Brigadier got everybody into their vehicles and drove off just as the Arabs started to appear over the distant sand dunes.

"Quickly everybody, there's a whole tribe of them coming. In fact several tribes, judging by the different colours I can see." Larter shouted, and for the vehicles to speed away out of danger.

Chapter V
Listening

The expedition made their camp inside the circle of the half-buried remains, so as to protect themselves from the hordes of Arabs that were seen to descend on the remains of the Lost Legion.

"Why aye man! They'll get a reet surprise when they start tampering with any of the tanks or howitzers. Those are top rate metals that fetch a good price you know, but just so that they cannot be used on us, I've booby trapped them." Catchpole chuckled, watching the Arabs through his binoculars with eager anticipation.

"You've done what? You bloody fool Catchpole! If any of them get killed then they'll be after us for revenge instead of leaving the site quietly." Larter said angrily.

"Yes! You'd better pray Catchpole, because if they get hold of us god knows what they'd do to the women among us!" Fahey warned, as others offered their opinion on the matter.

"By the time they're finished playing around over there, it would take a canny man to mount even a pony charge against us." Catchpole scoffed.

"If this gets ugly and out of hand, it will be your bloody fault Catchpole. Not only do we risk getting murdered where we stand but it will also create such a bloody row with the political wallahs in the Foreign Office. No doubt our friend Belverley will have something to say about it too." The Brigadier fumed, watching the Arabs closely with his binoculars.

John was busy digging out a strange machine that he had found, and did not hear the furore going on in the camp.

'A double engined four track vehicle, with a vehicle on skis hitched onto it. Just look at the size of the tracks. I wonder if the military boys can shed light onto it.' John mused, and examined the strange vehicle more closely, until he was satisfied.

"Brigadier, Mr Hartman can you come over here and see what I've found. Maybe you've seen vehicles like these before?" John shouted over to the group of men.

The Lost Legion

They came over to see what it was, and were amazed at what was found.

"Look at the size of the tracks, and all four of them." Catchpole said, suitably impressed with the vehicle.

"I could use a few of them no problem!" he snorted, gazing at the vehicle.

"So that's what it was. I was conducting aerial reccies to find the beast that made these tracks, but couldn't find any. We thought it was a super tank, much more powerful than their Leopards and Tigers. We had no answer to them, and we certainly wouldn't have the answers had these been tanks." The ex-pilot said in wonderment.

"Yes, we thought it was a super gun that was self propelled!" the Brigadier retorted, staring at the vehicle.

"Mind you though! It's a very clever idea to put skis onto the towed vehicle, as it must have saved a lot on their fuel. And judging by the size of the tracks, the weight of the vehicle would have been greatly reduced as it went over soft sand." John added.

"I knew we had invented something like this I but was not able to see a real one. According to my research, it was a special vehicle for carrying its own weight in supplies, or towing broken-down tanks that got stuck in the sands." Hartman conceded.

The balding ex-soldier looked at the vehicle and announced that it was also very well armed, as he uncovered a well-protected heavy machine gun on the top of the vehicle.

Sinclair and the other ex soldiers whistled at the almost brand new quality of the weapon, considering it must have been buried under the sand for a decade or more.

"By the looks of it, whoever the commander of this site was, he had all his armour and heavy weapons on the outside, and as the circle got decreased, the trucks and other soft vehicles were protected on the inside." The Brigadier opined.

"In which case, we should find some sort of command vehicle in the middle. And that lump of sand in the middle must be it." Sinclair said, pointing to the mound of sand in the middle of the circle.

"How convenient that the women should set up the cookhouse next to it." The ex-pilot replied as he agreed with Sinclair's theory.

Hartman grabbed a shovel and started to dig the mound away to reveal the doorway of the vehicle. All the other men helped him to uncover the vehicle completely, to find that it too was one of these new machines.

Hartman pulled hard at the sliding door which opened in jerky movements, and peeped inside once the fresh air had wafted out the stench of death.

"These men must belong to my unit, and now I know what happened to it, despite being reported as being wiped out at Wadi Birani. That Colonel's ID tag says Kretshmer, yet the only person of that name was my old Sergeant. How did he become Colonel when Luchens was the regimental Colonel and in charge of the unit? This other officer is a Captain, named as Kramsfeld but I don't know him. The person at the radio is called Lutz. I remembered him as a corporal, so he must have been promoted to Sergeant according to his stripes. It appears that somebody must have upgraded this unit for some reason. It had to be somebody like a two star General such as Stummell over there. But why?" Hartman asked.

"Here's the radio operators log, and he must have been keeping a diary too as he'd been entering events into it for some time." Larter said, and handed over the two books to the Brigadier and Hartman.

"Mr Werner and you can translate for us if you would." The Brigadier requested, and handed over the books.

"It says that they were on a gold shipment retrieval mission to the Spanish Sahara, and had to wait for the Colonel to arrive. In the next page it says that the Colonel, Luchens that is, had disappeared and that General Stummell had visited them. I can't read the next bit, but it mentions promotions all round and something I can't quite make out, but it's something to do with their gold shipment and the Generals Eagle." Werner translated.

The Lost Legion

"According to this radio log, there was a huge storm that created too much static for any signal to get through. He was still trying four days later but no more entries after that." Hartman read from the log

"Yes! There was a huge storm during that year due to some El Niño effect or whatever, and it turned out to be the worst one for decades. That sort of storm would affect the whole Saharan desert." The ex pilot stated, peering over the large map that was still stuck to a makeshift wall on one side of the vehicle.

"Here, look at this gentlemen. Look at all these special star marks. They are in two straight lines but cross in the centre at this point here. Now that could either be a reference point or where the General had his legion based before they were ordered out." Sinclair shouted, pointing out the details.

Everybody looked closely at the map but gave different reasons as to what the lines meant.

"No, we're almost on top of this spot, so it must mean a collection point or some sort of supply dump that the Germans had and we didn't." the ex-pilot said quickly.

"Yes it's called the Baerlitz system, that we used in preparation for, or during any protracted campaign in every theatre of the war." Hartman conceded.

"Then that centre point is probably where the gold is and probably where the General kept his Eagle too." Werner said eagerly.

"No wonder the Arabs are frantic to find it. There was reported to be at least 200 tons of it. But that point is in a mountainous area, so lord knows where it might be hiding." The ex-pilot added.

The men looked around the command vehicle again, picking up all the artefacts and items of interest, and had the vehicle tidied up for re- use.

"I'll see if I can get the radio working, if somebody can get me a power supply." Larter volunteered.

"I'll get you that Bruce. Come on Catchpole, you're an ex-mechanic, you can give me a hand." John added.

"Not before you eat. Food is now ready boys, so put your toys away and get it now while it's hot." Farrington announced, poking her head into the crowded vehicle.

The suggestion gave way to the unanimous agreement that food was definitely next on the agenda.

Their meal was a swift affair as the men were anxious to start their tasks, but during their repast they heard several faint explosions coming from the other site.

"Listen to that! As soon as you hear the last explosion then you can bet your bottom penny that those Arabs will be coming this way to try and find us. If they do, then we can all look out." Sinclair said, and finished his after-meal cigarette.

"We have enough military men here to cope with a few smelly Arabs, so let them come if they want to. I for one will be laying a few surprises for them." Catchpole said bravely, clutching a handful of stick grenades.

"Yes! I too have been very busy since arriving. My forte was weaponry, so I have managed to get some of those heavy cannons cleaned up and ready to fire. Maybe if Mr Grey can get one of those strange machines working, we could use it as a counter attack weapon instead of defending our perimeter." The balding ex-soldier said, pointing to one of the recently cleared vehicles.

"We shall dig in here and defend the camp. If the Arabs want us that badly they'll have to ruddy well come and get us." the Brigadier declared, taking control of the situation.

"Mr Grey, you get our generators going and you Mr Larter will get the radios working to call for help. Mr Catchpole and the rest of you men will man a heavy machine gun each. Except for you Mr Fahey, you will observe and record all that goes on. Lady Farrington, you and the women will keep the fires going to provide food and any medical aid should any of us be wounded or whatever. I shall be keeping watch on the entire camp from on top of the command vehicle."

"Once I've got the generators going, I shall be available for ammo duties if needs be and help protect the women." John volunteered.

"Besides, I'm used to handling a weapon anyway, so if the worse should happen, then I'll be our last defence."

"I'm a good shot too! I can handle a rifle." Lady Farrington responded.

"Thank you Lady Farrington. It's nice to know, but we need you to take charge of the camp whilst we're on the parapets." The Brigadier said patronisingly.

"When you men are dying at our feet and the Arabs are raping and murdering us, you'll wish you had more fire power. My ex-husband always said that the more fire power you had the better chance you stood at winning." Lady Farrington said glumly as she joined the waiting group of women.

"Now that is out of the way." The Brigadier said, turning round to speak to the men.

"I want one outer perimeter of mines or explosives at about 500 yards and another at 200 yards." He began, but was cut short by Sinclair.

"Hold on a minute Brigadier, before you get carried away. The war is over now and is supposed to be peace-time for everybody, so don't get any ideas that we are a full lighting legion like you probably commanded in the past. We are just twelve men and eight women on a peaceful mission. You are supposed to be the 'Man from the Ministry' to prevent such unwarranted intervention into what we're doing. If you can't overcome our difficulties by peaceful means, then you will be considered the one responsible for starting another full-scale war. Besides, all this armament and munitions are more than dodgy to handle. We have enough ammo to last maybe a day providing the guns perform. But what then?"

The Brigadier nodded his agreement to that statement but reminded everybody that it was Catchpole who sabotaged everything with his stupid booby-trap plot. It was the outcome of that, which would determine their fate, not plain words of sorry."

"This being so, I want everybody to do the following!" he continued, giving orders without further interruptions.

It took a full two hours before all the Brigadier's arrangements and preparations were made and the team braced to meet their fate.

The hue and cry of the massive horde of Arabs were louder and much closer than anticipated, before the first cordon of explosives were triggered off by the oncoming tide of Arabs.

"Get ready with those mortars Catchpole! Ernie, on my signal, start your crossfire with those two heavy machine guns. The rest of you stay out of sight." The Brigadier commanded from his lookout position.

The Arabs came into the gully as predicted and got blown to pieces by the booby traps and the mortar fire, which made them retreat to re group.

"Up the range of the mortars by 1000 yards and fire shrapnel for effect!" the Brigadier shouted, keeping his eye on the Arabs with his binoculars.

The 'whump' of the mortars were plainly heard but when the devastating shrapnel exploded amongst the charging Arabs, the screams and yells of agony and death drowned the noise of gunfire.

The Arabs charged into the gully again and were decimated once more by the withering fire of the machine guns, before they finally retreated.

"Hah! That surprised them!" Catchpole scoffed, standing up above the ramparts, and was nearly shot by some unseen sniper.

"They were only testing our strength, and found that we're blind on our left flank and to our rear. That's why Catchpole was almost shot. They've got snipers on that sand dune over there, and by the look of it over to our right flank too." Hartman said, and fired off his weapon killing the man who shot at Catchpole.

"We've used up our surprise perimeters Brigadier. Its getting dark now so they won't try anything until the moon starts to come out again. They like the dark but they need the moonlight in case they get killed so that their soul can follow them back afterwards." Sinclair announced.

"Then what?" the Brigadier asked.

"Simple, Brigadier. We use this stand-off time to plant a few more surprises that will be even more devastating than dynamite." Sinclair replied, with a cunning and wicked look.

"Whatever you've got up your sleeve I'll go along with Andy! But let's all into your secret." John said quietly, as everybody gathered round to hear Sinclair's dastardly plan.

"By 'eck Sinclair, you're one canny lad." Catchpole remarked in his broad Geordie accent, and started to chuckle at the fiendish plot about to be undertaken.

It was almost completely dark outside the camp, although the campfire lit up the interior, and the people creating shadows around it as if nothing was happening.

"No sign of our friends Sinclair, so good luck!" The Brigadier whispered, as four of the men slithered their way under the trucks and down the slope towards the killing fields before them.

It took about an hour before they all arrived back safely behind their defensive screen, and reported to the Brigadier that their mission was complete.

"I'm sure my old Sergeant, er Colonel Kretshmer would have approved of what we did Brigadier. I was pleased to find that Sinclair knew of similar delaying tactics that Kretshmer had told us about during our lengthy trip in a canal barge. " Hartman whispered, as the men were given a hot cup of tea to keep them warm from the plummeting temperatures of the desert nights.

"We'll soon know how well we've done in about half an hour from now. But remember, no firing or they'd pinpoint our positions." Sinclair stated, tipping some brandy into his tea, and offered some to John who went with him.

"How goes the radio Bruce?" John whispered, not daring to break the almost deafening silence.

"Got it working and have managed to contact Cairo.

Catchpole has got his trucks arriving soon to cart off the scrap over there, and Belverley is on his way with them. And should arrive in about two days from now providing the weather holds out." Larter replied softly.

"Maybe we'll get out of here and back to normality on board our ship then, Bruce." Sinclair replied, hearing the whispered conversation.

Everybody was listening intently to pick up any sounds from the desert, and was pleasantly surprised by the faint muttering and whispering sounds coming from Catchpole and Hartman.

"Listen! We planted a couple of those listening devices we found, to give us warning of our so called invisible attackers." Hartman whispered.

"This was one of our more successful tricks against the Allies and one of the reasons why we nearly won the African campaign." He added, as they listened to the Arabs talk amongst themselves as they tried to creep up on the camp.

"We found out your little secret about two weeks before El Alamein, and fed you with false information, that's why we won it, not you lot." Catchpole whispered back, but with a grin towards Hartman and Werner.

Everybody listened to their unseen attackers, and Sinclair started to count slowly up to ten. As he got to ten, there were several loud shouts followed by little popping noises, then loud piercing screams that seemed to disappear into the night, before all went quiet again.

"It seems that the Arabs don't like meeting their own kinfolk at night, or getting their fingers or whatever it was into contact with our little booby traps." Sinclair laughed.

"Surprising what a bullet case of gunpowder can do to a mans' privates. Let alone what he saw to help him go mad!" Hartman chuckled.

The same performance happened almost two hours afterwards, but from a different side, and again one hour later, from yet another different approach.

"I don't think they'll try another one until its daylight. So we might as well get some sleep!" Sinclair declared, which was accepted unanimously.

The camp managed to have a leisurely breakfast, before a group of Arabs were seen approaching the camp.

"They've got a black and white flag up which says they wish to parley." Larter said, handing over his binoculars for the Brigadier to see.

"What do they want this time! They must know that they can wipe us out many times over, so what is it they want?" the Brigadier asked to nobody in particular.

"They must know that we're sitting over a water hole, and they want to use it. They will want to parley for the use of it, and will probably offer us a safe passage out of here if we do. Otherwise they'll try and bully us into submission to give them the water rights. At least that's my own assumptions." Larter announced, and Hartman voiced his agreement with the statement.

"Cheeky bastards! They'll get no water from us that's for certain!" Catchpole said indignantly.

The small group of Arabs stopped several yards from the front of the camp before a black-robed man on his camel came forward and shouted his request loudly to the defenders.

"We are a people who are without water. As you have enough to share with us, we will take the waters, and in return we will let you go unmolested. Your life for our water." the Arab said in pidgin English, and brandished his long rifle that glinted in the sunlight.

"We have water enough only for ourselves. You find your own water, and may Allah be merciful to you." the Brigadier replied, taunting the Arabs by holding up a cup and pouring the water out onto the sands before him.

This action taunted the Arabs to such a pitch that they started to fire at the defenders before they turned and ran away.

A burst of machine gun fire chased them on their way so that they dared not return and repeat their challenge.

As the day wore on, the Arabs attempted several times to over-run the camp, but each time they were beaten back by merciless machine gun fire.

The desert sand in front of the camp was littered with the dead bodies of the attackers and their animals, and as the day finally ended, the stench was almost unbearable.

"Luckily we are up wind of that lot. But come nightfall they'll sneak in and take them all away. We shall let them do so, but if they decide that we're sleeping and try to sneak up on us like last night then they'll get the same as this!" Sinclair chuckled, rolling a dead man's head towards the campfire, maing the women scream with terror.

"Shush! He won't say anything, so why should you!" Sinclair laughed.

Lady Farrington came over and slapped Sinclair hard across his face saying.

"We are not amused. We've seen dead bodies before, but not the ones you seem to find!" She said nastily, as the other women started to calm down from their shock.

"Whassamatter? It's a standard practice where I come from! It's what kept the Arabs from your bedside last night, so be thankful you're still around" Sinclair replied defensively.

The men looked at the grotesque head and discovered that instead of a tongue poking out of the mouth were the erstwhile owners genitals, with the penis as the tongue.

"Where did you learn that trick Andy?" John asked anxiously.

"My brother Ronnie's company of the Gordon Highland Regiment managed to escape to Borneo from the debacle of Singapore. The local natives who were head hunters, showed him the trick which they used to great effect to harass and kill loads of the Jap forces that arrived there shortly afterwards." Sinclair explained.

The Lost Legion

"At least they know not to try any more tricks again tonight in case they get turned into one of these 'dick heads', so be thankful for, shall we say 'small' mercies."

"No wonder they were spooked, and you certainly stopped their heretical ways!" Larter smiled, and told them what the Arab words meant last night.

"Well let's hope we hear a lot more if it keeps us all safe then." Lady Farrington concluded, and turned her head away in disgust when Sinclair retrieved the sample and replaced the genitals back into the head again.

Sinclair's ruse worked a treat yet again, and the booby traps kept the Arabs guessing as to where they would step next.

The defenders were ready for the Arabs, who were surprised to find that they were out-guessed by the so-called 'effendis with camel breath'.

The red-hot barrels of the machine guns glowed in the semi-darkness as the Arabs finally disengaged themselves from the slaughter and left the field of combat.

They had a peaceful night and whilst the dawn was breaking, they discovered that all the dead were removed from the battlefield and no signs from the rest of the Arab camps.

"It seems that they've cleaned up and buggered off!" The ex-pilot declared, peering over the parapet and over the empty desert where the Arabs had their campsite the day before.

"They took us for a bunch of un-armed civilian archaeologists, probably wanting to capture us and hold us for a king's ransom. I've known it to happen before." Fahey said with relief, looking at the empty desert.

"We can now finish off our expedition by cataloguing all of this site too." Werner said to Moorhouse, who agreed with a nod.

"We have a signal from Lord Belverley who says that he'll be with us in two days. But according to the Met Office there's another big storm due any day now, so I dare say he'll be delayed." Larter announced.

"If that's the case, then we'd better start getting prepared otherwise we'll end up like my poor friends here." Hartman joined in.

"We have enough water and food for another two days, but after that I don't know." Lady Farrington added.

"If this is supposed to be one of those supply dumps then we should at least find out exactly where it is. That or we start drinking the water from the engines." Sinclair said to the Brigadier.

"The supplies would be contaminated and less than useless. Our only survival plan is to stay here until Belverely arrives, and in the meantime, filter off as much water from the vehicles as possible. But from now on, we'll have to start on half rations until I say otherwise." the Brigadier announced, after hearing the comments from the rest of the team.

"Maybe that's what happened to Kretshmer and all the others. But I think they all died of suffocation and of course being buried under all the sand and not knowing which way to dig themselves out again." Hartman concluded, which brought the team back down to earth and reality that replaced the euphoric victory feelings they had over defeating the Arabs.

Chapter VI
Too Late

The storm lasted almost two days before blowing itself away leaving the expedition team almost totally buried under a fresh sand dune to compliment all the other ones.

"I've picked up a signal from Belverley. He's coming along with Catchpole's heavy recovery gear, and has got extra supplies for us. I've given him an exact map reference from your own map Brigadier, and he says that he'll be here in about eight hours." Larter announced, handing the Brigadier the signal to read.

"Well done Mr Larter. We shall go and meet him instead." He replied.

"Meet him?"

"Yes. Your friend Mr Grey has got two of those mechanical monsters working, and it looks as if we can take a sleigh ride on them and bring all our equipment with us too."

"Well fiddle-de-dee! We finally get to ride on them." Sinclair said with total surprise.

"I knew it was wise to bring you three seaman officers with me. Between you, you have saved our bacon more than once."

"Well now. Don't go telling Belverley or he'll have us volunteered for more cock-a-mamie adventures like this one. Thanks, but no thanks Brigadier."

"What's that Bruce?" Sinclair asked as he came into the tail end of the conversation.

"Oh nothing Andy! Just have your steaming bag ready for when Belverley meets up with us. We're getting out of here pretty damn quick or even sooner."

"Amen to all that, Bruce. In the meantime, we three officers must have a confab like and now would be the best time." Sinclair said, beckoning Larter to join him.

* * *

The three friends were sitting on the sand under some remnants of the wartime tarpaulins, when John handed them something to look at.

"I thought it was a bar of lead with those two gold painted roses on the side of it. But I dropped it onto one of the steel tracks of this vehicle and look what fell out of it." John whispered, and held out a little purse containing three large and several small precious stones.

"Where did this come from John" Larter asked with surprise as they looked and felt the stones.

"This is not just a lead bar. It's the outside case for a small bar of solid gold with a hollow inside to contain these stones. Whoever made this knew what he was doing. I've looked everywhere, but can't find any more." John whispered back.

"Are you sure John? Better not let the others know." Sinclair said aside as someone passed close by them.

"I'll have the emerald, green for Ireland, You Andy can have the sapphire, blue for Scotland, and you Bruce can have the ruby, red for England. We will also have two diamonds each and I'll cut the bar up into three equal shares for us, is that fair?" John asked.

"Judging by the ingot, we'll have a good £400 apiece let alone the value of the stones." Larter said as he weighed up the ingot.

"This makes it worth our while coming on this stupid trip then. Maybe we can get a bonus from Belverley for our troubles as well." Sinclair stated, pocketing his share of the treasure.

"We say nothing of this to anybody and keep it a secret for eternity. All friends together and all that, is it?" John asked, looking into his friends' faces.

"Our handshake in Belfast was enough for me John, and I'm sure Andy feels the same." Larter replied as they held out their hands and avowed their friendship anew.

The three friends got themselves sorted out and ready to move off as Catchpole and the balding ex-soldier started up the two large vehicles with a cough and a splutter before the engines

The Lost Legion

purred gently and were ready to be used again after their enforced ten year sleep.

"I'll be back for the jeeps and lorries afterwards!" Catchpole shouted over the throaty growl of the engines.

The two big machines moved quickly and gently over the soft sand and making a soft *ziffing* sound as they went. Each machine towed two sleighs that skated almost silently over the sand, as the expedition moved off towards their relief column.

"The name on the front says it's a *Ziffer*, and made by Kretshmer. He was a racing car driver and mechanic before the war. Pity he is dead because this invention of his could be worth a fortune for any oil prospectors coming out into the deserts." Hartman volunteered.

"Yes! It's an apt name if you listen to the sound it makes." John appreciated, as did the others when they associated the noise with the name.

It was a surprised Belverley who had to stop his column when he met the Brigadier's small convoy head on.

"What in heavens name have you got there? I've never seen such an ugly vehicle, yet one that seems to eat up the desert." Belverley stated with amazement, looking over the *ziffers*.

"I'm the salvage master of this part of the desert and these belong to me. So get your thieving mitts off them!" Catchpole said quickly and proudly, stepping down from the driver's seat.

Belverley looked at the expeditionary team and shook his head in disbelief.

"I should have guessed that the three ' no good officers' who were involved in your expedition, were non other than 3rd Engineer Grey and his two friends, Brigadier. Why didn't you tell me?" he said with a grin.

"Now that's gratitude for you, Brigadier. Not so much as thank you for your services and here's a special bonus payment for your troubles. Oh no!" Sinclair said in mock disgust, grinning mischievously at Belverley.

"These men have given me an exemplary service, which you should be very proud and grateful for. You could do with a few like them, eh what?" The Brigadier replied and was joined by most of the other men.

"Stow it gentlemen! I think Lord Belverley has already sussed things out." John said, looking into Belverleys face.

"Yes, these officers certainly know how to keep me on my toes. Glad you all arrived back safely." Belverley conceded, nodding cheerfully at everybody.

"I was the one on the other end of your radio. Did you get a message from the local Sheriff in Tunis about your shipping agent?" Larter asked flatly.

"Yes! He's banged up for a long time, but I'm moving my operations to Tripoli or even Alexandria."

"Speaking of which, we were supposed to join the *Orchard lea* there. But as you can see we got slightly delayed. Is it still there?" John asked.

"Your ship in Alexandria? You're too late by at least five days. The strike is over now, so you three will return to Gibraltar and rejoin your ship again. See Mr Burford here, who will give you your papers and orders." Belverley said as he handed them over to Burford then turned back to the Brigadier, which Catchpole took exception to.

"Now just a minute Mr hoity-bloody-toity. You can't just dismiss them like that! They've saved our lives and Mr Grey here saved the Arabian Express train in Kalfa. You must be a reet wassock not to know that you've got three very canny men working for you." Catchpole said angrily.

"Unless you shut your uncouth Geordie mouth I'll see that you'll not get another gram of scrap off these sands. Do I make myself clear!" Belverley snarled, turning his back on the man.

Catchpole flicked two fingers at Belverley and told him in no uncertain terms what he could do with his ships, as he went back to his machine.

The Lost Legion

The Brigadier turned to the rest of the expedition team and told them that the expedition has just been concluded, and that everybody would be returning to Kalfa for the train back to Tunis. The news was greeted with a muffled cheer as everybody was now feeling the strain of the past two weeks out in the desert.

"We've had a torrid time out there, Belverley. I shall be making my report to the Foreign Minister in Whitehall, once I arrive back. But in the meantime, we have an Arab problem on our hands that I have to inform Cairo about, that not even you can fix. You might as well join our little convoy back to Kalfa as there's nothing out there now to concern yourself with." The Brigadier said off handedly, climbing wearily back into the *ziffer* and ordered the little convoy on.

The journey back to Kalfa was not as long as the outward trip, as the powerful *ziffer* machines gobbled up the miles in rapid haste.

The vehicles finally came to a halt alongside an awaiting train to take them all north again.

The Brigadier and the two War Graves' men left with Belverley and his team, on Belverley's private aircraft whilst the rest of the team enjoyed themselves in relative comfort on the train, which thankfully had an uneventful journey back to Tunis.

"Well here we are at last, and there's our plane landing." Larter said as the three friends made their way down the pontoon jetty to board the plane.

The flight back to Gibraltar was a quick one but eventful, as they found that some passengers were pressmen returning from a big to-do in Cairo, who were all talking animatedly about it.

"What was it in aid of?" Larter asked one of the pressmen.

"Some retired Brigadier and some Lord has got the Government into deep water with the Arab League of Nations." the reporter said, scribbling furiously into his notepad.

"Oh is that all! Now I wonder if that was Lord Belverley!" Sinclair said teasingly, which instantly stopped everybody talking.

The silence and the atmosphere was so that you could have cut it with a knife, and heard the proverbial pin drop, before the pressman gathered round the friends like opposing rugby scrums and firing questions at them in quick succession.

"What do you know about Belverley then?"

"He's our shipping line boss!" John replied nonchalantly.

"What was Belverley doing in the desert?"

"He was probably looking for the cement." Sinclair retorted with a grin.

"Did you see the Arab king? Who shot him?"

"I saw maybe the odd Sheik or two, but an Arab King getting shot? That wasn't me! Not guilty! So don't know anything about that!" Larter replied with a deadpan expression on his face, which incensed the pressmen even further.

"Then what the bloody hell do you three know that you're not telling us? We've a right to know." one irate pressman bellowed, shoving his face into John's.

"In fact, why the bloody hell were you three seamen in a bloody desert in the first place?"

"Yes, tell us about it!" the reporters shouted, as they posed several questions that were not being answered.

John stood on a chair and held his hand up for silence, which the reporters did, in anticipation of getting some answers.

"Why aye man! There's a reet lot of Nazi gold in them hills!" John shouted

"But you'd better speak to the reet wassock Sheik-Allah-bin-flippin-Sheik about that!" as he mimicked Catchpole, then climbed down off the chair and left the buffet with his friends in the quietness of the dumb struck reporters.

"We'd better get some rest before we arrive in Gib. As I fancy we've got a bloody good run ashore there before we get sent off into the wild blue yonder again." Larter said, as the three friends settled down into their seats and slept.

* * *

The air stewardess, who told them that the plane was about to land and for them to prepare to disembark, waked them up.

John looked wearily out of the porthole and saw the 'Rock' as large as life below him, as the plane circled it before swooping down then skidding across the water and halting at a pontoon bridge.

"Here we are again, happy as can be, I don't think! All fine fellows and jolly good company, so give us a bloody drink!" Sinclair sang as the other two stood next to him and gazed around at such a fine piece of British real estate.

"Now where's that git Armfield. I'll bloody well string him up by the bollocks when I get hold of him." Larter said nastily.

"Now what has he done?" John asked

"Thanks to him I've gone and lost my lighter in that bloody sand pit."

"Is this it Bruce?" John asked with a smile, and held out Larter's memento of his late father.

"Anyway, with what John found, you'll be able to buy several hundred lighters of your own." Sinclair chuckled as he saw the surprise on Larter's face as John handed him his lighter back.

"One for all and all for one is it Bruce? If so, give us a light!" John said, handing out the cigarettes.

Frederick A Read

The Lost Legion is the third book within the epic *Adventures of John Grey* series, which comprises of:

A Fatal Encounter
The Black Rose
The Lost Legion
Fresh Water
Beach Party
Ice Mountains
Perfumed Dragons
The Repulse Bay
Silver Oak leaves
Future Homes

All published by www.guaranteedbooks.co.uk

Fresh Water is due in May 2009.